Whispers
OF LOVE

A NOVEL

BLESSED ASSURANCE SERIES

LYN COTE

Whispers OF LOVE

A NOVEL

BROADMAN
&HOLMAN
PUBLISHERS

Nashville, Tennessee

0-8054-1967-5

Published by Broadman & Holman Publishers, Nashville, Tennessee
Editorial Team: Leonard G. Goss, John Landers, Sandra Bryer
Page Composition: Leslie Joslin

Dewey Decimal Classification: 813
Subject Heading: FICTION

Library of Congress Cataloging-in-Publication Data
Cote, Lyn.
Whispers of love / by Lyn Cote.
    p. cm.
ISBN 0-8054-1967-5
1. Great Fire, Chicago, Ill., 1871 Fiction.   I. Title.
PS3553.O76378W48   1999
813'.54—dc21

99-26539
CIP

1 2 3 4 5 03 02 01 00 99

To the teacher who taught me to write,
Mrs. Doris M. Crawford,
Waukegan Township High School, 1965
With fond memories and gratitude

Angels descending bring from above
Echoes of mercy, whispers of Love.

Watching and waiting, looking above,
Filled with His goodness, lost in His love.
—FANNY CROSBY, "BLESSED ASSURANCE"

"LET YOUR LIGHT SO SHINE BEFORE MEN THAT
THEY WILL SEE YOUR GOOD WORKS AND PRAISE
YOUR FATHER IN HEAVEN."
MATTHEW 5:16 KJV

HISTORICAL NOTE

The Great Chicago Fire, October 8–10, 1871, destroyed seventeen thousand buildings, left more than one hundred thousand people homeless, and took the lives of between two and three hundred people. There was never an actual body count. Many victims fleeing the flames drowned in either the Chicago River or Lake Michigan, and many of the missing must have been literally burned to ash.

In response to Mayor Mason's plea for help, Milwaukee's mayor sent three of his city's five fire companies. This was especially heroic since that left only one fire engine still in good repair to protect all of drought-ridden Milwaukee. Telegraphed news of Chicago's disaster prompted relief shipments by rail from as far away as New York City. Fifty carloads of food and clothing arrived in Chicago before sundown on Tuesday, the tenth.

The reactions of the fire survivors varied. One fashionable pastor rejected the offer of used clothing for his parishioners. He said they were accustomed to better. But one woman later recorded in her diary that on the night of the tenth as she lay down on the ground in a tent—with her husband and children around her—she had never felt richer in her life.

CHAPTER 1

April 9, 1871

THE BABY WILL LIVE. TENDERLY, Jessie Wagstaff pressed her white hand to his black angelic face framed by tight curls. The fiery heat had ebbed from his drawn cheeks. Trembling with fatigue, she sat slumped in an old rocker.

Across from her in the grayness of near dawn, she saw the outline of the baby's mother and father as they lay side by side on their narrow bed in mutual exhaustion. The way the black couple lay so close, so intimate, made her throat tighten. *No man is waiting for me at home.* She closed her burning eyes and scolded herself. Her six-year widowhood tormented her only at moments like these, times before chores and duties swallowed up each day.

Jessie felt the dark baby in her arms draw a deep breath. *Thank you, Father. I know it's not by my efforts alone that this child survived the night. Your hand healed him.* Leaning down, she kissed the baby's cool forehead. *Praise you, Father. Now, please grant me the strength to walk home.*

The awful dread of death that had oppressed her all night turned to gratitude. Like bubbles floating to the surface of a spring, a current of jubilation lifted her to her feet. "Ruth," she called softly to the sleeping mother.

The young black woman stirred and moaned, "My baby?"

"His fever's broken." Jessie waited for the woman to stumble to her side, then she shifted the child into his mother's arms.

The mother tentatively touched her son's forehead with the inside of her wrist. "Oh, you have the bestes' way with sickness."

Feeling as achy as an old woman, Jessie shuffled the few steps to the door and lifted her black cape and bonnet from a nail on the wall.

"Please, my husband will walk you home."

Jessie shook her head and wearily fumbled with the ribbons of her black bonnet and pulled on her gloves, noticing another seam was unraveling. More mending. She needed to hurry home before her gossipy neighbors saw she'd spent a night away from home. And if a young black man were seen with her, a white woman, it'd only add pepper to their scurrilous rumors. "Now don't give your baby anything but mother's milk. It's important. Promise me."

Cradling her baby son close to her breast, the mother nodded. "God bless you, Mrs. Wagstaff."

Jessie waved farewell and shut the flimsy door behind her. As quickly as her stiff limbs would let her, she started walking north along the railroad tracks. In her fatigue, she couldn't take her eyes off the tracks. She hated them, hated the prejudice they symbolized.

The parallel black metal lines separated the freed black slaves who had thrown together shacks on one side of the railway from the Irish immigrants opposite them. The gray-brown shanties, built from used lumber and tin, looked like heads bent in sadness, leaning close to one another as though sharing the sorrow. Still, a few defiantly faced away. How this shantytown would have grieved her mother-in-law Margaret's, tender heart.

Jessie could picture Margaret with a full basket on her arm going from door to door—on both sides of the tracks—dispensing food and herbal medicine. Caring for these needy people would have been as natural as breathing to her mother-in-law. Jessie sighed. *I miss you every day, Margaret.*

Jessie's long, black skirt and petticoats swirled around her ankles, and the weight of them seemed to grow with every step. Over the thud of her heels on the wooden Randolph Street Bridge, she heard the jingle of the harness bells and clattering hooves of the first morning bobtail trolley. *Oh, thank heaven.* She hated to part with the two-penny fare, but she couldn't walk any farther. She hurried to the corner and flagged it down.

Lifting her skirts discreetly, she climbed up the wooden steps. While she looked for a seat among the day-maids and workmen who were riding to jobs at this dreary hour, the trolley jerked to a start. She stumbled and sat down abruptly, then fidgeted on the hard seat till she positioned herself more comfortably on her bustle.

She'd make it now before the gossips were up and snooping. She closed her eyes, letting herself sway with the trolley's curious effect of going forward while rocking side to side. In spite of the contrary motions, she felt herself dozing.

She snapped her eyes wide open. If she missed her stop, then needed to ride back, it would cost another penny and minutes she couldn't afford to lose. Blinking to keep her eyes open, she glimpsed the skyline of downtown and saw dawn had come.

The rising sun cast a rosy glow over the squared, ornate parapets of the limestone hotels. Her Will had called them imitation castles. After giving her an engagement ring, Will had taken her to visit each one, trying to decide where to spend their wedding night. Will's face surfaced in her memory, smiling as always, blonde and blue-eyed. He whispered to her, "Come here, Princess." He drew her into strong arms and his warm lips touched . . .

Ring! Jessie sat up. Jolt-stop! The woman next to her hurried to the rear exit. Jolt-start! With a growing sense of urgency not to miss her stop, she anxiously read each northward street sign. At Ontario Street, she pulled the bell cord with relief and stepped down at the corner. Her step quickened—she was so near home. The familiar, white frame houses crowded so close together showed little sign of life yet. But the lowing of a few cows and the clatter of a milk pail told her some people had already risen.

Mistiness filtered the rosy sunshine around her. A curtain of fog had settled itself across the middle of the street, and she walked into the cloaking vapor. Early morning fog in spring was one of the prices she paid for living just a few blocks from Lake Michigan. Today she welcomed its concealment.

April rains had left her alley sticky with mud. Though she lifted her skirts and stepped around murky puddles, the thin soles of her worn shoes let moisture leak in, wetting her cotton stockings.

At last, through the thick grayness, she picked out her own alley shed and gate. *Almost there.* From the shed, she heard the reassuring hollow clang of her goats' bells and the tut-tut of her hens. Walking up the fog-surrounded path, she could see only the bottom steps of her back porch—looking like an island in the surrounding mist.

She felt like a rag doll moved by unseen hands, but God had brought her all the miles home in time. Feeling as though sliding into a trance from lack of sleep, she listened to the crunch-crunch rhythm of her shoes on the coal-cinder path. Longing for her first cup of coffee, she lifted her foot to the first step.

CHAPTER 1

"Jessie?" a sleep-filled voice muttered out of the veil of mist.

A man's voice. A cold needle of shock raced up her spine. She screamed.

The man, no longer sounding sleepy, asked anxiously, "Jessie, Jessie Wagstaff?"

Her eyes focused on the male figure looming above her on the porch. But the slender man with dark hair and eyes, dressed in a well-cut black suit, did not appear threatening to her. Indeed, his startled reaction must have mirrored her own. "Who . . . who are you?" she stammered.

"Smith. I'm Lee Smith."

Now all her hurry and worry would go for naught. Even if no one had seen her in the fog, surely every neighborhood gossip must have heard her scream. Anger flashed through her. "Why are you on my porch at this hour!"

The man just stood there staring at her.

The door behind him hit the outside wall with a crack like a gunshot. Susan, Jessie's black friend and partner, bolted toward the stranger, brandishing a broom. "Get! Get! You leave Mrs. Wagstaff 'lone!"

The man ducked just in time to avoid the swat aimed for his head.

Jessie felt so tired. She couldn't make herself react. As the man swerved to deflect the next blow, he stumbled down the few steps to her side.

"Susan!" Jessie finally shouted over the black woman's continuing stream of agitated threats, then Jessie captured the end of the broom. "Stop! I'm unharmed!" There was instant silence.

Jessie glared at the stranger. "Explain yourself, sir. You have just sixty seconds to persuade me that you have a lawful reason to be here before Susan and I run you off." Her quelling tone had some effect. He removed his slightly cockeyed hat, but still made no effort to reply.

Her patience snapped. *"Sir?"*

He began in a soothing tone, "I apologize to you both. I did not mean to alarm you. I must have dozed off while I waited for your household to waken—"

"I asked you a simple question." Her control was slipping again. Jessie gripped the end of the broom as if holding onto her temper. "Answer it now or I will summon the police."

He gave them a contrite look. Appearing unimpressed, Susan scorched the man with her gaze. "If this is Wagstaff House, I am looking for a room."

"You want a room!" Jessie couldn't keep her voice down. Her fatigue made her tremble.

He went on, as though gaining confidence. "This is a boarding house. I need a room—"

"It's only 5 A.M. Who would look for a room at this hour?" Her exasperation mounted. She gave him a look of distaste.

In a smooth voice, he said, "I'm so sorry, Mrs. Wagstaff. You are Mrs. Wagstaff, are you not?"

"Yes, I'm Mrs. Wagstaff," she admitted to him grudgingly. Did he really think she was so easily swayed? Susan began to mutter under her breath again, sounding dangerously like a locomotive building up a good head of steam.

He seemed to hurry on, trying to calm them both. "I'm sorry to have startled you. I arrived at the railway station downtown only about two hours ago. I didn't see any sense in taking a room, so I asked directions and walked here—"

"Here?" she demanded. "Do I know you?"

"No, your house was recommended by the conductor on my train."

Liar! "You expect me to believe that?" she snapped. "Chicago has over 300,000 people, and you expect me to believe that some train conductor gave you my address. I don't know any train conductors."

"Well, he spoke highly of you." His smile held.

In spite of the fog-muffled morning air, the hooves of a fast-approaching horse clacked sharply on the wooden street out front. Soon, only a few feet from Jessie, a uniformed officer dismounted. "Police! What is the disturbance here? We received a summons."

Jessie felt her face go red. *Police!* The gossips would have a heyday with this!

Jessie deftly dropped the broom and turned to face the policeman, pulling herself together. She had to head off the rumors. "Oh, officer, I'm so sorry you were called. Yes, I did cry out. The fog veiled Mr. Smith from my sight and he startled me. That must have prompted the summons."

"You're certain you do not need any assistance, madam?" The policeman stared at the stranger.

"No, but thank you for coming so quickly." She glanced up the steps at Susan.

Astonished, Lee felt Jessie link her arm in his, then she glanced back at the policeman. "Officer, it does my heart good to know that such a minor disturbance brought such quick action. Thank you again." Lee allowed her to lead him up the back steps to the door. Standing so close to Jessie, he was fascinated by her appearance—a young woman with ivory skin; dark, serious eyes; and soft, wavy brown hair. She had changed little from the worn daguerreotype he still carried in his pocket.

Over his shoulder, Lee nodded civilly to the policeman. He let Jessie lead him through the back door into a large kitchen. As soon as the door closed, she dropped his arm like a hot coal.

With his hat still in one hand, he stood stiffly, wishing he had taken time to have his suit freshly brushed and pressed.

The two of them remained, facing each other in tableau, listening to the officer's departure. Coming inside, Susan closed the door behind her. "He's goin', Jess . . . Mrs. Wagstaff."

Jessie released a deep sigh. "That takes care of that."

Lee's curiosity forced him to ask, "How did anyone alert the police so quickly?"

"Someone must have pulled the alarm on the corner and then pointed out our house when he arrived." Jessie untied the strings of her bonnet.

"Alarm?"

"Yes, didn't you know Chicago has alarm boxes every few blocks which are connected by wire to the nearest police station?" She turned her back to him. "Susan, who do you think called in the alarm?"

"It got to be dat Mrs. Braun or Mrs. O'Toole," Susan said, her hands perched on her hips.

Grimacing, Jessie nodded. "What would they do for diversion if we didn't live here?"

Lee detected only the barest touch of humor in Jessie's tone. Then he found her gaze on him once more, and he fought the urge to tug nervously at his collar.

"I suppose you'll have to stay," Jessie grumbled, with a look that made him feel as though he were a child who had come to her table with dirty hands. "At least, 'til breakfast is finished. One of my nosy neighbors will certainly stop the officer and ask him about you. It would look suspicious if you were seen leaving too soon."

"Old biddies," Susan muttered.

Stifling a mocking grin, Lee bowed. "Thank you for your charming invitation. I am free for breakfast."

"Humph." Jessie walked away from him.

Lee bit back a retort while she took off her very threadbare, dreary-looking bonnet and cape. She then tugged the gloves from her fingers and tucked them inside the cape pocket. A startling fact suddenly occurred to him. At 5 A.M., she had been coming up the steps, not out of her door. Where had Mrs. Jessie Wagstaff been all night?

The black girl was tying a red calico apron around herself when she put his thoughts into words. "Do you think dey saw you was comin' *in*, not steppin' *out*?"

CHAPTER 1

Jessie, donning a full white apron, frowned and shook her head at Susan. For a moment, Lee considered repeating the hired girl's question. However, he wasn't prepared to call further attention to himself.

Jessie motioned to Lee, directing his gaze toward a long table beside the kitchen window. The stark white curtains that fluttered over it suited the sparsely adorned, whitewashed room and it all seemed to go with the cheerless woman who stood near him. She said abruptly, "Sit yourself." With clenched teeth, he obeyed, balancing his hat on his knee. How long did this woman think she could get by with treating him like a pesky bill collector?

Ignoring him, the women went on with their obvious morning routine. *Fine. Just as long as breakfast is good and comes quickly.* Susan picked up a milk pail and left by the back door. Jessie filled a wall-mounted coffee mill and began to crank it. The aroma of freshly ground coffee beans wafted through the room, making his mouth water.

He asked, "Do you have a room for rent?"

"I have no vacancy; and even if I did, I never take in male boarders. A widow can't be too careful when it comes to gossip."

"I want a room—not a widow," he snapped back.

She glared at him.

Suddenly he didn't like Jessie Wagstaff one bit. Only his reason for coming compelled him to remain seated. Instead of retorting, he reverted to his usual tactic, charming nonchalance. It had always infuriated his family but had given them no opportunity to continue berating him. He gave her a languid smile and dusted the top of his hat with careless fingers. "I'm merely looking for a clean room and good food. You were recommended and—"

"I said before that I find it hard to believe that some railroad conductor pointed you to my house."

"Mother!" A young lad with tousled blonde hair, still dressed in his white nightshirt, rushed through the curtained doorway into the kitchen. The sight of the boy made Lee's heart skip a beat. As Jessie unhooked the jar of freshly ground coffee from the mill, the boy grasped her forearms. "There was a policeman and a horse. I saw them from my window."

Jessie balanced the coffee jar to keep it from spilling. "Well, why not? Policeman often come down our street, Linc."

The boy dropped his hold on his mother and turned to Lee. "Who is this?"

Lee looked into the face of the boy—so new to him, yet so familiar. Without warning, the innocent face unleashed an avalanche of wrenching, often reoccurring memories inside Lee. Phantom cannon roared in his ears, and the sweetly putrid smell of gangrenous flesh made him gag. Fighting the urge to retch, he clutched his hat brim with both hands. Susan came in and set a heavy milk pail on the edge of the sink. "Mister, you be all right?"

He could not answer. He fought free of the haunting sensations and they began to pass. "I'm fine." Both women were staring at him. "I'm fine," he repeated, his voice firmer. "Lincoln, I'm Lee Smith." He stretched out his right hand and grasped the youngster's palm in his. As they solemnly shook hands, Lee put his reassuring smile back into place.

"Linc, Mr. Smith is staying for breakfast. He is new in town and wanted to rent a room from us. But since we don't have any rooms available, he will have to look elsewhere."

Linc moved closer to Lee. The boy's scent of cornstarch powder and soap blotted out the lingering odors in Lee's memory.

"Mr. Smith, I wish you could stay. I'm the only boy here."

Unused to being around children, but touched by this confidence, Lee clumsily stroked the boy's hair. "I'm happy I was able to meet you, Linc." *Poor kid—defenseless in a household of "skirts."*

CHAPTER 1

Their few moments together ended. Again Lee observed the mother and son together. Jessie came up behind the boy and turned him by the shoulders, then swatted him gently on the behind. "Young man, you need to get yourself ready for breakfast. You remember what happens today, don't you?"

"The game! It's today, isn't it? It's April 9th!"

Smiling, Jessie bent and kissed the bobbing forehead. "Yes, Linc, it is finally the ninth. Go mark it off on the calendar."

Lee grinned as Linc jumped straight up. When the boy's feet hit the bare wood floor again, he charged toward the calendar beside the pantry doorway. He lifted a pencil, dangling from a string, and marked a large "X" through the date.

His mother touched Linc's shoulder. "Get more wood please. We barely have enough to finish heating the water, and I need to start brewing the coffee."

Groaning, the boy padded back out of the room.

Lee sat down while Jessie went to the sink and began filling the two large coffeepots with water.

"What game?" Lee asked, searching her face.

"Today is the first exhibition game of the new Chicago White Stockings Baseball Club. My son is an avid supporter."

"Is he?" Lee grinned.

Jessie began spooning coffee into the pots. "Yes, he will tell you all about them and the new National Association of Professional Baseball Players." He liked the way her voice softened as she spoke of her son.

Susan added with a grin, "Five games dey play with da other teams. Five with each one." Carrying a wire basket, the hired girl started out the back door.

"Yes, would you like us to recite the names of the other nine teams, Mr. Smith?" Jessie surprised Lee by actually chuckling.

Emboldened by this, he replied, "Thank you, no. But when do you think you might have a vacancy?"

"You are persistent, Mr. Smith. Listen, *even* if I had a vacancy and *even* if I rented to males, I still would never rent to a stranger. I cannot, will not, rent you a room, Mr. Smith."

Lee gritted his teeth behind smiling lips.

A young woman's voice from the other side of the curtain interrupted them: "Mrs. Wagstaff, is the wash water ready? Some of the boarders are fussing."

Lee watched Jessie grimace, but her voice did not betray her. "Please tell them it won't be long."

The young boarder murmured indistinctly and retreated.

Linc came into the kitchen pulling his suspenders into place. Jessie motioned her son to the back door. "Hurry, Linc, we are running late."

A querulous voice issuing from the hallway surprised Lee. "How long is a body supposed to wait for a small pitcher of warm water?" A very old woman, leaning heavily on a gnarled wooden cane, made a good effort at stomping into the room in spite of her advanced age and evident rheumatics. She reminded Lee of his own Great Aunt Hester. Out of common politeness, he rose to his feet.

"Who is this man? Why are you entertaining a man in this kitchen at this hour? What is he peddling?"

"I'm not a peddler, ma'am," Lee cut in, holding back irritation.

The old prune ignored him and spoke to Jessie, "Is he an army comrade of Will's? I thought we were all done with that sort of chicanery. They start by making women believe they are army friends of their husbands, and in the end, the ninny-women have bought worthless shares—"

"I'm not—," Lee started, nearly stepping forward. Not trusting himself, he let Jessie override him.

"Miss Wright, Mr. Smith arrived this morning looking for lodging and employment. He is staying for breakfast."

"Humph. Too poor to buy his own breakfast. . . ." Sounding exactly like his Aunt Hester, she grumbled one accusation after another at Lee.

Linc brought in an armload of wood. Miss Wright scolded him, "You there, boy, why didn't you bring in enough wood last night? Are we to wait for breakfast while you gawk at this stranger?"

Lee, though bristling himself, was impressed by Linc's composure while under attack. The boy carefully, but swiftly, loaded the wood into the stove.

The irritating old woman went on, "If his father were here, he would take a strap to this boy—"

"No, he wouldn't—" Lee and Jessie, who had spoken at the same time, stopped and stared at each other.

"Humph!" the old woman declared. "Send that worthless black girl up with my water! I don't know why I put up with the inconvenience of living here. If only Margaret were still alive!" Miss Wright continued her tirade, thumping her cane petulantly all the way down the hall.

The thought of facing this old crow dimmed slightly Lee's anticipation of breakfast. "Why did you say that about my late husband?" Jessie asked him.

He looked at her squarely and lied through his teeth, "No particular reason. I just don't like grouchy old women."

Susan entered with the wire basket now full of brown eggs. When she glanced darkly at the curtained doorway and grumbled to herself, Lee was certain Susan had heard everything the unpleasant old woman had said.

As he watched, Jessie and Susan poured the wash water for the boarders. He noticed that while Susan shot inquiring glances his way, Jessie never turned her eyes toward him. Her ability to ignore him grated on his tender nerves. Why couldn't he ignore her?

Susan carried out the warm wash water and Jessie began cracking eggs. Soon the aromas of bubbling coffee and sizzling bacon and eggs made Lee's mouth water and his stomach rumble in anticipation. When Susan stood at the stove toasting bread on long-handled forks over the fire, Jessie removed her white apron and nodded in his direction. He followed her into the long, roomy dining room as she carried the large tray, laden with a covered blue-and-white tureen filled with oatmeal and a matching platter of the bacon and eggs. *Breakfast, at last!*

Lee scanned the room, which gave him a feeling of austerity. The rectangular table of dark walnut, though simply covered with a white oilcloth, stood out as a showpiece with its ornately carved legs. Three women sat around it, the old one with her cane, a middle-aged redhead, and a pretty young blonde. *This will be interesting,* Lee thought.

He bowed to them. After nodding to him in reply, the young, stylish blonde politely looked away. The middle-aged redhead ogled him, while Miss Wright scowled at him. He smiled what he knew was his most irritating smile at the old biddy.

Jessie supplied the introductions, "Mr. Smith, you have already met Miss Wright. This is Mrs. Bolt and Miss Greenleigh."

Mrs. Bolt, the redhead, simpered, "Your place, I believe, is next to mine, sir." She indicated the empty chair to the right of hers.

Lee bowed to the ladies once more and sat down. Linc welcomed him with a grin. As Lee spread the crisply starched napkin across his lap, he heard the old lady grumble loudly. He looked up. Everyone, except for the old woman and him, had their heads bowed for morning grace. *Scold me, will you?* He waggled his forefinger as though chastising her for not bowing her head also. Then smiling inwardly, he folded his hands in his lap formally and bowed for the prayer. After Jessie's brief blessing, the meal began.

While he savored the combination of hot coffee and crisp toast with crab-apple jelly, Mrs. Bolt, who immediately informed him she was a war widow and taught eighth grade, kept him busy dodging each of her questions. Interspersed between the coy widow's chatter and Linc's occasional comments about the afternoon game, the old spinster grumbled at him. But overall, Jessie's silent, unwelcoming perusal discouraged him most. How would he break through the wall she'd built to surround herself?

The meal ended all too soon. Linc dashed upstairs to get his books. Miss Greenleigh and Mrs. Bolt, in bonnets and gloves, departed to the local school where they both taught. The old woman, thumping her cane as though still scolding Lee, crossed the hall to the parlor. He and Jessie were left alone at the table.

"What kind of work will you be looking for in Chicago, Mr. Smith? Or do you already have a position?" Jessie asked him in a cool tone that daunted him.

"Clerking," he mumbled vaguely.

"The McCormick Reaper plant is nearby at the corner of Rush and Erie, but there are many offices downtown—or at the grain elevators along the river or the lumberyards. I'm certain you will have no—"

Saving Lee from more of this dismal information, Linc rushed in. "Excuse me, Mr. Smith, Mother. I'm ready for school." The boy halted beside her, his hair slicked back with water. "Remember—I'll be going to Drexel Park to see the White Stockings."

"*After* school." Jessie smiled and tugged his earlobe playfully.

"Aw, Mother." He headed out the kitchen door, calling over his shoulder, "Bye, Mr. Smith, I wish you were staying."

Sincerely touched in spite of himself, Lee waved farewell. He stood up. "Mrs. Wagstaff, I'll be off now."

She accompanied him to the front door as though to make sure he left the premises. He walked outside and down the front steps. He paused at the bottom, looking up at her standing in the doorway of the simple white frame house. "Thank you for a fine breakfast, Mrs. Wagstaff."

"You're welcome. Please let me know how you get on, Mr. Smith." Her face wore a warning expression that did not match her polite words.

But the Widow Wagstaff would see him again, and soon. He'd purposely left his valise on her back porch.

CHAPTER 2

After sending Mr. Smith on his way, Jessie returned to the dining room. Susan was clearing away the breakfast dishes. Jessie read the question written plainly on Susan's face. "Yes, he's gone."

"What that man here for anyway?"

Jessie shrugged her shoulders. The stranger's presence in her kitchen and at her table had been disturbing, as disturbing as a crowing rooster among a brood of fluttery hens. The War for Emancipation had taken such a dreadful toll on the population of young men that no man under the age of forty had sat at her table for over five years.

This man in particular had disturbed Jessie in a way she couldn't name. "We'll probably never see him again." She cleared the table with Susan in companionable silence.

However, when Jessie and Susan entered the kitchen, Susan set her stack of dishes down with a thump. "Humph!"

"I know," Jessie murmured. "You heard Miss Wright—"

"Worthless black girl. After the war, when I come North free, I think Chicago goin' to be my promised land. But I work here for more'n five years and I still that worthless black girl.'"

Coming to Susan's side, Jessie pressed her cheek to Susan's rich ebony one and tucked one arm around her friend's waist. "I know it's hard to forgive and forget again and again, but she's too old to change her ideas."

"I don't 'spect her to change her ideas about all colored folks, just me. I work hard—"

"And I thank God for you every day."

Susan laced her arm through Jessie's and sighed deeply. "Don't you think I feel da same way?"

Jessie smiled. "Susan, you've been a blessing straight from heaven. I couldn't do all this work by myself and still have time to spend with Linc."

"God bless me with you."

"We were both blessed to find each other. You needed work and a home and I needed help." Straightening, Jessie drew away.

"I got more'n a home here. I got a friend, a friend who teach me how to be free."

"And you're the best friend I've ever had. But I know what you mean about learning how to be free." Jessie looked lovingly around the simple kitchen. "When I was twelve, coming to this house to be Margaret's hired girl set me free too."

"You talkin' about gettin' away from that stepfather of yours?"

Jessie wrinkled her nose. "Let's not spoil this beautiful day by mentioning that man."

"I don't know how you turned out so sweet when you raised by such a hard-hearted man."

"Well, my mother taught me how to love. No one could doubt my mother's Christian love, even for someone as unlovable as her husband, but Margaret taught me how to show my love to others."

Susan drew away and began rinsing dishes in the dishpan. "Well, she did a good job. Everybody know you got a heart a pure gold. And that's da trouble with you. You do too much extry. I bet you didn't get two hours sleep last night."

Jessie yawned and stretched her arms overhead, wiggling out the kinks in her back. "I'll be all right. 'I can do all things through Christ which strengtheneth me.'"

"I know that, but do he want you doin' everythin'?"

Jessie sighed and reached for a dishcloth.

Susan pulled it right out of her hand. "You go take a nap. I can do these dishes by myself."

"I'll help you, then go lie down."

"You go now or I'll do da shoppin' and you won't get to see your mama today."

Jessie gave Susan a crooked smile. "All right, Miss Susan."

Susan slapped a washcloth into the basin and poured water from the hissing kettle onto the cups and silver. "How's Ruthie's child?"

"His fever broke just before dawn. If Ruth can get him to nurse today, I think he'll mend," Jessie replied as a wave of fatigue washed over her.

"I am surely glad to hear he all right, but you can't go on, workin' all day at this house, then go nursin' all night."

Jessie felt as though Margaret stood beside her. She heard her mother-in-law's gentle voice quoting Jesus' words, *"Inasmuch as ye have done it unto one of the least of these my brethren, ye have done it unto me."*

"Susan, how can I say no?"

✼ ✼ ✼ ✼ ✼

With a large oak basket on her arm, Jessie walked briskly down Lake Street to the open market at the north end. From Lake Michigan blew a cool wind, but the stalls were filled with farmers' early lettuce and rhubarb, eggs, milk, fresh meat, pre-serves, and more. Jessie enjoyed being part of the bustling crowd of women in bonnets and heavy capes who carried similar bas-kets to hers on their arms.

"Mrs. Wagstaff, your boy need any pencils today?" The dou-ble amputee sat on a homemade wicker wheelchair at his regu-lar spot on the corner.

"Mr. Tyson, he goes through them like lightning." She pulled out a penny from her pocket purse.

He tossed the bright yellow pencil into her basket.

A breeze off the nearby Chicago River blew over them, making Jessie press a lavender-scented handkerchief to her nose. The stench surprised a comment from her. "That awful odor! I'm sorry to mention it, but it's even more abominable now that the weather is warmer. How do you stand it all day?"

"I smell it when I first come. Then my nose must get used to it."

"They can't fix that river soon enough for me," Jessie spoke through her handkerchief. "I dread it when the wind switches and I get a trace of *that* in my own backyard."

He pointed a yellow pencil at her like a teacher with a pointing stick. "Do you really think they can change a river's flow by digging a deep ditch? I can't see it myself."

"We'll know soon. Isn't the day they're to finish in July?"

"Jessie."

She turned to greet her mother, a slender woman with the same dark hair and eyes as her own and a handkerchief pressed to her nose also. For a moment, Jessie hoped her mother would open her arms and pull her in for a quick hug. But, of course, her mother merely offered Jessie her hand. Hiram Huff had taught them never to show affection in public—or private for that matter. Just thinking her stepfather's name caused a ball of fire to shoot through Jessie's veins.

God, free me from this anger, she prayed, but the fiery resent-ment flamed on.

Jessie's mother cleared her throat and blushed. "Mr. Tyson, my husband said this pencil broke because it's poorly made. He wants you to return it to your supplier."

Jessie sympathetically observed her mother's face turn even brighter pink. Only Hiram Huff would return a pencil to a crippled Union Army veteran.

"I'll do that, ma'am. Tell your husband I stand behind my pencils." He took it and gave her a new one.

"Oh, I forgot," Jessie said. "Miss Greenleigh asked me to pick up two red pencils." She handed him a nickel. He tossed two red ones into her basket.

With parting nods to him, they walked away side by side.

"Thank you, dear," her mother murmured.

Jessie nodded. They didn't have to discuss it. Hiram Huff made his wife account for each penny, even those spent for charity. The breeze changed and they were able to move their handkerchiefs down from their faces.

"You look tired, Jessie. Have you been up late again nursing someone?"

After Susan's lecture on the same subject, Jessie hurriedly changed topics. "I had an unexpected visitor this morning—at dawn."

"At dawn? Who was it?"

"A stranger. He actually tried to make me believe some train conductor recommended my boarding house."

"Why would he choose your house if someone hadn't recommended you?"

"Just my luck." Jessie gave a half-smile.

"But . . . that's so odd. Please be careful."

"After meeting Miss Wright, I doubt he'll be back."

They halted near the egg stall. Her mother asked, "Do you have any extra eggs, Jessie?"

"No, we're using all the hens give."

Her mother spoke to the buxom farmer's wife wearing a simple poke bonnet, "A half dozen please—your large white."

The woman motioned her to pick out the ones she wanted. Then the woman wrapped them in newspaper one by one and tucked them into the basket for Jessie's mother.

As they walked away, her mother glanced at Jessie. "How is Miss Wright? That poor woman."

"Poor woman with a razor sharp tongue. She sliced that stranger up like the bacon for breakfast."

Her mother shook her head. "I'm happy you're able to take care of Miss Wright. Margaret loved her so."

Jessie nodded. A sensation of tenderness swelled in her heart. "You had one of the sweetest mothers-in-law I've ever known."

"Yes, I did." Jessie looked away. Losing Margaret less than a year after Will had died in the final months of the Civil War still had the power to hurt her. Margaret's sweet temper and kindness had freed Jessie from her stepfather's harshness.

How often she still yearned to lean her head on Margaret's soft bosom and listen to her honeyed voice soothe every problem with a prayer. Willing the pain away, Jessie took a deep breath and felt her stays press against her ribs.

Then she heard it, the idle clang of a fire bell. With terrible apprehension, she looked up at the shiny red, black and brass fire wagon coming down Lake Street.

Her stepfather in his highly starched, blue fire captain's uniform hopped down from it, looking at her with grim satisfaction on his square face. He waved the wagon to go on without him and stepped in front of them. "Hello, Jessie, Esther, I thought I'd find the two of you here."

"Hiram, I . . . ." Her mother pressed her hand to her heart. "You surprised me."

"I knew you'd probably be shopping about now, and I wanted to have a word with your daughter."

This didn't surprise Jessie. She prepared herself for disapproval. He wouldn't have stopped if he didn't have something to scold her about. "I'm sure I don't need a word right now," she murmured.

"Jessie, please." Her mother touched Jessie's sleeve.

"We already know, Esther, that your daughter doesn't have a teachable spirit."

"What is it you want to tell me, stepfather?" Jessie forced herself to speak politely for her mother's sake. He had planned this meeting so that it would force her compliance. He knew how much her mother hated any confrontation, however mild.

"Very well. You were seen leaving that shanty town at an ungodly hour this morning by a fellow fire captain of mine. I thought I told you I didn't want you going there anymore."

"I had to go. A sick baby needed me," Jessie spoke quietly.

"Your actions reflect on us. There is no reason for a decent woman to go there at any time, but certainly not at odd hours of the day and night."

"The baby might have died if I—"

"I expect this odd behavior to stop *now*, Jessie. Esther, I'll be home a little late this evening." He tipped his hat and marched down the street.

Jessie fumed in silence, trying to get her anger under control. But like a flash fire, resentment flamed through her. She tried to call up some of the phrases that Margaret had taught her about being persecuted, but they'd deserted her. Why had her mother ever married this man? In a low voice, Jessie said, "Mother, I am doing the work God has given me. No one will turn me from my purpose."

Painful crosscurrents of love and shame showed on her mother's face.

To end the silent impasse, Jessie took a step closer to her mother, who grasped Jessie's elbow gratefully.

"Daughter, will you come to Field and Leiter's with me?" Her mother's voice was rich with feeling. "I need to buy the twins new shirts."

Jessie was touched. Calling her "daughter" sounded like a commonplace; but in their unspoken code, using this term was an endearment that had slipped by her stepfather's net of interference. Even now, when Jessie was grown and no longer under her stepfather's roof, these brief daily shopping trips were the only way they saw each other regularly. "No, but I'll walk you there."

Through the crowded streets of shoppers, Jessie enjoyed strolling beside her mother the few blocks west. At the corner of Washington and State stood the five-story, fairy-tale edifice. How Will would have enjoyed Potter Palmer's "marble palace." If Will had survived the war and lived to see the gala grand opening night in the fall two years ago, he would have drawn her arm through his and escorted her like his princess through the aisles of exotic rugs, Balmoral petticoats, silks, and more.

Instead, she'd only read about it in the *Tribune*.

Her mother coaxed, "Jessie, won't you please come in this time. Just admiring the counter displays—"

"There's no reason for me to look at what I can't afford." She smiled reassuringly at her mother's crestfallen expression. "Linc and I are making ends meet, but I have to save for Linc. Even more than pretty things, I want Will's son to go as far in life as he is able."

"I know, but you're only twenty-six! You're only young once. I'd like to see you enjoy life more while you can."

My joy died with Will. He'll never walk the marble floors of Palmer's "palace." "Mother, as long as I have Linc, I'll always have fun. Why, I'm going to my first baseball game today. What could be more fun than that?" Jessie was rewarded with a deep, genuine smile from her mother.

"Then I won't keep you. I'm sure you have much to do so you can make the game in time." With a wave, her mother walked through the door held open by a boy in a royal blue uniform with bright brass buttons. Stylishly dressed and still

24

handsome, her mother looked exactly right walking into the elegant store.

Will had always said that Hiram Huff's only redeeming characteristic was that he was a good provider and he always demanded that his wife wear the very best. Which only proved what Will had believed was right; happiness didn't lay in finery.

I have Linc, a home, and Susan—God's given me all I need.

Jessie hurried to her favorite butcher shop to purchase pork chops for supper. Out of the corner of her eye, a slender man in a dark suit caught her attention. The way he moved—a kind of cocky nonchalance—had caught her eye. It was Mr. Smith. That indefinable feeling zigzagged through her again. She brushed it away. What if it were he? She'd never see his face at her door again.

*　*　*　*　*

Lee wearied of roaming the unusual wooden sidewalks of downtown Chicago. In the main shopping district around State and Randolph, the streets and sidewalks were flush with each other. But a few blocks away, though the street and first floor of a business were even, often the entrance was by means of a staircase to the second floor. It made no sense to Lee.

As he walked, several windows with signs saying "Help Wanted" had beckoned him, but crosscurrents inside him had kept him walking by. What did he really want to do while he set everything up? He'd planned to start by getting a room at Jessie's. But he'd failed at that so far, so a new plan was necessary.

His stomach rumbled. Just ahead of him on the south side of the river was a tavern, "The Workman's Rest." Its sign also proclaimed "Free lunch with nickel beer." His mouth watered at the thought of a long draught of ale. But as he approached the double swinging doors, he frowned. He couldn't go in.

Suddenly two burly men crowded one on each side of Lee and carried him along with them into the tavern. One of them called out, "Pearl, brought you a new customer! He's wearing a suit!"

Lee halted, shocked at finding himself where he didn't choose to be.

"He's welcome!" the woman behind the bar called back without taking her eyes from the two tankards of ale she was filling at the tap. She thumped them down on the bar, then wiped her fingers on her white apron. "Welcome to the Workman's Rest, stranger. I'm Pearl Flesher. Put her there." The woman thrust out her hand.

Lee took in the sight of her with pleasure. She was tall, blonde, good-looking and thirtyish. He accepted her out-thrust hand. "A pleasure, ma'am."

"A man with manners! What can I do for you, mister?"

Lee was stumped. He knew he was expected to say, "A beer, Pearl," but he couldn't.

"He wants a beer just like we do, Pearl!" the workmen on both sides of him declared. "Come on, we only have a short lunchtime!"

Lee cleared his dry throat. "Really, I would prefer a barley water." The words brought a stunned silence to the two workmen.

"Barley water!" one exploded.

"Yes, my stomach, you see." Lee felt all eyes turned on him.

One of the men started to speak, but Pearl cut him off. "If he wants barley water, it'll be barley water. You jugheads could digest nails!"

The men around him laughed and Lee felt intense relief. Soon he was having a congenial exchange with them as he sipped his barley water and enjoyed a thick sandwich of sliced sausage on fresh bread.

An older man farther down the bar pointed his pipe in Lee's direction. "You sound like you come from out East. What do you think of our Chicago?"

"I admit I am surprised—and pleasantly so. It is truly a modern city—policemen, fire hydrants, gaslights on the street corners. I thought it'd be a frontier town."

The man hooted with laughter. "Mister, you'd hafta go a ways west for that—maybe Abilene. It makes me laugh how Easterners always think we're punching cows and fighting Indians here."

"Personally, I did not fear Indians or cattle when I arrived." Lee bowed with mock formality. "Now can you answer a question about your fair city for me? Why do some sidewalks here go up and down like hills and why do some businesses have second-story entrances?"

The old man took a draw on his pipe. "Chicago was built on a swamp, you know. It were muddy, and they couldn't do nothing about the land being so low, so they shaved off a hill nearby and used it to fill up the main part of town—to make it level."

Lee paused with his glass to his lips. "They filled it in? With the buildings already there?"

"Pullman did that," Pearl broke in while she refilled a glass. "I seen it when I was a girl. He had a thousand men put large wooden screw lifts under each part of the foundations."

The old man caught Lee's eye. "Like the Hotel Tremont. That Pullman fella, he blew a whistle and they'd all give one turn. Another whistle, another turn."

"You're kidding me," Lee said with a grin.

"No, he did it. With people staying in the hotel the whole time," Pearl cut in, "just like nothing was happening."

"And, mister, as to why places got entrances on the second floor—see, in some places the sidewalks used t' be higher. They finally made most sidewalks level, but left some entrances where they was—higher up." The man demonstrated the different heights with his pudgy, white-haired hands.

"But what about the few sidewalks that still go up and down?" Lee asked.

"Some stores didn't get raised. Not everyone could afford Pullman's price!" The old man chuckled.

Lee shook his head and took another sip of barley water. The conversation around Lee turned to baseball and some bets were wagered between the men over the White Stockings' chances. The tavern was small, clean, and felt homey to Lee. Most of the men mingled around the bar near him though there was a row of small tables against the wall. And instead of pictures of racy women as he would have expected, only a few posters announcing today's ball game were pinned on the back wall.

Lee stared at the posters and suddenly he pictured Jessie this morning in her kitchen talking about her son and the boy's interest in baseball. She'd actually smiled. That smile had lifted her face from pinched and plain to attractive. An idea came to him. *The son is the key to the mother. And baseball is the key to the boy.* Lee stood up straighter. "Where's the baseball field from here, Pearl?"

"Down by the lake, near the river," she answered. "You can't miss it."

The hour passed and the lunch crowd trickled out on their way to nearby factories. Finally, Lee handed Pearl a dime. "Keep the change."

"Thanks, mister. Come in for another barley water any time."

Lee tipped his hat and walked out whistling.

※　※　※　※　※

That afternoon at Drexel Park, the breeze from the choppy waters of Lake Michigan was brisk. Lee sized up the park's wide open view of the lake from a block away. The blue, white-capped waves and the vital green of early spring were dazzling in the sun. At first glimpse, he momentarily forgot where he was and thought he was looking at the Atlantic. The Chicago lakefront sported the same tall masts of ships, but they rose above

Great Lakes shipping vessels, not China traders or whalers. And his Boston boasted no tall grain elevators standing like towers along the waterfront. But the gulls screeched overhead—just like home.

The first pitch of the baseball game had already taken place when Lee reached the field. He looked for Linc, but since school hours were still on, he saw only a few very scruffy-looking truants. While he waited for Linc to arrive, he leaned back against a sturdy elm and surveyed the Chicago White Stockings at their first exhibition game. They wore striking white cotton stockings that covered their calves up to the bottom of their spanking white knickers. Very professional.

The crack of the bat uncorked a rush of undiluted nostalgia which overcame Lee. How many impromptu baseball games had he played in the army? Days of waiting between battles and campaigns . . .

A wagon on the nearby street creaked loudly over a bump. A picture flashed from Lee's memory: a rough horse-drawn ambulance bumping over a rutted road and a steady trickle of blood spilling from inside the wagon bed onto the dust—garish scarlet on brown clay.

He shuttered his mind against the images. *I am alive and in Chicago. I have eight dollars in my pocket. It won't last very long, but I'll take care of that soon enough.*

Lee turned back to the game. The batter had reached first base. Inning followed inning. At last, Lee recognized Linc's blonde head near the front of a surging wave of schoolboys heading for the field. Lee lifted his hat and motioned to Linc. When the lad left the other boys behind and headed directly to him, Lee's heart unexpectedly warmed.

"Mr. Smith!" Linc exclaimed with a wide smile.

"Linc." Lee offered his hand, and the two shared one quick handshake. "It's the fourth inning. The White Stockings have two outs."

Linc told him, "I seen that hitter last year at a game. He always gets a run."

"The White Stockings need it. They're down by two." Standing side by side, both man and boy awaited the pitch, their attention riveted on the man at bat. It came. The bat caught the ball with a satisfying crack. Lee joined the rising crescendo of shrill, enthusiastic voices and deeper bellows urging the runner to first base. The player made it with only a second to spare. A cheer surged through the onlookers. The mood was infectious. Lee found himself grinning.

In quick succession, two more White Stockings made it off the plate. With three men on base, the contagious excitement lifted Lee's spirits. Then, as though uttered by one voice, a moan went through the crowd—the White Stockings' batter struck out.

Linc threw his hat to the ground. "Three men on base. How could he let that pitcher strike him out?" With a half-smile, Lee retrieved the hat and placed it on Linc's head.

With his hand on Linc's shoulder, Lee watched the game. In swift order, the White Stockings' pitcher struck out the first two batters, but the third opponent proved to be a challenge. As the pitcher took his time reassessing the batter, Lee idly scanned the crowd and caught sight of Jessie Wagstaff approaching. Why had she come?

A stiff black bonnet, completely without feather or orna-ment, covered her warm brown hair. Its black brim paled her rosy complexion. After six years, why did she still dress in deep mourning, totally in black with not even a touch of gray? Mourning clothes and her stiffly upright posture made her look older than the young woman Lee knew her to be.

For a fraction of a second Lee envisioned the face and form of the girl his father had recently chosen for him to marry. She was a confection of creamy white skin, rosy lips, fluffy blonde hair—and even fluffier ideas. To Jessie's credit, he doubted she would ever have the kind of malleability his father had desired in a daughter-in-law.

He felt Jessie's glance of recognition pierce him—like a well-aimed dart. He bowed slightly in her direction, reading disapproval in the set of her chin. He waited for her. Standing with military straightness, he prepared himself for a thorough jousting. The bat cracked. Lee's glance darted back to the play. Foul ball. As Jessie reached them, a faint fragrance of lavender wafted from her. Perhaps there was a soft, feminine woman inside the widow's armor.

Jessie stepped between Lee Smith and her son. "Lincoln, why didn't he run to base?" She kept her irritation at finding this man here with her son out of her voice. It wasn't Linc's fault. But more irritating to her was her own reaction at seeing this stranger again. His gaze on her affected her like a bold touch.

"Hello, Mother. The ball went outside the bases. See?"

"I do see." She glanced at Mr. Smith, but he said nothing. The player hit another ball that popped upward and was caught. Linc cheered as the handheld scorecards were changed. Jessie stepped behind Linc.

Lee said, "The White Stockings are back at bat now, ma'am."

She looked sideways at him, out of the seclusion of her severe bonnet. *Was it by coincidence or design that this man kept appearing today?* She felt a pinch of concern and prayed silently for wisdom. *Why had he popped up in their lives?* "You are a baseball enthusiast then?" She used her tone to make it clear she wasn't pleased to find him here with her son.

"I am."

Jessie heard a man shout, "Strike three!" When Linc groaned with disgust along with the rest of the audience, she asked, "He shouldn't have done that, son?"

Lee answered, "You must be new to the game. I thought Linc would have instructed you in baseball."

"One of my neighbor's sons began bringing him to amateur games only at the end of last summer."

"I see."

An activity across the field attracted her interest. "What is that man doing over there?" A man was nodding fast and taking greenbacks, then giving slips in return.

Lee's gaze followed hers. "He's taking bets on the game."

She frowned at him. "I didn't realize that men gambled on the games."

"There will always be gambling, Mrs. Wagstaff," Lee pointed out. "I've seen men bet on how many fleas another soldier could pull from his shirt to the count of thirty."

She stared at him for several moments, then relaxed her stance slightly. "A point well made. Do you gamble?"

"Not recently."

She nodded once, disposing of the topic. Trying to ignore the man beside her, she watched the game without further comment for about fifteen minutes. Then she bent her head as she read the face of her pendant watch. "Linc, I must be getting home."

"Yes, Mother."

Jessie smiled to herself at her son's complete attention on the game, but remembering the stranger made her add, "Come straight home, son."

"Yes, Mother."

"Supper will be at six as usual."

"Yes, Mother."

"Make sure you come in quietly so Miss Wright won't scold you."

"Yes, Mother."

Even in the midst of her concern about this stranger, she swallowed her amusement at her son's sanguine personality. He was so like his father. Nothing spoiled his enjoyment of life. She turned to face Lee. "I will bid you good day." She emphasized her words, making "good day" mean "depart forever."

"Good day to you, Mrs. Wagstaff." He bowed slightly and rested his hand on Linc's shoulder. The boy looked up with a grin at him. Jessie walked away, frowning.

✹ ✹ ✹ ✹ ✹

"*He* was at the game!" Jessie let the kitchen door slam behind her.

"That man?" Standing in front of the stove, Susan turned to face her.

"Yes, *that man.*" Jessie whipped off her bonnet and jerked it down onto the hook on the wall.

"What he doin' there? He with Lincoln?"

"Yes." Impatiently Jessie tugged open her wrist buttons, folded up her sleeves, then reached for her apron. "I don't like it. He shows up this morning sitting on our porch at a time that no man should be anywhere but in bed."

"I'm agreein' with you." Susan began turning the potato slices sizzling in the hot fat.

"I mean, who is he?"

"And is he really a *Mistah Smith*?"

"Exactly. And why did he pick our door?"

"'Xactly."

Jessie set a large gray stoneware bowl onto the table by the window. She reached into it with both hands and lifted a thick clutch of dandelion greens out of the cleansing salt water and laid them on a fresh white towel beside the bowl. Picking up a paring knife, she began to slice off the tough ends of the greens. Suddenly she wished instead she could be kneading a large bowl of bread dough and punching it down—punching, pushing, and rolling the dough to suit herself.

Her own reactions nettled her. How could she have felt a flush of giddiness at the sight of Mr. Smith? That man had flustered her twice in one day!

Susan's words sliced through Jessie's thoughts. "You keep usin' the knife that way and you gonna cut a finger into the greens."

Jessie sighed. She stilled her hands and slowly rolled her neck to loosen her muscles. "Seeing him there got my goat. I didn't want to leave Linc with him, but I couldn't bear to make him come home before the end of the game."

"He been countin' the days till that game."

Jessie consciously relaxed her shoulder muscles and began to make the salad. "I suppose Linc will be safe enough in the crowd and he'll be home well before dark."

"God will take care of him."

"I know."

Susan shook her finger as though scolding a child. "But if dat man comes 'round here one more time—"

"I'll send him off with a bee in his ear!"

Jessie and Susan chuckled. Then amid the arrival of the two schoolteachers, Jessie lost herself in the flurry of preparing supper. When Jessie left the kitchen with the kettle of warm water to fill the washbasins in the boarders' rooms, she was surprised to find Mrs. Bolt waiting in the foyer.

"I'll take that up, Mrs. Wagstaff." Mrs. Bolt tittered. With a grin of anticipation on her face, the redhead hurried toward the stairs. Jessie cast a questioning glance at Miss Greenleigh, who had just come in the front door.

Miss Greenleigh, stylishly dressed as always, carefully pulled off tan kid gloves. "I believe she saw someone on our way home and is expecting company for dinner," the pretty blonde announced cryptically. Loosing the lavender ribbons on her fashionable bonnet, she went to join Miss Wright for their usual after-school chat in the parlor.

Jessie paused, then turned back to the kitchen. She never knew what Mrs. Bolt might do next. *And I don't have time to wonder now.*

Soon she was crumbling bacon onto her dandelion salad. Linc burst through the back door. "We won! We won!"

Jessie turned to applaud the White Stockings' triumph. Her hands froze in midair.

"Good evening, Mrs. Wagstaff, Susan."

Jessie stared in disbelief. The last man on earth she wanted in her kitchen was standing there with a "cat-in-the-cream" grin on his face.

Mr. Smith removed his hat and bowed to them. Jessie's hands itched to strangle him.

CHAPTER 3

"Mr. Smith!" Mrs. Bolt swished through the curtain. "I thought I heard your voice."

Seeing the coy redhead deigning to enter the kitchen for the very first time since she came to live at the boardinghouse robbed Jessie of speech.

"Mother, I brought Mr. Smith home for supper," Lincoln said from the washbasin where he was scrubbing his hands and face with the bar of her homemade, yellow soap.

"Lincoln—"

"How thoughtful," Mrs. Bolt gushed. "Lincoln's such a dear boy. Here, Mrs. Wagstaff, I'll carry that bowl to the table and show Mr. Smith where to hang his hat." As though helping in the kitchen were an everyday occurrence, the schoolteacher picked up the bowl of pungent salad and led the grinning man through the curtain.

Jessie's mouth formed a perfect O.

"All done, Mother," Linc announced proudly, holding up his clean hands.

Jessie turned a stern face to her son while his innocent eyes gazed up at her.

"Lincoln, why did you bring Mr. Smith home with you?"

"You said I could bring a friend home for dinner if his mother gave her permission. Mr. Smith is my newest friend, but he's too old to ask his mother. Mother, he knows *everything* about baseball!"

What could she say to that? Jessie pursed her lips. "We will talk later, Lincoln. Go in and take your seat." The boy nodded happily and hurried out. Fuming, Jessie marched to the back door, whipped off her apron and flung it on a nail, tugged down her sleeves, and buttoned the cuffs with two quick twists.

It had been bad enough to have Mr. Smith return to her kitchen like the proverbial bad penny, but he had caught her with her face flushed from the heat of the stove and her clothing disheveled. Taking a deep breath, she patted her hair back into place, then pressed a wet cloth from the washbasin against her flaming cheeks.

At last, she looked up and whispered heatedly to Susan, "He better enjoy supper. It'll be his last meal at my table!"

"Amen to dat."

Grimly resolute, Jessie headed to the dining room. Susan, carrying a tray of fried potatoes and pork chops, brought up the rear.

Greeting all of her boarders and Mr. Smith with a curt nod, Jessie sat down at the head of the table. After grace, Susan moved the steaming dishes from the dark, ornately carved sideboard to the table.

"Oh, dandelions! So early!" Miss Greenleigh smiled prettily as she scooped some onto her plate.

"Yes, they are especially tender this spring." Jessie eyed the unwelcome man, wedged in beside the Widow Bolt, at her table.

CHAPTER 3

"Dandelions," Linc echoed, quiet dismay evident in his voice.

When the bowl came to Lee, he spooned a modest helping onto his plate, but only a dab onto Linc's. "Be brave," he murmured. "This too will pass."

"You're so good with children, Mr. Smith," Mrs. Bolt cooed.

Jessie frowned at the woman.

"Don't talk twaddle." Miss Wright glowered at the widow and the man. Mrs. Bolt flushed an alarming red.

For once Jessie silently agreed with the old spinster.

Miss Greenleigh asked soothingly, "Were you successful in finding a position today, Mr. Smith?"

"I'm afraid not."

"I'm sure—," Mrs. Bolt began.

Miss Wright snorted in disgust. "Any fool can find a job in Chicago."

"I hope to prove you correct," Mr. Smith said.

The man's smooth flippancy set Jessie's teeth on edge. While Mrs. Bolt scowled at Miss Wright, Jessie observed Miss Greenleigh swallow a chuckle. If it weren't this particular man, she might find this exchange amusing also, but she didn't feel up to it now. Her fatigue was catching up with her.

Stifling a weary sigh, Jessie lay the back of her hand to her forehead. The light from the oil lamp over the dining table hurt her eyes, and the odor of the kerosene bothered her much more than was usual. Just as the long night before it, the day had gone on and on—picking dandelions from several yards; planting early lettuce, onions, and radishes; doing the marketing.

As she accepted the platter of pork chops from Miss Greenleigh, Jessie's hands trembled slightly. She tried to pass the platter on to Susan without taking a helping. Susan crossed her arms over her breast. Only when Jessie slid the smallest remaining chop onto her plate did Susan accept the platter, curtsey, then disappear through the muslin curtain. Jessie stared down at the food on her plate. A wave of vertigo made it impossible for her to begin eating.

"Mrs. Wagstaff, are you well?" Miss Greenleigh's soft voice roused Jessie.

"I'm just—"

Miss Wright thumped her cane on the floor making Jessie's nerves jump. "She's exhausted from staying up all hours."

"How was your day at school, Mrs. Bolt?" Lee asked smoothly.

Jessie was grateful for his unexpected intervention. All the starch had gone out of her.

"The children are busy memorizing the latitudes and longitudes of the capital cities of the world."

Mrs. Bolt's self-satisfied voice grated on Jessie's taut nerves.

"How interesting." Lee looked at Linc.

"What good will that do them as adults?" Miss Wright demanded.

Jessie took a small bite of pork and tried to chew it. *Why couldn't everyone just be still and eat?*

"Every adult should know the location of major world cities!" Mrs. Bolt retorted.

Miss Wright impaled the redhead with her gaze and hissed, "You're not teaching them geographic locations, you ninny. You're just teaching them meaningless numbers by rote."

Red stained Mrs. Bolt's cheeks again.

"I'm certain the principal and parents approve," Lee said.

Jessie stopped trying to eat and stood up. "I'll be right back." She stumbled through the kitchen curtain. Her right temple pounded and she felt nauseated.

By dim lamplight, Susan sat at the kitchen window having her supper. She looked up at Jessie's entrance. "You don't look good." Rising, she hustled into the pantry. "I gonna make you a cup of that chamomile tea your mother-in-law always made."

While Susan bustled around the stove, Jessie sank into the chair and rested her head on the nest of her folded arms.

She heard Susan pour the hissing water into the teapot, then leave to carry another pot of coffee into the dining room to freshen everyone's cup.

Sitting in Margaret's kitchen, Jessie recalled her mother-in-law standing beside her, showing her the different herbs and explaining each one's healing properties. *Jessie, dear, God has given us the cures for most illness, but never forget the best medicines are love and prayer.* Then she felt Margaret's gentle touch on her cheek.

Muted voices from the other room floated to Jessie until Susan returned and quickly poured the tea. Jessie sipped the heavily honeyed cup of chamomile. Gradually, the muscles in her neck loosened and she sighed. "Thank you, Susan. What would I do without you, my friend?"

Susan patted Jessie's hand. "What would I be doin' without you?"

Jessie squeezed Susan's hand in response.

"Mother?" Linc peeped into the kitchen between the folds of the plain, muslin curtain. "Are you all right?"

"I'll be in again soon, Linc." Jessie stood up, and her son left the doorway. "I have to go back, Susan."

"I'll be in soon with pie. Maybe that'll shut 'em up."

Jessie gave a half-smile, but shook her head at Susan's saucy words. She straightened her shoulders and smoothed the stray tendrils of hair off her forehead and neck. A rapping on the back door halted her.

"I'll get it." Susan passed her and opened the door. Ben with Ruth stood in the doorway.

Ruth, who held their son in a blue blanket, rushed past Susan. "You have to help us, Mrs. Wagstaff!"

Jessie flew to Ruth's side and lifted the baby from her arms. "He's burning up again. Susan, turn up the lamp."

Susan turned up the flame in the oil lamp hanging over the table, casting a golden circle of light. Jessie lay the child on the table and stripped away the ragged blanket. By the light she saw what she dreaded—dull eyes sunken in a tiny, drawn, emotionless face. Dismay squeezed her, nearly making her gasp. "Ruth! Wasn't he able to nurse today?"

Ruth pressed her folded hands to her mouth.

Ben, who stood behind his wife, shook his head. "Ruth's lost her milk completely."

Jessie looked up, the terrible truth streaking through her like iced lightning. "Oh, no, I warned you. You promised me! At only nine months, he's not old enough to be given cow's milk."

Ruth trembled visibly. "We didn't have anything else!"

"I brought it home at lunch." Ben pulled his wife close and put his arm around her shoulders. "It was fresh and sweet. We warmed it. What else could we do? Let him starve?"

"What is all this?" Miss Wright demanded as she struggled to walk into the kitchen.

Jessie stiffened. "Miss Wright, there's no need for you—"

"You people are going to be the death of this woman." She gestured toward Jessie. "She can't work all day and take care of you all night—"

With both hands outstretched like a mother hen gathering her chicks with her wings, Jessie crossed the room to intercept the old woman. "There's no need for you to trouble yourself."

Miss Wright resisted her. "If Margaret were still alive, she would put a stop—"

The mention of Will's late mother intensified Jessie's resistance. How could Miss Wright twist memories of Margaret to suit her needs? Her mother-in-law would never have turned anyone who needed help from her door. How Jessie longed to throw this into the old woman's face.

But Margaret had loved this woman. So, instead of shouting, Jessie gritted her teeth. "Miss Wright, this doesn't concern you." She placed her hand under the old woman's elbow to urge her out of the room.

Miss Wright pulled away from Jessie's grasp and glared at her. "I'm not a child. I don't need to be led around like one. I see the toll this nursing is taking on you. What if you contract an illness and are carried away before your time? Who will be left to raise your son?"

Jessie froze. Her heart stilled.

"Do you want to leave your son an orphan? That's what will happen. Do you want your son in an orphanage? Your stepfather would never let your mother take Lincoln in."

"Mrs. Wagstaff!" Susan called out.

Jessie swung back to the table. The baby began gagging violently. Jessie scooped him up. "Convulsions!"

Ruth moaned and dropped to her knees.

"It's the fever." Jessie held the baby close and tried to think. The baby was dangerously near death. This thought almost paralyzed her. *God, help me. They're counting on me. But what can I do?*

An overwhelming urge to go for aid came over her. "I need help."

"Just tell us what to do!" Susan took hold of Jessie's arm.

"This baby needs a doctor," Miss Wright snapped.

Ben shouted in an agonized tone, "No doctor I know will take colored folk."

"Take the child to the charity hospital on Kinzie," Miss Wright urged. "It's less than a mile away."

"Yes, we'll go," Jessie said. "Ruth, get my hat and cape." Without waiting, Jessie hurried out the back door with the quivering child in her arms.

"Jessie!" Miss Wright called after her. "You can't keep on doing this! Come back here!"

Through the deep twilight, Jessie rushed heedlessly around the house and out onto the wooden sidewalk. Ben and Ruth ran after her.

Jessie didn't stop until she burst through the double doors at the old hospital. Her heart pounded from running. As she stepped across the threshold, the child in her arms went limp. She sprinted forward. "Help me—please!"

A matron stood up from her place by an old, scarred table with a feeble lamp on it. "Your servants will have to leave, ma'am."

"What?" Catching her breath, Jessie looked at the woman without comprehension. "I need a doctor. This baby's had convulsions, high fever—"

The matron peered into the blanket. "This baby's black!"

"Is there a doctor here? I need a doctor." Jessie pushed past the woman.

"Ma'am, come back here!" The matron caught up with Jessie and seized her arm. "Stop!"

Still trembling from running, Jessie wrenched away. "I need a doctor! I don't know who you are, but I'm not leaving until I see a doctor."

The two women stared at each other for a moment. The matron swelled with indignation. "If these people don't leave now, I will summon the police."

Jessie stood taller. "Go right ahead and call the police. If you send this sick child away and he dies, you'll be liable for murder."

The matron turned an ugly red and began to sputter.

"What is the problem?" a cool voice asked. An imposing man in a long, black frock coat stepped out of the shadows.

Surprised, Jessie walked swiftly toward him. "Are you a doctor? Help me, can you help me—please? This baby's dying!" She held the child out toward him.

The man briefly stared into her face, then bowed slightly. "I am Dr. Gooden."

At Jessie's elbow, the matron burst out angrily, "These people can't stay here! Colored aren't allowed in this hospital."

The doctor spoke to Jessie, "The parents must wait outside. I think no one will object to the baby, but . . ."

Jessie pivoted. "Ruth and Ben, wait outside. I'll see that everything possible is done."

Ben drew Ruth close and tugged her toward the door, obviously against her will. The sight nearly broke Jessie's heart, but the baby's life was all that mattered now.

The doctor touched Jessie's sleeve. "Come."

Jessie hurried beside the doctor down the dimly lit passage, leaving the blustering matron behind.

"What is your name, please?"

"Mrs. Wagstaff, Jessie Wagstaff." She sped up to keep up with his long stride.

"Tell me the condition of the child; what do you know?"

"He's just a baby, not a year yet."

"He has been sick how long?" His voice intrigued her. It held the barest hint of an accent.

"He began to be feverish at night over a week ago."

"Diarrhea?"

"Yes," Jessie said as she trotted after him down another corridor. She turned the corner sharply, still keeping up with the doctor.

"The mother stopped nursing; isn't that it?"

"Yes, I warned them not to use cow's milk with a baby this young—"

"It is most likely milk fever, that you know. A mother loses her milk in the warmer part of the year before a child is a year old or more, so she gives the child cow's milk . . ." He lifted his hands in a gesture that said, "What can be done?"

"I know. I know," she said desperately.

The baby jerked in her arms and began gagging again. Dread filled Jessie. "He's started again!" *Oh God, help us! I don't know what to do!*

The doctor sprinted the last few feet into a small examining room. Jessie ran to keep up with him. He paused just long enough to turn up the gas lamp on the wall. "Lay the child on the table." He hurried to a bowl and laver in the corner and washed his hands.

Within seconds he was with her again, turning the child to its side. He probed the quivering child with deft fingers, checking the pulse, fever, and listening to the heart with his stethoscope.

"Isn't there anything we can do?" Jessie twisted her hands together.

"Will you act as my nurse?"

"I'm not trained."

"It does not matter. The male night nurses here will not help with a black child."

"I'll do whatever you tell me to." *Father God, bless this doctor. Save this child. How can I tell Ruth her baby's gone?*

"We start with an alcohol bath."

Soon Jessie was sponging down the naked baby with the cool, pungent alcohol. The child went limp again, but it was his appearance that terrified her. His little jaw hung slack, and under his dark skin, an ashen undertone was seen, even in the low light. "I feel so helpless," Jessie whispered.

"I know."

At the touch of empathy in his voice, Jessie finally looked at the man who stood across from her in the dimly lit, sparsely furnished room. He was tall, as tall as her late husband, Will. He was blonde with blue eyes, like Will, only much darker blue. A surge of loneliness tightened around her heart like a tourniquet. *If only Will had been spared.* She mercilessly pushed down the familiar vacant feeling.

"This maddens me." The doctor raked his hands through his hair, then leaned over the table studying the child. "He could go into convulsions again and again."

The stark words of desperation sent a chill through Jessie. "Isn't there anything else we can do?"

"I ask myself over and over—why does this happen? What is the cause? What is the cure?"

He stepped away from her, moving swiftly around the room gathering items, then brought a tray to the table. "Both of us believe this child has been exposed to something in the cow's milk. That something caused this high fever and diarrhea. But what is it? To prevent or treat it, I don't know how."

In spite of the dire situation, for just a moment, Jessie was thrilled to have him speak to her as though she were an equal. Before this, only Will had believed in her intelligence.

The doctor went on, speaking forcefully as though he thought his words could subdue the child's disease, "What is in cow's milk that is not in mother's milk? Older children drink cow's milk without bad effect—why? I need to know the answers!"

She looked at him wonder struck. "I've felt that way myself."

"I thought so." His gaze connected with hers, then dropped back to the baby.

Jessie eyed the items he had arranged on the spotless tray: a very thin, glass tube several inches long, a small tin funnel, and a pint bottle of clear liquid. "What are you going to try?"

"Two ways liquid has to enter the body, through the mouth and the anus. I have tried this before. Introducing a mild salicin—"

"Salicin?"

"A powder from willow bark dissolved in boiled water. It could lower the fever."

"What do you want me to do?" *God, help this doctor. Help me do what is right.*

"Move the bathing things away. Elevate the child's bottom. I will do the rest."

Jessie obeyed, drawing strength from the doctor's firm voice. His voice intrigued her. She watched him handle the simple instruments with precise confidence.

Painstakingly, the doctor dribbled water through the funnel into the tube, then into the baby. Minutes crawled by. The water trickled silently down the clear tube.

Nearly mesmerized as she watched, Jessie supported the baby with her left arm, holding his bottom at a sharp upward angle. Finally, the small bottle of water was empty. "He hasn't gone into convulsions again. Maybe it's working." *Please, Lord, let it be so.*

"I promise you nothing. I could be doing exactly the thing that is wrong."

His honest words shocked her. She had never heard a doctor admit to not knowing something. He offered her no comfort, but she felt an easing of tension. At least they'd tried something. She watched the small chest taking in and letting out tiny breaths. *Keep breathing, Little Ben. Keep breathing. Don't give up.*

"I must make rounds. If you need me, just step into the corridor and call."

"Yes, Doctor." Jessie lifted her eyes briefly, then focused again on the infant in her arms. The doctor's footsteps faded down the hallway.

Jessie remained bent over the table, leaning against it for support. Each moment the child drew an even breath felt like a blessing. The night minutes ticked away, measured by the ponderous clock in the hall. Her vigil stretched on.

※　※　※　※　※

"Mrs. Wagstaff, feel his brow."

Jessie roused herself. "I must have been dozing."

"While you stand?"

Jessie nodded as she touched the baby's forehead. "He seems cooler."

Dr. Gooden came to stand across from her. "It's after dawn; did you know?"

Jessie noted that the infant's eyes had lost their unfocused look. Little Ben looked up at her. "That isn't important. He is cooler, isn't he?"

"*Ja,* he survived the night."

Though her head weighed heavily on her neck, Jessie finally looked up. "Will he live?"

"I don't know. He survived the night. Neither of us thought
he would."

"But will he live?"

"God only knows that."

Jessie sighed and pressed her fingers to her burning eyes.
"Thank you, Doctor."

"I did so little. I cannot really take credit."

"At least, you didn't turn me away." She opened her eyes and
looked at him steadily.

He grinned. "My mother taught me never to contradict a
lady."

Jessie smiled, but shook her head at his modest humor.
Ignoring a dull ache behind her eyes, she carefully wrapped the
sleeping child into his blanket. "I must take him out to his parents."

"Tell the mother to give him nothing but water boiled with
rice. Rice is an old remedy for diarrhea. If she gives him anything else, he won't survive. In about two days, she can give him
a little of the rice also."

"I'll tell her. Thank——"

"Do not bid me good day. Would your husband mind if I
drive you home?"

Startled, Jessie looked to his face again. "I'm a widow, but
that's not necessary."

"It is. I need not be a doctor to diagnose that you suffer
from exhaustion."

"I'll manage. I . . ." Jessie suddenly felt limp. "I need to sit
down."

Dr. Gooden hurried and assisted her to a chair. "Let me have
the child. I'll take him to his parents, then I'll bring my gig."

Jessie felt numb. She couldn't even speak. From that point
on she was aware of voices, of fresh air on her face as she was

being lead by the arm, and of the clipclop of the horse's hooves on wooden streets.

"Mrs. Wagstaff?"

Jessie sat up straight on the gig seat. The sun struggled against the morning mist. "Where am I?" Her mind felt like a roll of cotton batting.

"I hope at your front door."

Jessie looked around her, surprised to find herself at home.

"Ben told me it is the white house with green shutters on Pine Street near the corner of Ontario."

"Yes, this is it." She turned to him. "I can't thank you enough, Doctor."

"My pleasure, Mrs. Wagstaff." He helped her down and stood in front of her. "I'll walk you to your door."

Ever mindful of the spying neighbors, she shook her head. "Thank you. I'll be fine. Good day." She tried to step away.

Dr. Gooden reached for her. "Good day to you." He bowed over her hand.

Bemused by his escorting her home, Jessie walked up to the house and followed the sidewalk toward the back door.

Dr. Gooden watched the diminutive widow walk away, but in his mind he pictured her entering an ornate drawing room. She would wear amber silk with cream-colored lace, a great deal of creamy lace at her throat.

She would sweep in and charm all the gentlemen with her attractiveness and her sensible conversation. No society matron would be able to wither her with a superior glance. A woman who could threaten the crochety old matron at the charity hospital with a charge of murder could stand up to anyone.

This woman had starch, yes—but also a heart for the sick. And a level head. She hadn't fainted when he discussed body parts and treatment. She'd done her part without any vapors or airs.

CHAPTER 3

He'd been looking for a woman like her for a long time. And she'd come into his life now, just when he needed her.

CHAPTER 4

April 10, 1871   "JESSIE, I BEEN SO WORRIED!" Susan hurried down the back steps.

"Little Ben is all right. He made it through the night!" Jessie shivered slightly in the spring-damp air.

"I've been praying all night."

"Your prayers were granted." Jessie's fatigue weighed her down like dragging an invisible load of rock. Trying to gather her heavy skirt to climb the steps, she half-stumbled.

Susan caught her by the arm.

Jessie sagged against Susan gratefully. "I need sleep. Will you help me upstairs to bed?"

"I'm helpin' you right to da kitchen table."

"I'm too tired to eat."

"You are eatin', then sleepin'. That's final." Susan tugged her along, nearly carrying her to the long kitchen table, then nudged her into the hard wooden chair by the window.

"I'll fall asleep before——"

"It don't take long to scramble up some eggs! Here's coffee." Susan pushed a cup into Jessie's hand. "Now drink that. No arguin', hear?"

Jessie sighed. The cup warmed her hands and its aroma lifted her spirits slightly. "I'm not very hungry, really."

"You ain't had an appetite for months now. You gotta eat to live. So I'm cookin' and you're eatin'."

"You certainly will eat!" Miss Wright stumped into the kitchen. "You didn't take two bites of your meal last night!"

Setting down the cup, Jessie leaned her head into her palm. *Oh, no.* She couldn't face another tirade.

"The child?" Miss Wright asked with a scowl.

Jessie looked at the old woman, but speaking up to defend her actions for Little Ben would cost her too much energy.

"Ruthie's child made it through the night, ma'am," Susan said over her shoulder.

"Well, that's good," Miss Wright muttered. "But you can't go on like this, Jessie. As I said last night——"

Taking a deep breath, Jessie looked straight into Miss Wright's pointed finger. "You were right. I couldn't have saved that baby on my own." Jessie glanced up as Susan put a plate of eggs and toast, fragrant with butter, in front of her. "I need to find a doctor to help your people, Susan."

"I'm glad you are finally listening to good sense," Miss Wright grumbled. "Now you eat every bite of that."

Jessie glimpsed Susan's half-grin before her friend went back to the sink where she started doing dishes quietly. Jessie began taking small bites. Why did chewing take so much energy? *I'll never eat all this.*

"The charity hospital took the child in then?" Miss Wright prompted.

"The matron didn't want to, but I wouldn't leave. And then a doctor came out of the shadows and he . . ." Jessie's voice faltered. She tried to chew more, but her jaw went numb.

"Are you sick?" Miss Wright touched Jessie's hand.

Jessie shook her head and forced herself to take another bite. *I have to eat.* Her eyelids drooped and felt heavy. She batted them open again.

"Susan, does she look pale to you?" the old woman asked.

"Ma'am, maybe she just too tired to talk now," Susan suggested gently.

Nodding, Jessie sighed with relief and continued chewing laboriously.

"Well, it's about time you eat. Go ahead. Eat." Looking like a watchdog who would make sure Jessie ate every bite, Miss Wright folded her hands on the top of her cane.

Jessie heard a polite tap at the back door, but she was too tired to care. Susan wiped her hands on her red apron and went to the door. "Mr. Smith is here, Mrs. Wagstaff."

The man walked in.

Miss Wright sat up straighter. "What are you doing here?"

Jessie wearily smiled around another mouthful of egg. For once, she was grateful for Miss Wright's outspoken ways. *What is this man doing here this morning?* She felt defenseless. She didn't have the strength to deal with his worrying effect on her.

He paused a few steps into the kitchen. "Oh, Mrs. Wagstaff, you're home! I was concerned about you."

"Yes." Her eyes blurred a little. She blinked to bring him back into focus.

"Did Mrs. Bolt get you that room, Mr. Smith?" Susan glanced from her place at the sink.

"Yes, I'm rooming with Mrs. Crawford over on Ontario Street."

"She has my sympathy," Miss Wright snapped. "I suppose that means you'll be underfoot day and night."

Aware of a floating sensation, Jessie felt as though she had taken a step away from the kitchen.

Lee bowed to the spinster. "Thank you for being concerned about a lonely newcomer, Miss Wright."

"Humph!" the old woman fumed.

Jessie looked down and watched the fork slide from her fingers as though her hand belonged to someone else.

"Shouldn't you be out finding a job, Mr. Smith?" Miss Wright demanded. "Or didn't Mrs. Crawford feed you enough breakfast?"

The old biddy reminded Lee of Great Aunt Hester more and more. He opened his mouth to answer back, but he suddenly caught sight of Jessie as she dropped her fork. *"She's fainted!"* he shouted.

"Catch her!" Susan exclaimed.

Lee rushed to rescue Jessie's unconscious form that was slipping from her chair. As he caught her limp body, the elusive fragrance of lavender still clung to her and a curious sensation slid through him at her nearness.

Miss Wright thumped her cane on the floor. "What's wrong?"

Lee quickly took Jessie's faint pulse. "Did she get any sleep last night?"

Miss Wright leaned forward anxiously. "She returned home only minutes ago. It's just fatigue, isn't it? She could have caught some contagion at that hospital."

Lee scanned Jessie's pale face. "Her heartbeat is slow, but that would be expected with a case of exhaustion." He swung Jessie up into his arms. The incredible lightness of her body surprised him. With her full skirts and stiff posture, she'd appeared more substantial. But maybe it was only that he was more accustomed to the weight of men on stretchers, not a woman.

"Is she gonna be all right?" Susan wrung her hands. "I can't recall her ever faintin' before—not ever."

"Why are you asking him?" Miss Wright blustered. "He's no doctor."

Lee smiled. "Even if I'm no doctor, I can tell whether a woman is feverish or not. Mrs. Wagstaff is not." He turned to Susan. "I'll carry her to bed."

Susan pointed toward the other end of the kitchen. "Please, just bring her to my bed. It just through here. I wanna be able to hear her if she need me."

Lee let the young black woman lead him through the pantry to her tiny room off the kitchen. Glancing at Jessie's face, so relaxed and soft in repose, Lee waited while Susan turned back the blankets, then he lay Jessie down gently and stepped back. Susan stepped around him and began unhooking Jessie's shoe buttons.

Unexpectedly, Lee felt himself moved by the stark contrast of Jessie's slight form, dressed all in black against the white sheets. She looked crumpled and frayed, like an autumn leaf after the long winter.

He had a sudden urge to gather her into his arms. With his cheek against hers, he would whisper that he would take care of everything, that she wasn't to worry anymore.

A gnarled finger poked him in the back. "Stop gawking, Mr. Smith. It's time you left. Go out and find that job you need. Mrs. Crawford doesn't need a charity case on her hands."

Lee pulled himself together and bit back a retort. *This crone could make a preacher swear. And I'm no preacher.* "I'll bid you good day then." He turned toward the back door through the pantry.

Susan's voice followed him. "Thank you, Mr. Smith!"

"My pleasure, Susan." Outside, he strode away, letting the cool morning breeze clear his head. *If Jessie Wagstaff wanted to stay up all night nursing sick, probably thankless people, it was her business, not his.*

He walked briskly toward town. A good night's rest in a pleasant, but reasonably priced room at Mrs. Crawford's plus a delicious breakfast had given him new hope he would find work today. He didn't want a job, but he needed one—after all the years without one . . .

Thoughts of Jessie intruded, however. *That fool woman. Up all night!* He shook his head. Jessie Wagstaff was obviously an inveterate do-gooder. He blocked these thoughts from his mind. *Like it or not—I'm going to find a job today. I'll stop at the first Help Wanted sign.*

That first sign came quicker than he had expected. A warehouse on Lake Street sported a notice in its dusty window—"Bookkeeper Wanted." Lee stepped inside before he could talk himself out of doing so. He hailed a workman, "Who do I talk to about the bookkeeping position?"

A voice came through an open door. "You talk to me."

Lee stepped inside the door. "Sir?"

The man motioned him closer. "How long have you worked as a bookkeeper?"

Lee stepped to the desk and held out his hand. "Lee Smith, at your service, sir."

The man stood up and shook Lee's hand, repeating, "How long have you worked as a bookkeeper?"

This is how they do business in Chicago? So abrupt? "I have no formal experience, but I am very good with figures."

"Sorry, I need an experienced bookkeeper. This is the beginning of our shipping season. If I could afford two bookkeepers, I'd take you on as assistant and the main one could train you. Sorry." The man sat back down and immediately began leafing through papers.

Out of ingrained courtesy, Lee bowed and left.

Outside, the morning was still very young, but Lee felt his confidence slip a notch. *Well, that's strike one, but I'm not out yet.*

By the end of the morning, he had been turned down for three more jobs. He had more than struck out. His budding confidence withered.

CHAPTER 4

He needed to find someplace familiar, soothing. Soon, inhaling the scent of ale, he pushed through the swinging doors at Pearl's.

"Hey, the suit's back!" a familiar-looking workman shouted.

Within minutes Pearl had poured Lee his barley water, and he was spinning an action-packed account of yesterday's baseball game for the workmen who crowded around him. Two men tried to buy him beers, but he waved them away with his glass of barley water.

All too soon the workmen went back to their jobs and left Lee alone at the bar with Pearl.

"Why the long face?" She swabbed the bar with a large white washcloth.

Lee looked up. Behind the bar, she paused in front of him. The edge of genuine concern in her voice loosened his tongue. "I'm new in town and looking for a job."

She looked him over for a long minute. "Ever tend bar?"

Lee shook his head.

"Want to?"

"Here? You mean work *here*?"

"Yes, here." She stared at him as though daring him to insult her offer.

Caught between competing tides of relief, caution, and shame, Lee's thoughts raced. Wouldn't a saloon be the worst place for him to work? "I don't know . . . what to say. I've never worked as a bartender."

Her tone softened. "It ain't hard."

Lee clenched his jaw. He was surprised at the depth of his embarrassment. *Bartender.* Of all the jobs he had pictured himself taking up, the trade of bartending had never occurred to him.

"It pays only four dollars a week for six days' work. Eight A.M. to seven P.M. Not much to raise a family on."

"I'm single."

She nodded. "Too good to tend bar?"

"No, I just—"

"I noticed you stuck to barley water. I can't have a souse working behind the bar, especially during the day. That's when I need to be taking care of things at home. If you've got a problem with drink, tell me now."

Lee imagined the Widow Wagstaff's reaction to his telling her that he was a bartender at the Workman's Rest. Everyone knew Chicago was prominent in the budding temperance movement. If she found out, it would raise another wall between them. Then again, since he would not be living under her roof, she need never know where he worked.

"Well?"

He recalled the rejections of the morning. If he turned down Pearl, he would be forced out onto those lonely streets to begin again. "We could try it and see how it works out for both of us."

"Can't say fairer than that. Remember, I don't allow my barkeeps to drink while working their shift. If someone wants to buy you a drink, just toss the nickel in your mug and tell them you'll drink it later. Can you abide by that?"

A silent sigh of relief vibrated through Lee. "Yes, ma'am."

"All right then." She held out her hand to him. Her handshake was firm and direct. "Come into the back and I'll show you the layout."

※ ※ ※ ※ ※

Jessie slowly came awake. For a moment, she was lost in time. But then she remembered the night before and this morning. *I must have fallen asleep at the breakfast table.* She yawned and stretched languidly. Her body still felt leaden. She gazed around the room, noting the little touches that made it Susan's room: a palm pinned to the wall from Palm Sunday service, a string of red beads on the bedside table.

Life was strange. Years ago, waking in the bed in the little room off the kitchen had been an everyday occurrence for her. *This little room was mine when I came here as a hired girl.*

In her memory, Jessie saw herself at the age of twelve, leaving home with one small valise in hand; her stepfather had marched her brusquely up to Margaret's back door, then left her there without a wave or backward look. Just the week before, she had overheard him telling her mother no girl needed more than a sixth-grade education and it was time to put Jessie out to earn her own living. He'd supported another man's child for nine years. He had done his duty.

So on that cold, dreary November day, Jessie had stood stiffly on Margaret's back step. Feeling a sinking sensation in her stomach, she had sneaked a look up at Margaret's plump and smiling face. With a gentle touch, Margaret had drawn her in and shown her to the little room. The room's new pink gingham curtains had snared Jessie's attention.

Margaret commented, "I thought you might be partial to pink." Tongue-tied, Jessie'd only nodded. After her few possessions and clothing were arranged on the small bedside table and the pegs on the wall, Margaret escorted her back to the kitchen where they spent the morning baking ginger cookies. Those sweet, spicy ginger cookies had tasted like manna from heaven, and those few hours of gentle welcome had made all the difference to Jessie. She had loved Margaret from that day on.

Three years later, on November 7, 1860, Jessie had married Will, Margaret's only son. Will, ten years older than Jessie, enlisted a year after their marriage and left his wife, his widowed mother, and, after a furlough home, his only son.

Now lying on the once familiar bed, Jessie breathed a sigh which quivered through her. *Margaret and Will made all the difference in my life. Thank you, God, again and again. I never knew laughter. I never knew freedom until I came into this house.* Will's smiling face came to her memory, sweet and teasing as always. His teasing voice said, *"Still in bed, princess?"*

Susan intruded on Jessie's daydream, "You awake den?"

Jessie looked over at her in the doorway. "I need to freshen up. What time is it?" Looking at Susan brought the frightening incidents of the night before back to mind. She'd been terrified Little Ben would die. What was she going to do the next time a colored child nearly died? *Dear God, I need to know what to do.*

"You can get up, but you ain't doin' much today. I got my eye on you."

Hiding her concern about a problem for which she had no solution, Jessie swung her stocking feet down and sat up, the bed ropes creaking under her. She spoke lightly, "How did you get so bossy?"

"Been watchin' you." Susan grinned.

This unexpected "sass" hit Jessie's funny bone, lifting her heavy spirits. She tried to pout comically, but went into giggles instead. "Oh, Susan, what would I do without you?"

April 11, 1871

Jessie sat on the back porch, watching Mr. Smith rolling up his sleeves. The man stood, facing her, with his back to the small, whitewashed shed that housed her goat and chickens. When he finished rolling up his sleeves, he patted the leather baseball glove on his hand.

"Throw it, Linc. Right into my glove," Lee urged.

Linc, with his back to his mother, wound up and threw the softball. To Jessie, it seemed a feeble imitation of what she'd seen that day of the first White Stockings game at the ballpark.

Still, Lee lunged forward and caught it. He grinned broadly at Linc. "That was a good try. Catch this." Lee moved forward a few paces. He sent the ball back in an easy toss.

"Got it!" Linc did a bouncy jig; Jessie celebrated, too, with a smile.

Though it was still early spring, she had chosen to sit outside in the last sunshine of the day and watch Linc play catch.

CHAPTER 4

With a dark shawl around her to ward off the lingering April chill, Jessie rocked in an old Windsor rocker, sipping her cup of sweet tea while she inwardly experienced a civil war of emotions over the man in her backyard.

Half of her couldn't help rejoicing. This was the very first time a man had offered to play ball with Linc. Never in her son's seven-year life had any man taken an interest in him. Linc's face had glowed with excitement when Mr. Smith arrived after supper with a baseball and a leather glove. Jessie had felt the excitement herself.

How many times in the past years had she suffered silently along with Linc as they caught sight of a father and son playing catch in a park or splashing into the waves at the beach? Since she never intended to marry again, having a man who would willingly spend time with Linc had been only an unanswered prayer, a dream—till Mr. Smith had arrived.

But the other half of her was galled at the man's intrusion into their lives. Why did it have to be this man? Lee Smith used his handsome face and glib charm entirely too much. No matter what she said to him, he always had a smooth reply. What's more, having a handsome, eligible man around would only lubricate the jaws of the neighborhood gossips. In order to be trouble-free, Mr. Smith should be near sixty and have a pronounced paunch, and even then the gossips might not ignore him.

As Jessie rocked in a steady rhythm and watched, she tried to get the better of her antipathy to this stranger who had forced his way into their lives. Though she'd warn Linc that as Mr. Smith became acquainted with more people he'd probably have less time to play catch, why shouldn't she let her son enjoy tonight? Why shouldn't she enjoy watching him experience it?

Over this joy hung the unresolved, knotty problem of Little Ben's illness. What if the next time this type of crisis occurred a child died? Jessie wasn't a doctor. All she knew was what Margaret had taught her. She felt as if a steel band circled her head, tightening a notch every time she went over this same insoluble worry.

"Mrs. Wagstaff?" Susan stepped out on the back porch. "You got a caller. I ask' him if he'd please wait for you in da parlor, but—"

"But who would sit in a parlor on a balmy spring evening like this?" A familiar male voice came from behind Susan. Dr. Gooden strode forward.

"Dr. Gooden?" Jessie nearly dropped her teacup.

"Mrs. Wagstaff, forgive me. I startled you. But I finished early this evening, and I wanted to see if you were well after staying awake all night."

"I'm fine. I took a long nap this morning. Please, won't you take a seat?" Jessie motioned to the other rocker beside her.

"Thank you. I can stay only a short time." Moving the rocker next to hers, he sat down and smiled at her.

"Would you care for some tea? The pot is still warm."

The doctor nodded, and Susan went in to get it.

"How are you, Doctor? Did you get any sleep?" Her gaze ran over him, taking in more than she had last night. He had an honest face and a firm chin. She found herself smiling at him.

"I slept this morning also. Then I go to my practice. I finished my calls just now."

"I can't thank you enough for your help last night. You saved Little Ben." Impulsively, Jessie reached for the doctor's free hand.

He gripped her hand in response, then let it go politely. "That was my reason for becoming a doctor. Too many children die and we have no inkling even of what causes the diseases. Sometimes I feel like a man stumbling in the dark."

Jessie felt his likeness to Will again. This man didn't speak in polite nothings. He spoke to her of important concerns as though she could understand them, not treating her as a mere woman who wouldn't comprehend serious matters. How well she recalled Will's long crusade for abolition. How thrilled she had been to be thought worthy to be included in his discussions and work.

"Have you seen the baby today then?" Dr. Gooden asked as he unbuttoned one button on his suit jacket and sat back comfortably.

Coming through the back door again, Susan cleared her throat and caught Jessie's attention. "Pardon me, Mrs. Wagstaff, you was nappin' dis afternoon when Caleb called."

"What did Caleb say?"

"He said Little Ben is doin' better. They bought the rice, and Little Ben is drinkin' the rice water fine."

"Good." The doctor accepted the heavy white mug filled with creamy tea.

"Susan, you should have brought out the china," Jessie said.

"No, no." The doctor took his first sip.

Susan apologized, "I thought 'bout usin' the china. But I figured a gentleman want a *full* cuppa tea."

"The girl's right." He nodded his thanks.

"Who's Caleb?" Mr. Smith's voice intruded lazily.

Jessie turned an unwelcoming glance to him, then felt a twinge of guilt. *I should be grateful to this man.*

Topping the final step, Mr. Smith repeated, "Who's Caleb?"

Jessie forced herself to answer in a perfectly polite tone. "He's the black minister's son. He often brings us messages."

"Got an eye for Susan, eh?" The man winked at Susan.

Susan suppressed a grin. "Can I get you a cuppa tea, too, Mr. Smith?"

Lee bit back a groan of dismay. *Barley water at Pearl's. Now tea at Jessie's.* He'd never thought he'd drink such pap.

"If you're not partial to tea, there's buttermilk in the icebox," Jessie offered.

Lee swallowed hard. "I'll take tea, please."

Linc had followed Lee and stood beside him. "May I have buttermilk, Susan? Please?"

Susan nodded and turned back to the kitchen.

"I'm Lee Smith." Lee held out his hand to the stranger. He hadn't liked the man on sight. For a stranger, the doctor had insinuated his chair too close to Jessie. *I'll have to keep an eye on this one.*

"Oh, I apologize," Jessie said. "Dr. Henry Gooden, Mr. Lee Smith."

Lee shook hands with the man.

"Who is this young man?" the doctor asked, looking toward Linc.

"This young fellow is Jessie's son, Linc." Lee ruffled Linc's hair. The boy smiled up at him. Glancing at Jessie, Lee saw that his implied intimacy with Linc irritated her. Although he'd done it to goad the good doctor, it had come so naturally, so easily, that he'd surprised himself. He'd never taken an interest in a child before.

"Lincoln," Jessie said, sounding very formal, "make your bow. This is the doctor who helped Little Ben last night."

Linc bowed, but stayed close to Lee.

Jessie went on, "Mr. Smith has just arrived in Chicago."

"Indeed?" The doctor sipped his tea.

Lee leaned back against the porch railing. "Indeed."

Linc leaned against the railing, mimicking Lee.

"Did you find work today, Mr. Smith?" Jessie asked.

"I did."

"Where?" the doctor asked.

"I'm clerking at one of the many offices downtown," Lee lied. "Finding a job in Chicago is not much of a challenge."

Susan came out bearing another cup and a glass of buttermilk. She handed the glass to Linc. Before Lee's eyes, Linc downed the glass in one long, noisy draught.

Lee found himself laughing out loud. "Slow down, sport. You'll get the colic drinking that fast. Won't he, Doc?"

The doctor smiled at Linc. "You have a healthy thirst, don't you, Linc?"

"Yes, sir," Linc replied politely, then he looked up at Lee. "Can we play some more now?"

"I thirst and I need my tea. Go practice your pitching form."

"What's that?" Linc demanded.

"It means practicing to throw the ball *without* the ball." Lee sipped his hot tea cautiously.

"Really?"

Lee nodded. "Really."

"Linc, it's nearly time for you to wash up for bed," Jessie said.

"Aw, Mother, *please*. I need practice. We're playing ball at recess now, and I gotta do better or I won't get picked."

"Very well, Linc, but just a little while longer."

Linc scrambled off the porch before his mother had finished her sentence. Lee took a long sip of the sweet tea. Tea wouldn't have been his first choice, but it was wet and tasted better than barley water.

"Jessie!" Miss Wright clumped out onto the porch. "That boy needs to get up to bed. The sunlight is nearly gone. Dampness is coming up out of the ground. And you need to get to bed early yourself."

Out of politeness, Lee stood up straighter, then gritted his teeth. Unpleasant memories of Great Aunt Hester came again.

Dr. Gooden also rose politely. Jessie quietly introduced him to Miss Wright.

Miss Wright's greeting to the doctor was as unwelcoming as any Lee could have hoped for. "Well! It's about time someone helped this woman. She can't go on staying out all hours nursing. She'll ruin her health."

Dr. Gooden smiled and bowed. "I must be leaving. I haven't been home yet."

Wise man, Lee said to himself. "I must go also."

The evening came to an abrupt halt. Irritated by Miss Wright's high-handedness, but too tired to argue, Jessie wished both gentlemen good night, then she and Linc started climbing the steps to their attic room. Fatigue and the headache had dogged her all day. Now her arms and legs felt as though they had been weighted down with wet sand. By the time she reached the top of the second flight of stairs, she could barely shuffle along. But her mind was busy with Miss Wright's words: *It's about time someone else helped this woman.*

Susan bustled up the stairs behind Jessie and Linc.

Jessie wanted to ask Susan what she thought of the possibility of finding a doctor who would take blacks as patients, but Linc was there. "Oh, Susan, I thought *you* were going to help Miss Wright get to bed tonight. I just don't have the strength."

"She told me to help you first. You sit while I watch dis boy wash up—"

Linc protested, "I can do it myself, Susan! I'm almost eight!"

As Jessie sat down wearily on the side of her bed and began slipping pins from her hair, Susan chuckled and swatted Linc's behind. Sunk deep in thought, Jessie fought to stay awake long enough to watch Susan monitor Linc through his getting-to-bed routine.

Jessie's tired mind still wouldn't give up the problem she faced. How could she make certain Susan's people had medical care? Just because no doctor had been found by Susan's friends yet didn't mean some kind doctor might not be persuaded. Surely she could find one. At this thought, she felt a load of worry float off her spirit.

After Linc said his prayers, she preceded Susan behind the dressing curtain where Susan undid the buttons down the back of Jessie's dress then loosed her corset laces. Jessie sighed at the sudden release, "Ah . . ."

"Jessie," Susan whispered insistently, "I want you asleep in that bed all night, you hear?"

Jessie pulled on the worn cotton gown and slid between the cold sheets of the bed she hadn't slept in for two nights. She wanted to whisper her thoughts to her friend, but she was suddenly too tired to speak.

CHAPTER 4

Susan stopped beside Jessie's bed. "Now you sleep as long as you want."

Jessie yawned. One last lucid idea flitted through her mind. *Why haven't I asked our own Dr. Miller?* Smiling, she closed her eyes.

"Your nights nursin' and then days workin' be over." Susan patted Jessie's arm and left, the door open behind her. "From now on I'm gonna take better care a you."

April 12, 1871

Jessie woke. The room was chilly and damp in the gray light just before full daybreak. A glance at her son told her that he needed to be covered better. She eased out of her warm cocoon and dragged the faded crazy quilt from the bottom of Linc's narrow bed up to his ears. Then, shivering, she slid back into her sheets.

She knew she wouldn't go back to sleep. Lying back, she reached into the drawer in the bedside table for one of her treasured letters from Will. She kept them close at hand and read them in her few private moments.

"Dear Jessie," it began. She read each line intently, trying to picture the battle scene Will was describing. Then a name caught her eye, "Another ambulance driver, Smith, joined our medical troop today. He seems a bit sly, and he had a run-in with Dr. Smith right off."

"Mother!"

"What, Linc?"

"I'm really hungry! Can Susan make pancakes and sausages for breakfast?" Linc sat on the side of his bed, rubbing sleep from his eyes.

Jessie folded the letter. Her day had begun. She gave one last thought to the fact that a man also named Smith had just come into her life. But the chances that Linc's friend, Mr. Smith, was the same Smith who had served with Will was too much of a coincidence to be considered. After all, Smith was a common name. She shook her head and slid the letters back into the drawer.

CHAPTER 5

April 12, 1871

J ESSIE, STANDING OPPOSITE HER
guest, glanced once more around the parlor with satisfaction.
Margaret's china tea service, decorated with a tiny band of hand-
painted violets around the rim of each cup and saucer, set just
the right tone.

"Thank you, Jessie." With a smile, Dr. Miller, her family's
longtime physician, accepted the thin china cup of coffee from
her.

"Thank you for stopping before starting your rounds today."
Jessie sat down across from him, comfortable in the confidence
her parlor gave her. She remembered the praise her mother-in-
law had showered upon her when Jessie had successfully
reupholstered the sofa and chairs in the sprigged rose and white
chintz. The polished oak floor shone in the morning sun. The

day was warm and she had opened the windows. The tied-back, floor-length damask rose curtains moved gently in the breeze. "It should be a lovely day—"

"It's already a lovely day."

"The lilacs will be blooming—"

"Jessie, please," Dr. Miller chided her with obvious affection. "Are you ready to tell me why you sent Linc over with a note asking me to stop by? I've known you since the day you were born, and when you get nervous, you chatter. You've talked my ear off about nothing since you opened the door for me."

She blushed and smiled. "I don't know why I'm nervous. I know that when I explain the situation, you will want to help." Despite her brave words, she quivered inside. Five years ago when she had begun to help Susan's friends, she had crossed an invisible line. The War between the States had brought about emancipation and citizenship for Negroes—but little else.

"Oh?" Dr. Miller responded questioningly.

Jessie cleared her throat. "You know Susan, don't you, Doctor?"

"I've seen her here. Yes." He took a sip of his coffee.

"When I got to know Susan's people, I found out that they have no one to provide medical care—"

"Your dear mother has told me that you have been helping them. A fine work for you. True Christian charity."

She drew herself up. "But I'm inadequate, Doctor! I try to do what I can. I use everything my late mother-in-law taught me about nursing the sick. But it's not enough! Miss Wright made me see that a few days ago. She said that I'm not what they need. They need a doctor." Surely kind Dr. Miller wouldn't turn his back on people who needed him.

Dr. Miller pressed his lips together and gently set his cup and saucer onto the small round table. "Jessie, my dear, you don't know what you're asking."

"I only want you to accept Susan's people as patients. They aren't beggars. They would pay—"

"Jessie." The tone of his voice grew steely.

She bit her lip. Quiet reigned, then she looked up at him. "They *need* a doctor."

"I cannot help them directly." He moved forward on his seat and reached for the wallet in his back pocket.

Jessie touched his arm, halting him. "Why can't you?" Her pulse leaped as she contemplated that she might fail to convince him.

He frowned. "If it becomes known that I'm treating blacks, I'll lose all my white patients. It could destroy a successful practice it has taken me thirty-five years to build. I can't risk it."

Her fingers tightened around his arm. "People will understand. Negroes are human beings too. After all, doctors volunteer to go to the mission field—"

"That's all right in foreign parts, but not in Chicago." He stood up. "You're young. You don't understand the depth of the feeling here that colored people should've stayed where they belonged."

Jessie rose to her feet. Temper flashed red-hot through her. "Do you mean Africa? Well, the slavers didn't allow them that choice!"

He let his irritation with her show on his face. "I have to get on with my round of patients." He took a five-dollar bill from his wallet and lay it beside his discarded cup. "That's to help buy medicine. Good day."

He strode out, leaving Jessie fuming in her parlor. She heard him close the front door firmly. Her face stung as though she'd been hit by the door, but it was the doctor's indifference that hurt most.

"Well, that's that," Susan said as she stalked into the room with her arms crossed over her breast.

"You heard?"

"Course."

"I'm stunned. Dr. Miller is one of the kindest men I know."

"Kind to white folks."

"I just can't believe it."

"I can."

Jessie'd known she was taking a chance. She'd never asked anyone else to cross the invisible color line and join in her work. Maybe Dr. Miller wasn't the man for such a challenge. It took a man with a larger vision. "Maybe I was meant to meet Dr. Gooden," Jessie said in a thoughtful manner.

"You think he might help my people?" Susan's doubt was clear in her tone.

"The Lord doth provide. I think I'll send Dr. Gooden an invitation to dine with us Friday evening."

Susan smiled and nodded. "I'll make an extra rhubarb pie."

"That should help." Jessie nodded with a grin. "Who can resist your pie?"

Susan came over and hugged her. "Come on. We got work to do."

April 15, 1871

Dr. Henry Gooden stood on the front porch of the Wagstaff house. The young woman of color answered his ring. He was pleased with the girl's neat, sober appearance. "It is Susan, isn't it?" Dr. Gooden handed her his hat.

"Yes, sir. Will you step into da parlor, please?" Susan showed him to a chair, then curtseyed. "I'll tell Mrs. Wagstaff you're here."

From the comfortable wingback chair, Henry examined the parlor. The room, decorated in shades of rose and white, was spotless and harmoniously arranged. The oak floor and wood-work gleamed in the lamplight. Only the oil lamp on the table, instead of gaslights on the wall, denoted the modesty of the home. Everything else spoke of a notable homemaker.

"Dr. Gooden, I'm so happy you could come." Jessie swept in, her hand outstretched to him.

CHAPTER 5

He stood, took her hand, and bent to kiss it. The scent of lavender floated from her. He smiled. He favored the scent of lavender on a woman, especially a young woman with pretty, brown eyes. "For the invitation, I thank you."

"Please, have a seat."

As he waited for her to be seated first, he gazed at her with admiration. She lowered herself delicately, then perched like a lady with her spine held straight, not touching the back. She folded her hands demurely in her lap.

"Have you had a busy day, Doctor?"

He liked the way she politely focused her attention on him. And her question was the perfect social start to a conversation. Tonight, she was dressed all in black, but this dress was obviously newer. Though simple to the point of plainness, it was cut in the latest mode with the skirt swept toward the rear in a modest bustle. Excellent style. "A day of usual cases. But I never tire of it."

"I understand."

Her two quiet words touched him. This woman did understand. He felt that. Nodding, he smiled at her.

"Are you a native of Chicago, Doctor?"

"No, I was born in Ohio." He heard halting footsteps approaching. Out of the corner of his eye, he saw the old woman he'd seen on his first visit coming through the foyer toward them.

"Who is this you're sitting with?" the old woman barked.

Deferentially, he stood up.

The old woman glared at him. "That doctor? What is he doing here again?"

"Miss Wright, do you remember Dr. Henry Gooden? I've invited him for dinner."

As he bent over the old woman's hand in the continental way, she grumbled, but Jessie's quiet, firm tone had its effect. The old woman said no more. His hostess was definitely the mistress of her home.

"Mother?" Linc scrambled into the parlor. "Dinner is served."

"Thank you, son." Jessie stood up. "Lincoln, please tell Susan we're coming right in."

Henry wanted to offer his arm to Jessie, but good manners dictated he offer it to the elderly spinster first. When she rebuffed him, he was relieved. He entered the dining room with Jessie's hand featherlight on his arm.

The dining room impressed him much as the parlor had. For a modest home, the furniture was well kept and distinctive. "The carving on your sideboard, it is beautiful."

"My late husband's father was noted for his fine wood-working."

"He was an artist." Henry seated Jessie at the head of the table and waited while she introduced him to her other two boarders. The young blonde was a treat to behold, but the red-head was mutton dressed as lamb. A widow schoolteacher, obvi-ously over thirty, should be dressed in navy, gray, or some sober hue. He had been a bit surprised to see Jessie still dressed in widow's black, but seeing Mrs. Bolt in pink ruffles made him value Jessie's discretion.

He took his seat at the foot of the table and at Jessie's request, gave the blessing. "God, thank you for this home and this meal. Amen."

"It's so nice to hear a man say grace," Mrs. Bolt enthused.

Dr. Gooden nodded to her.

"So have you family, Doctor?" Miss Wright asked tartly.

"My father has been gone more than two years. My mother lives in Cleveland with my elder brother and his wife." He paused. "This is fine stew, Mrs. Wagstaff. You're lucky to have Susan."

"My mother cooked the stew," Linc said with obvious pride.

"You are a fortunate young man. Your mother has many talents."

"Sir, what made you become a doctor?" Miss Greenleigh, the young blonde, asked him.

"When I was only eight, my sister nearly died. With the diphtheria. A doctor saved her life. After that, I became his shadow."

"You began your avocation early then?" Jessie asked.

He liked the way her voice sounded so sure, so confident. The meal went on just as he'd hoped, good food in a genteel dining room. He passed over the old woman's grumbling and the redhead's tittering and flirting. He kept his attention on the self-contained lady at the head of the table.

He ate his final bite of tart rhubarb pie with sweet whipped cream. "Delicious. Lincoln, your mother, did she make the pie also?"

"No, sir, Susan makes the pies."

Susan came through the curtain. "Mrs. Wagstaff, could Lincoln be 'scused from da table now?"

"Why?"

"Mr. Smith is here. He wanta know can Linc come out and play ball?"

Henry was pleased to see that though Linc eagerly sat up straighter, he did not bolt from the table. A very well-brought-up son. Only when Jessie nodded did the boy disappear in a flash behind Susan.

Mrs. Bolt stood up. "Dr. Gooden, perhaps you'd be interested in attending a temperance meeting with me tonight? You, too, of course, Mrs. Wagstaff."

Henry looked at the red-haired, plump woman in the unflattering ruffles and shook his head. "So sorry, ma'am. Already I am involved in much charity work. It takes up all my extra time."

"Very well." Her mouth primmed up.

"Perhaps Mr. Smith would like to accompany you," Miss Wright said piously.

"Why I hadn't thought . . . I'll ask him." Mrs. Bolt headed for the curtain and disappeared through it.

The old woman snorted.

Miss Greenleigh shook her head as she rose. "Miss Wright, that was very naughty of you. Anyway, I have time to read awhile tonight. Would you like to hear more of Dickens?"

"Aren't you going to visit that sister of yours this weekend?" Miss Wright asked with a growl.

"No, I'm relaxing this weekend."

"Well, if you haven't got anything else to do, I could stand a chapter or so." Sounding disgruntled, the old woman got up and the two of them turned toward the parlor.

Jessie smiled at Miss Greenleigh. Having the cheerful young woman in her home was a true blessing.

Making a sudden decision, Jessie rose. "I'm sorry, Doctor, but would you mind spending the evening on the back porch? I should support Linc in his efforts to master baseball. It seems to be his ruling passion these days."

"In this balmy weather, it would be a pleasure. A lovely meal, Mrs. Wagstaff."

Jessie inclined her head and smiled. Again, his trace of accent caught her ear. But he said he was born in Ohio, not Germany. But just as she'd hoped, everything about the meal seemed to have mellowed the doctor. "We're happy you enjoyed it. Why don't we go out through the front hall? I need my shawl."

At his nod, she preceded him into the foyer. When she reached for her shawl on the hall tree, his hand bumped hers. He lifted the shawl and draped it carefully around her shoulders. She stood perfectly still and felt herself blush. No man had done that for her since Will had gone to war that last time, seven years ago.

"Is that satisfactory?"

"Yes, thank you." She let him open the front door for her. When he offered her his arm, she stiffened, but accepted it without demur. She had invited this man tonight to ask him for his help, but she had overlooked the fact that he might misinterpret her intentions. Did he think she might be pursuing him? Her mouth went dry.

They walked down the steps. Mrs. Bolt hurried past them, her mouth in a grim line.

The doctor murmured to Jessie, "Mr. Smith preferred a game of catch to a temperance meeting, do you think?"

"I suppose so." Jessie led the doctor around the side of the house. As she did, she recalled racing over this same walk with Little Ben limp in her arms. Yes, she did want something from him tonight, but she smiled up at Dr. Gooden. If this man never did another favor for her, he had saved the baby's life and she would never forget that debt.

As she and the doctor approached the backyard, she saw in the twilight that Mr. Smith stood behind Linc moving the boy's arm forward, obviously demonstrating how to pitch. The sight of Linc with a man who cared about him still moved Jessie. For a second she wished she could rest her hand on Mr. Smith's arm in silent thanks.

No matter how his cocky attitude grated on her at times, she owed him so much already. His nightly visits had given her son an extra bounce to his step these days. And she'd heard Linc bragging about "his friend Mr. Smith" to the neighborhood boys. Only the presence of Dr. Gooden held her back from the emotional pull that drew her to Mr. Smith.

Then she looked up and saw Dr. Gooden smiling at Linc. Yes, this man had a kind heart too.

At the sound of footsteps, Lee looked up. *Oh, the good physician has returned? And Widow Wagstaff is actually smiling at me.* Lee called to them, "We meet again, Doctor. Good evening, Mrs. Wagstaff."

Jessie nodded.

The doctor replied, "Mr. Smith."

Lee didn't let the doctor's unwelcoming tone bother him. As Linc babbled to Lee about the ball game that day at school, Lee overheard the doctor seat Jessie on the porch. *I don't want to miss a word Dr. Gooden says to Jessie.* "Okay, Linc, tonight you go stand with your back to the shed, and I'll stay here, close to the porch."

Linc ran where Lee had pointed, leaving Lee close to the porch. Listening to the doctor trying to charm the Widow Wagstaff would make an entertaining evening.

The doctor cleared his throat. "Mrs. Wagstaff, you recall our discussing the possible causes of milk fever?"

Lee grinned to himself. *His approach is unusual all right.* How many men after dinner would discuss milk fever with a lady?

"Yes, I've often wondered why milk is good for children Linc's age, but harmful to infants."

"And the factor of the time of year is significant also, don't you think? Milk fever comes with the warm weather."

"Yes."

"Have you ever heard of Louis Pasteur?" Dr. Gooden asked.

Lee answered silently, *Yes, I have. What about him?*

"No, he sounds foreign."

"He is a French scientist. For the past decade he has been studying diseases and their causes. He believes disease is spread by bacteria or germs."

"Germs?" Jessie didn't sound like she favored the word.

"Yes. The idea, I think, is to liken the term *germ* to the germ in a seed—the part of the seed that makes the plant grow. A microscope—have you ever seen one?"

"No, but I know what it is."

Now Lee's interest had been caught too. What was the man's angle?

"Looking in the microscope, Pasteur has identified germs or bacteria that he says are alive and cause disease. He has experimented with heating milk to boiling. With thirty minutes boiling, all the bacteria in the milk are destroyed."

"Then if mothers boiled the milk before they gave it to their babies, they could destroy the bacteria that causes the diarrhea? Is that what it means?" Jessie sounded excited.

"Yes."

"But what about the age difference? Why does this bacteria harm infants, but not children?"

Good question, Jessie. Lee caught the ball and tossed it back to Linc.

"If a person has a disease and survives, that person develops an immunity—"

Jessie asked, "You mean like being poked in the arm, so you don't succumb to smallpox?"

"Exactly. Jenner proved that over fifty years ago."

"But what about the warm weather? How does that make the bacteria worse?" Jessie's interest came across clearly.

Lee strained to hear the answer to this question. He had to admit, the widow knew how to delve into a subject without dithering about the constraints of polite conversation.

The doctor's voice showed his excitement at Jessie's interest. "Look around you. When the weather warms, everything grows. Why not bacteria?"

"Of course!"

Lee caught another pitch. "Good pitch!" He tossed the ball back to the boy. Everything the good doctor said made sense, but would it impress half the doctors in Chicago? *In a pig's eye.*

"You've given me a lot to think over," Jessie said.

She definitely sounded impressed with the man.

She went on, "I've never heard a doctor talk about these ideas. Why don't they?"

"A lot of doctors have no interest at all in these new theories. They don't want to deal with all the new ideas this century has spawned. They don't bother to read the foreign journals."

"That's wrong."

That's right, Jessie. Lee wound up and threw a slow curve to Linc.

"At the very least it is shortsighted. That is why my goal is to run a teaching hospital," Dr. Gooden said.

"You want to teach medicine?"

"At first, but later I want to direct a hospital that trains doctors in the latest discoveries, the newest medicines. The old doctors won't change, so teaching new doctors must be my goal."

Lee heard the enthusiasm in the man's voice and pitied him. His passion of the innovative would make him an easy target for lesser men.

"That sounds so exciting. I knew when I met you, you were different from other doctors. You have ideals, a passion for your fellowman." Jessie leaned forward, her voice eager. "I believe you were sent to me by God. Dr. Gooden, I need your help."

"My help?"

You walked right into that one, Doc. Lee grinned and tossed a faster ball back to Linc, who yelped happily as he caught it.

"You witnessed yourself how cruel the matron at the charity hospital was. She would have let Ruth and Ben's son die in my arms the other night—"

"It is unfortunate, yes."

"Susan's people need a doctor." Jessie rushed ahead. "Will you consent to be their doctor?"

Silence fell on the porch.

Lee grimaced to himself, *Go ahead, Doc, talk your way out of this one.*

"This is a deep concern of yours, isn't it?" Dr. Gooden asked cautiously.

Tell her you can't do it, Doc.

"It is. I was terrified that night. I couldn't think of another thing to do for him. If he had died, I would have been culpable."

"You? No! How can you say that?"

"Because my skills are inadequate, and I haven't found them someone who has the skills they need!"

"But why are you responsible for them?" Dr. Gooden asked.

"My husband, Will, worked for abolition from his boyhood. He enlisted in the U.S. Sanitary Corps to help the wounded as soon as it was organized. He died in the war that freed the slaves. But his work isn't finished. What good is freedom to Susan's people if they can't even find a doctor who will treat them?"

Lee felt his face draw down and become stiff, grim.

"What's the matter, Mr. Smith?" Linc gazed at him with the ball poised to throw.

"Nothing. Toss that ball here, sport!"

Dr. Gooden replied, "I understand your concern for them, but some problems are too big for one person to solve. Your late husband didn't end slavery all by himself."

"No, he didn't," Jessie admitted. "But he did what he could. And so will I."

"I cannot do what you want for me to do."

At the doctor's simple statement, Lee stood up straighter. *I can't believe he had the guts to tell her the truth.*

"Why not?" Jessie's voice sounded tremulous.

Did you really expect him to just say yes, Jessie?

"If I do what you ask, I put in danger—or worse—destroy all my chances to succeed in reaching my goal of establishing a teaching hospital."

"Why?" Jessie asked.

The doctor explained, "Hospitals cost money. A good hospital costs a good amount of money."

"Yes?"

Lee tossed the ball. "Catch this, Linc?" *So Dr. Gooden's a realist after all?*

"I need sponsors, wealthy contributors. I cannot do anything that will endanger my impressing these people with the importance of the work I've been called to do."

You mean impressing them plain and simple, don't you, Doc?

"I would think you'd be taken more seriously," Jessie said.

"This world we live in is not perfect."

"I know, but . . ."

Lee waited. The Jessie Wagstaff he knew didn't take no for an answer.

She said, "I don't believe that our goals oppose one another. We both want only the best. And I can't believe you would turn your back on a person, white or black, who needed you."

A brief silence transpired.

The doctor broke it. "I tell you what. I will give you medicine and the information you need to nurse them."

Lee heard the rocker creak. He glanced over his shoulder and saw Jessie take hold of the man's hand.

She said, "Thank you, Doctor. That makes me feel so much better. You don't know how many times I've felt so helpless, inadequate."

"You think I don't know how that feels?"

Lee's stomach clenched. He walked toward Linc. "It's time we take a rest."

Linc frowned. "I'm not tired."

"I am." Lee lowered his hand to rest on Linc's back. Doing this was starting to feel natural, comfortable. He and Linc walked up onto the back porch and leaned back against the railing side by side.

Jessie drew her hand from the doctor's. "It's nearly bedtime, Linc."

"Mother, please. It's Friday night."

"Well, young man," the doctor said, "your catching and pitching, they're improving, I can tell."

"Did you play ball when you were a boy, sir?"

Lee hung back and let Linc take a step forward.

"Yes, but I was not as good as you or Mr. Smith." The doctor grinned.

Linc stepped back to where Lee rested against the railing.

The doctor stood up. "Linc doesn't have to get up early for school, but I am on duty at Rush Medical Hospital early on Saturday mornings."

"Thank you for coming, Doctor." Jessie rose.

The doctor bent over her hand, refused her offer to walk him to the front door, and departed.

Susan walked out onto the porch. "I come for Linc. Time for bed, mister baseball player."

"Mother, please?"

Lee said, "I'm tired myself, sport."

Linc's face fell.

"But if your mother doesn't object, we'll continue our game of catch tomorrow evening."

"Hooray!" Linc jumped straight up.

"Come on, Linc, your bed be callin' you." Susan and Linc started toward the back door. "Oh, I forgot. Your mama stop and left you a note." Susan pulled it from the pocket in her apron and handed it to Jessie. Then she led Linc away. The boy looked back at Lee until the last moment.

While reading the note, Jessie stood facing Lee. He could see why the doctor might be intrigued by her. Even dressed in black and buttoned up tight as can be, Jessie Wagstaff still caught the eye. "So you're trying to find yourself a doctor?"

She surprised him by tearing the note in two and shoving it into her pocket. "So you were eavesdropping? Yes, I am looking for a doctor. My stepfather has just written me that my asking my own doctor to treat them was 'outrageous.' Is that what you think?"

Her vehemence didn't surprise him, but her naïveté about the deep prejudices in this ugly old world sharpened his voice. "Don't you realize no doctor in this city will take Susan's people as patients?"

"Dr. Gooden has agreed to help me."

"He'll give you medicine and advice, but don't expect him to visit shantytown any time soon." Lee couldn't keep the sarcasm out of his voice.

"It's easy to sneer at someone who has a higher calling, but what would an office clerk know about the pressures a man like Dr. Gooden faces?" With a swish of her skirts, she swept by him like Queen Victoria herself.

Lee stared after her. *I know all about men like Dr. Gooden. I used to know one like him a long time ago. Watch out, Jessie; a man like that can let people down badly.*

CHAPTER 6

Saturday, June 18, 1871 "Beer, *bitte*."

"Not pink champagne, Slim?" Though Lee grinned as he pulled down the spigot of the beer keg, he mentally tried to shrug off a restlessness that had gripped him for several days.

"Very funny, Smit'." The large, broad-shouldered German tossed a nickel into Lee's hand.

Lee aimed and expertly flipped it into the cigar box behind the bar that served as Pearl's cash box. Talking would keep him from thinking. "How's your day?"

"Six hours more work and tomorrow is *Sontag*."

Lee nodded along with the raucous but friendly agreement to this sentiment that rippled through the line of men along the length of the bar. With genuine satisfaction, Lee anticipated tomorrow, his day off from the Workman's Rest. But this Sunday was more than just an ordinary day of rest. For the first time, Jessie had invited him for Sunday dinner, to celebrate Linc's eighth birthday. Lee was making progress toward his goal.

Out of the corner of his eye, Lee saw his pretty boss enter from the rear of the tavern. Several voices around him called out greetings. One man ventured, "Hey, Pearl, you look grand!"

Lee grinned ruefully. He should have expected Pearl to drop in. He forced himself to use a light tone, "Checking to see if I'm pocketing some of the money from these gentlemen-about-town?"

More laughter approved his sally. One thing Lee had learned about bartending was that the rough men who came into the tavern were starved for amusement. The least he could do for the work-weary men was give them something to chuckle about.

As Pearl came behind the bar, she exchanged several teasing comments with the customers. Lee allowed his ironic gaze to rove over her. She wore a charming cranberry-red dress with wide bands of ivory lace across her bosom. He had noticed that whenever she visited during his shift, she always made herself a treat to see. That was the problem.

She turned to him. "I came in to pay you."

"So early?" He dried his hands on the towel tucked into the waistband of his white apron. "Are you sure I won't close up and take a nap in the back room as soon as you leave?"

"He's a sly one!" the men warned Pearl. "He's as lazy as a dog with a lame leg!"

"Pooh!" Pearl waved a dismissive hand to them. Lee listened with only half an ear to the banter that continued until the majority of the men reluctantly went back to their jobs in the nearby factories. Then Pearl took the cigar box into the back room where she had a desk.

While she was gone, Lee served the two drunks who were sprawled at a table in the back. They weren't carrying on a conversation. They were just sipping, slowly and steadily drinking themselves into their daily stupor. He didn't mind serving work-men beer with their lunches. Many of them were German immigrants who had drunk a glass of beer at lunch their whole lives. But these two drunken faces haunted him more every day.

"Mr. Smith," Pearl called him back to the bar. "Here's your wages." She handed him four one-dollar bills.

Outside, a wagon rattled by and a flume of dust floated over the double swinging doors. Pearl paused, just as he did, to watch the particles dance in the rays of sunlight and finally drift down to the tabletops.

"When will we get some rain?" Worry was plain in Pearl's voice.

"Who can say?"

"Yesterday a neighbor boy almost started his father's barn afire."

"Playing with matches?"

"He bought some firecrackers early. His mother heard them."

Lee shook his head.

Pearl's tone sharpened. "I used it as a chance to put the fear of fire into my two. A fire is just what I'd need about now."

Two widows had become important to Lee's new life in Chicago. Jessie had been left one son and a house as a means of support. Pearl had been left a son and daughter and a saloon.

"I'm off to the bank now, then home," Pearl said. "I needed extra money to pay my neighbor. My boy just broke another window playing that baseball."

Lee grinned. "Boys will be boys."

"That's what everyone says, but *this time* he's going to have to work it off. He'll be coming here every afternoon next week to mop the place."

Red flags waved inside Lee, but he said gallantly, "As you wish, ma'am. I will miss doing it myself, but . . ."

She chuckled. "I'd give anything to know who taught you such pretty manners—and how you ever let me hire you as a barkeep."

"It was my lucky day." He grinned more broadly to hide his uneasiness.

Pearl shook her head at him. As she left, femininely swaying her high and ornately beribboned bustle, he knew she was flirting with him. Pearl teased him with practiced subtlety and great finesse—in contrast to Mrs. Bolt, who launched herself at him like a lovesick adolescent.

Lee imagined himself telling the "prim" schoolteacher that a bar owner had better manners than she. Why hadn't anyone explained to the redhead that while no man turns from the attraction of a pretty woman, no man ever desires to be the object of such a blatant pursuit? Mrs. Bolt embarrassed herself and him every time they met.

Lee clenched his jaw as though forcing back these words while he swabbed the bar with a large wet washcloth, tidying up after lunch.

The heat from the blistering, noon-high sun weighed down the stagnant air of the saloon. One of the drunks lifted a hand. Lee turned away from the man and grimaced to himself as he picked up the whisky bottle, then walked toward them.

The odor of whisky no longer made Lee's mouth water. Instead, it made his pulse jump as though he needed to run. This and worrying lest he go to see Linc with alcohol on his breath kept him dry as a bone every day. Nothing must come between Linc and him.

He poured each of the drunks a shot of whiskey. Everything within him suddenly swelled with a deep repugnance. How had he let himself start work here? The walls around him suddenly felt like a trap. He wished to be anywhere—no, not anywhere. He longed to be in Jessie's backyard.

In his mind's eye, he pictured her image of a few evenings ago. For the very first time, Linc had hit a ball over the back fence. Jessie had leaped to her feet. Because of the heat, the top buttons of her high-necked black blouse and the buttons at her wrists had been loosed. Her wavy hair had come a little undone and wisps of hair curled in the faint perspiration all around her temples.

When he glanced at her face, he had been captivated by her animation and uncontrived beauty. Her pinched look of stern widowhood, which he had grown so to dislike, had vanished. In that moment he'd glimpsed the sweet, young woman she'd been before she'd put on widow's black.

Sunday, June 16, 1871

Jessie held herself rigidly, not allowing her spine to touch the back of the pew. To her right sat her mother, stepfather, and their twin sons. Jessie had tucked Linc to her left on the aisle. She wanted him to be able to see the front of the church. But more importantly, it would limit her stepfather's opportunity to scold her son.

Her stepfather's presence explained why she sat so stiffly. He always insisted this was how a lady should sit. She had learned to obey him early in life. Even now, if she didn't do just as he wished each time they met, he would wound her mother later by criticizing Jessie's "unladylike behavior" to her.

She never felt comfortable in this new church. Five years ago her stepfather had moved his family away from the old neighborhood where Jessie still lived. After his promotion to fire captain, he'd built a new home among the newer, more fashionable homes west of the Chicago River. He had moved his membership to this new redbrick church nearby. Other former neighbors of Jessie's had made the same choice. Jessie, however, had remained at the small church on Ontario Street where she'd worshiped as a child, where she and Will had married. And every Sunday she thanked God for this blessing, a place to worship without her stepfather's galling presence. Her conscience scolded her, but she couldn't seem to let go of her anger.

Jessie stood with the rest of the congregation to sing "Bringing in the Sheaves." She tried to keep her mind on the hymn, but it kept slipping back to Susan, who had stayed home from her own church service to make sure Linc's birthday meal was prepared perfectly. *Thank you, God, for Susan!*

Her mind deserted the church where she was singing and took her back five years to the day she had first met Susan. That Sunday morning she had walked to the Negro church that met on the South Side in a warehouse along the lakefront. Too poor to purchase pews, the congregation stood except for a few older men and women who sat on ladder-backed chairs at the front. Jessie remembered standing there among black people for the first time. It hadn't occurred to her that being the only white face in a room filled with dark faces would make her feel so conspicuous.

Linc, only three then, toddled away from Jessie's side, forward to one of the few older women who was without a child in her lap. In silent request, he held up his arms, but the grandmother looked over her shoulder to Jessie. When Jessie smiled and nodded, the black woman bent, picked him up, and settled him on her navy skirt.

Around her the congregation began singing, "On that great getting up mornin', Hallelu, Hallelu. On that great getting up mornin' . . ." Jessie stood thunderstruck. The people around her swayed to the rhythm. She yearned to follow their lead, but years of sitting beside her stepfather in church held her in check. Never had she heard such voices, lyrics, melodies, such joy! They stirred her beyond her imagining—awakening her blood, setting it to flow rich and sure through her veins, awakening her spirit from its deep mourning.

The mood of the music shifted, and a song about dying swirled into her heart: "Were you there when they crucified my Lord?" They sang this plaintive question—"Were you there when they crucified my Lord?"—over and over, letting it build, rise, soar. Surreptitiously she touched her eyes with her handkerchief. When the low chorus "Sometimes it causes me to tremble, tremble, tremble" was sung and sung again, she shivered from her head to her toes. The pain of losing Will, of losing Margaret, pierced Jessie's heart anew.

Then the old black preacher at the front led the congregation in song: "I must walk this lonesome valley. I got to walk it by myself. Nobody else can walk it for you, you got to walk it by yourself." His voice was cellar-deep, gravelly, powerful.

Her own loneliness welled up inside her. Silent tears coursed down her cheeks unchecked. *Oh, Margaret, Will, how can I go on without you?* Freshly opened grief made her regret coming. Despair pulled her down. She clasped her Bible to her breast— as though it were her heart and she had to hold it together or it might shatter.

Then a high soprano voice, joyous and true, broke over the congregation like a wave of cold, clear lake water: "Sing a ho that I had the wings of a dove. I'd fly away. I'd fly away!" Jessie felt shot through with excitement, feeling, sensation. Her body prickled with energy. "I'll fly away!"

She imagined Will and Margaret standing on either side of her, imagined how this song would have lifted them to joy. *All this will pass away in time. I, too, will fly away. I will fly away.* She let the song's harmonies carry her heavenward. *"Yes, I will fly away!"*

Then the singing came to a close. With a full heart, Jessie watched the pastor open his well-worn Bible. In his deep, charged voice, he read the last chapter of John, of Christ's appearing to the apostles as they were fishing in the Sea of Galilee. Jesus had made a fire on the sand and cooked a humble fishermen's breakfast in the chilly, gray dawn on the shore. The picture the pastor made so real took Jessie outside to the shores of Lake Michigan. She smelled the fresh lake air, heard the gulls screech, imagined the brisk morning wind on her face. Jessie tingled with the story of how Peter, when told he would die a martyr's death, turned and asked if that would be John's fate also.

"You see, Peter was the Rock. Christ had chosen him to be the foundation of his church. But Peter still was irritated that he wasn't the one Jesus loved best. And the Lord answered Peter, 'What is it to you, Peter, if John live till I come again?'" The pastor repeated the question. His voice dropped, "You see, friends, Peter's spirit was willing, but his flesh was weak. He wasn't happy with just being the top rung of the ladder. He wasn't satisfied. He wanted to be the one—not John—who rested his head upon Jesus' chest."

The pastor's voice rose. "Did Christ strike Peter dead for this effrontery? Did he?"

The congregation answered, "No!" It made Jessie jump. She'd never heard a pastor actually get a reply.

"That's right! No! And he'll show the same kindness to us! It's the same for all of us. Peter was there with the Holy Christ right beside him, yet he still could think small thoughts. Are we any better? Are we any better?"

Jessie was prepared this time for the "No!" that resounded around her.

"So, brethren, let's be kind when we judge one another. Yes, let us be kind one to another. You know we aren't even supposed to judge. No, we're not. But we judge anyway. Yes, we do! We're weak. So weak. Remember that and be kind. Are any of us worthy? No, not one."

A chorus of "Amen's" followed this. There was a simple prayer, and then the service ended.

The pastor went to the door to shake hands. Jessie, with Linc by the hand, was politely ushered to the front of the line. "Good morning, sister, I'm Reverend Mitchell." Feeling shy, she shook his hand, the first time ever she touched dark skin. His kind eyes eased her discomfort in this new place.

"I'm Mrs. Wagstaff. Reverend, I would like to ask your advice about a matter when you're free."

He replied, "Mrs. Wagstaff, you might as well speak plainly. No one here will go about their business 'til you state your reason for visiting our service." His words were direct, but spoken kindly.

Jessie blushed. "I'm sorry. I didn't mean to intrude, but I am looking for a woman to help me at home. I'm a widow and I'm going to take in two more boarders to support myself, but I need help—especially since my son takes up so much of my time."

"I see," said the Reverend. "You want someone reliable."

Jessie nodded, then leaned down to wipe a smudge off Linc's cheek.

A tall, young man at the pastor's elbow said sharply, "Ask her how much she's willing to pay."

The pastor frowned. "I intend to ask that, son."

"I don't know exactly." Jessie bit her lower lip. "I am receiving two dollars a week from my present boarder, so I'd probably be taking in about six dollars a week. But I don't know how much it will cost to feed six people."

The young man spoke up sharply again, "So you expect her to work for room and board like a slave?" The man's words visibly shocked his father and many of those standing around.

Jessie looked him in the eye. "No, I was thinking that since the money would be supporting three: the woman, my son, and me that I would pay her one-third of what is left after expenses each week. Would that be fair?" There was a moment of silence.

"Yes, ma'am, that sounds fair," the old preacher said. He then cast his eyes over the waiting assembly. "Susan, would you like to work for Mrs. Wagstaff?"

"Yes, thank you, Rev'rund." Susan came forward, clothed in a shabby gray dress with mended lace at the neck.

"How do you do, Susan?" Jessie offered her hand.

"How do, Miss Jessie." She curtseyed to Jessie.

"Please, call me Mrs. Wagstaff. I am your employer, not your mistress."

Susan's face registered a flash of happiness and she curtseyed again. "Yes, Mrs. Wagstaff."

The large church's pipe organ reverberated with the final chords of the hymn and jolted Jessie's thoughts back to the present. *I must find someone to help Susan's people. I will.* Jessie sat down amid sounds of skirts rustling, children being whispered to, and Bible pages turning.

In the discreet well-bred silence that followed, the minister read the New Testament Scriptures for the morning, Galatians 3:28: "There is neither Jew nor Greek, there is neither bond nor free, there is neither male nor female: for ye are all one in Christ Jesus."

Jessie nodded her agreement.

Then the minister read 1 John 2:9–10: "He that saith he is in the light, and hateth his brother, is in darkness even until now. He that loveth his brother abideth in the light, and there is no occasion of stumbling in him." Jessie drank in these words of purity and devotion and tried to let love blossom inside her heart for those sitting around her, many of whom she had known since childhood. Unfortunately, she didn't succeed.

Her mother's hand brushed Jessie's knee. Mother nodded in Linc's direction. Linc, sitting with his hands folded in his lap, was silently swinging his legs back and forth. Jessie knew this was not bothering her mother, but her stepfather demanded all children imitate statues in church. *This is why I can't rid myself of my anger. He never stops interfering.* For much less than two cents, she would have ignored her stepfather, but Jessie knew later he would lecture her mother about Linc's "misbehavior." For her mother's sake she touched her son's knee.

Linc looked up innocently. She pointed to his legs and shook her head. A sudden, tiny grin lighting his face, he wrinkled his nose, but obeyed. Inwardly Jessie was delighted. It was times like these that she most saw Will in his son. Will's son was undaunted by his step-grandfather.

At long last, the minister concluded his sermon. Jessie whispered a prayer of thanks. After two hours of adhering outwardly to her stepfather's strictures, Jessie felt stiff and choked. Any longer and she wouldn't have been able to breathe. *How did I survive every Sunday as a child?* Her stomach burned with her resentment. *Lord, forgive me. I hate him.*

As she rose with the congregation to sing the closing hymn, "Blest Be the Tie That Binds," she caught sight of the back of Dr. Miller's head a few pews ahead of her. Purposefully she directed her mind to the words she was singing. Because of the doctor's refusal to help Susan's people, her resentment toward him burned inside her. She didn't feel "her heart bound to his in Christian love" as she was singing. She was still deeply disappointed in him. Was "their fellowship like that above"? *No.* How could a good man be so blind to his Christian duty? Didn't he realize his heart was bound to Susan's because of their shared faith?

Whom do I ask next? Dr. Gooden's smiling face came to her mind. He hadn't refused her outright. He'd shown his charity the night he'd saved Little Ben's life. Perhaps she should try to persuade him once more.

At last, Jessie respectfully followed her mother as she worked her way down the crowded church aisle, out the double doors, and down the stone steps. Jessie smiled mechanically to everyone who greeted her, but it was a deceiving mask and she hated it. *Lord, I'm sorry.*

Shielded from the noonday sun by their white parasols, Jessie and her mother strolled home, side by side. Jessie smiled at her mother and enjoyed seeing her grin in return. Mother rarely smiled, especially when her husband was near at hand.

Jessie had been willing to endure a day in her stepfather's company and the anger he sparked inside her because it was the only way to have her mother with her at Linc's eighth birthday.

In honor of the day, Jessie had put off her "blacks" and worn her dove gray with ivory lace collar tatted by Margaret. She felt festive to be out of black, despite her stepfather's presence. Her mother and she ascended the steps of Wagstaff House. Her stepfather hurried forward to open the door for them. Jessie looked away from him as she and her mother folded their parasols and stepped inside.

"I smell fried chicken," Mother said.

"Yes, Susan stayed home from church to cook—"

"That's her job, isn't it?" Her stepfather hung his hat on the hall tree.

Jessie swallowed a stinging retort. *I won't give you any opportunity to leave early, stepfather. Mother and I are going to enjoy this day—come what may.*

While her half-brothers, Tim and Tom, followed their father's sedate example, Linc ran ahead toward the kitchen. Her stepfather frowned and shook his head over Linc's lapse of decorum. Pointedly ignoring the man, Jessie walked with her mother toward the parlor.

"Good morning, Esther," Miss Wright's voice from the parlor greeted Jessie's mother, one of her former pupils.

Esther entered the sunny room and pressed her hand into the old woman's. "It is so good to see you, ma'am, especially on such a happy day."

"Yes, it is hard to believe the little scamp can really be eight today. I was remembering Margaret's delight at receiving God's gift of a son, then a grandson. I've been enjoying memories all morning. Margaret and I were girls together, you know."

The spinster's mellow mood surprised Jessie, but Will's mother had been the old woman's best, nearly her only, friend. "I must check on dinner," Jessie murmured and rustled down the hall through the kitchen curtain.

"I heard ya'll come in." Susan lifted the black iron skillet's lid to pierce the sizzling chicken with a large fork, checking its doneness.

"Everything smells delicious. What can I help with?" Jessie reached for her apron.

"You put that apron back," Susan ordered. "Everythin's done and this is your day to cel'brate. Now shoo! Get out of this hot kitchen!" Susan matched her words by waving her hands toward Jessie in a shooing action.

Jessie chuckled. "In a minute. Where did Linc disappear to?"

"He went out to water dat pup Mr. Smith done got him. I'll sen' him back to da parlor when his hands is all wash' again."

Nodding, Jessie returned to the parlor, walking sedately in to sit beside her mother, who was deep in conversation with Miss Wright.

As usual, Jessie kept her peace in her stepfather's presence, but from under her lashes she observed him as his keen gaze measured the lack of dust in each nook and cranny of the parlor. Next he inspected the polish on her oak floor.

A complacent smile tugged at the corners of her mouth. She'd left no dust anywhere, and her floors shone like crystal. Her back and arm muscles still ached from a day spent on her knees polishing the floor. Nothing her stepfather could say now or later would spoil this day for her mother, Linc, and herself.

A knock sounded on the front door. Jessie rose to open it. She found Mr. Smith standing on the front porch. He held a bouquet of pink and white carnations.

"For my hostess." He laid them into her arms. "That dress is charming on you, Mrs. Wagstaff."

A tingle of exhilaration robbed her of speech as she stepped inside to allow Mr. Smith to enter. She stared at the blooms, then fingered the slender petals of one carnation. "Thank you. I can't remember when I last received flowers." She felt herself blushing.

Before she could compose herself she heard more footsteps on the porch. Jessie stepped farther inside and motioned Dr. Gooden in. He held out a bouquet of pink roses to her.

She sensed an instant restraint—or maybe it was tension—between the two men. She couldn't think why that should be. In addition, the experience of holding two bouquets from two different men struck her speechless for a moment. She silently scolded herself for being silly. Of course they would bring hostess gifts to her. They were just being polite.

Suddenly she recalled her stepfather sitting only a few feet away from her. That fact scouted all emotion from her, making her dry up and stiffen inside.

She cleared her throat. "Please come in."

At her request the two gentlemen hung their hats on the hall tree and followed her to the parlor. She introduced them as "Lincoln's friends" to her parents, "Mr. and Mrs. Hiram Huff." Under her stepfather's scrutiny, Jessie held onto her flowers, outwardly calm. "I'll have to find a vase for these," she murmured.

Sensing Jessie's insecurity, Lee diverted attention from her. He asked, "Where's the birthday lad?"

"He's out back watering Butch," Jessie said.

"Butch?" Huff repeated as though the word were as bitter as alum.

The man's negative tone instantly put Lee on guard. Probably without realizing it, Jessie made it plain she didn't like her stepfather. Lee watched the way she took a deep breath and composed her mouth into a forced smile. He couldn't recall Jessie ever behaving so unnaturally before.

"Butch is the puppy Mr. Smith gave Linc for his birthday," Dr. Gooden said approvingly. "He is a fine pup."

Lee glanced at the doctor, surprised at his support.

"A dog!" Huff blustered.

One of the twins asked in obvious awe, "Linc got a dog?"

"Children," Huff barked at his son, who flushed a deep red, "are to be seen and not heard." He glared at Jessie. "You have heard me say time after time, town dogs are just a nuisance. He'll dig up your yard, draw flies, and infest your house with fleas. What will your boarders say to that?"

"Butch *isn't* a house dog," Miss Wright spoke up.

Lee could hardly believe his ears. *I didn't know the old woman had it in her.*

Lee eyed Huff with distaste. "That's correct. Linc and I built a doghouse together for him, sir."

CHAPTER 6

Dr. Gooden nodded and added, "I heard Linc promise to walk him each morning and each evening, so the dog won't be at large. Some dogs do bite in the hot weather, so I told him he must keep Butch tied up and wet him down in the hot afternoons."

Reluctantly, Lee gave the doctor an imperceptible nod of thanks. The stepfather choked back his ire with evident displeasure. He might bully the women, but how could he argue with two men who approved of the pet? Hiram Huff's opinion of dogs matched Lee's father's opinion exactly. *That's why Linc is going to have his dog.*

"Mr. Smith, it's very good of you to take time for Lincoln," Jessie's mother said quietly.

"It's my pleasure, Mrs. Huff."

"Mother! Mother!" Linc burst into the sunny room, hugging a small brown-and-white pup. "Reverend Mitchell, Caleb, and everyone is in the backyard! You've got to see them! Come on!"

As Huff lunged toward the boy, Lee moved forward protectively. Ignoring his step-grandfather, Linc hopped excitedly from foot to foot. When his mother didn't move, Linc grabbed her hand and pulled her through the hall and kitchen.

Lee, followed by Dr. Gooden, had to nearly run to keep up. The four of them came to a halt on the back porch—next to Susan, who stood stock still on the top step, transfixed.

Lee surveyed the backyard where about a dozen of the black community had gathered. Lee recognized them, friends of Susan's whom he had seen come and go through Jessie's back door. In their midst, Lee picked out the face of the bent, but untroubled old, black preacher who had called on Susan just the week before. Beside him stood a very round, short woman with gray hair, peeking out from under a calico turban. The old woman's clothes were faded and tattered, and her wide feet were bare.

Suddenly Susan came out of her distraction and shrieked, "Ruby! Grandma Ruby!" As the girl raced down the steps, the old woman tottered forward. Susan threw herself into those open arms. "Grandma Ruby, I never thought I'd see you again! You're alive!"

"I been lookin' dese las' five years for you, my honey." Ruby wept and rocked Susan back and forth in her arms as though the young woman was just a child once more. "I's walk miles and miles and ask a thousan' people n'more—where be my girl, my onliest girl? Praise da Lord! Praise God! I found my girl at last!"

Lee felt his throat thicken. A homecoming. A reunion. He was not surprised to see Jessie wipe tears from her eyes. He was having trouble holding back his own.

Jessie stood like a statue, pressing both bouquets to her breast. She must have felt Lee's attention on her because she looked up at him. She murmured, "Susan was sold away from her only relative, her grandmother, when she was only thirteen."

Lee acknowledged her explanation with a subdued nod.

Dr. Gooden cleared his throat. "It is hard to believe that the Emancipation Proclamation was signed only eight years ago."

Lee nodded soberly, watching the two women cling to each other—kissing, weeping, and laughing.

Jessie hurried down the steps straight to the two women. Susan, her face ashine with laughter and tears, turned her grandmother toward Jessie. Without waiting for a word of introduction, Jessie gave the bouquets to the old woman and threw her arms around her. "Welcome. Welcome."

From behind Lee, Huff's outraged voice snapped, "What is all this commotion? Don't these people know this is the Sabbath?"

Lee glanced coolly over at him.

But Dr. Gooden answered, "Susan is reunited with her long-lost grandmother."

"That is all good and well, but she should have waited for Susan to be notified and then the girl could go to her in their neighborhood. These darkies have no business here, interrupting us." He clattered down the steps, headed straight for Jessie.

Lee couldn't help but smile. He often didn't like Jessie's determined ways, but she wouldn't tolerate this man ruining Susan's reunion. He followed Huff at a discreet distance. *I wouldn't miss this for the world.*

Keeping pace with Lee, Dr. Gooden leaned to speak close to Lee's ear, "That man doesn't know his stepdaughter very well, does he?"

"So it seems," Lee replied with a wicked grin.

Huff's voice boomed over the backyard, "Jessie, these people don't belong here!"

Jessie replied, "Stepfather, this doesn't concern you. Won't you return to the parlor? I will be right in."

Huff stopped directly across from her. "You must tell these people to leave now. What will your neighbors think?"

Lee watched Jessie straighten and lift her chin. *Now the sparks will fly.*

Jessie stared at her stepfather. "This is no concern of my neighbors or of you."

Lee suppressed a grin at the honed steel in Jessie's tone.

The Reverend spoke up quietly, "We'll be leaving then, Mrs. Wagstaff. We didn't come to cause friction. We just couldn't wait. When we learned it was Susan, our sister, who Ruby was searching for, we had to bring them together."

"No," Jessie said, putting out her hand to forestall him, "I want you to stay. There is no reason for you to leave on this happy occasion. I know Susan has made enough fried chicken and cake to feed a small army. You can celebrate Susan and her grandmother's reunion in my backyard while we celebrate Linc's birthday in the dining room." Jessie touched Susan's arm.

Lee said to himself, *That makes sense, Jessie, but Huff won't buy it.*

"But, Mrs. Wagstaff—" Susan began.

"Jessie!" Her stepfather grasped Jessie's arm. "This state of affairs will not do. Your neighbors will be appalled. These people know they don't belong here. Send them home. Susan can visit her grandmother when she has her day off."

Lee couldn't wait to hear Jessie's reply.

Jessie pulled away from Huff's grip. In a deceptively soft tone, she said, "This is my home. You are not the master here."

CHAPTER 7

L EE READ THE DESPAIR ON MRS. Huff's face. She hurried down the back steps where she had been standing beside her young sons and Miss Wright. White-faced, she opened her mouth.

Her husband silenced her, "We are leaving, Esther. Your stubborn daughter doesn't care that she is making a spectacle of herself, and I won't subject you and our sons to such goings-on."

"Goings-on?" Lee heard himself say. "She just wants Susan's friends to eat cake in her backyard."

Huff glared at him, then reached for his wife's arm. She pulled back, eluding his grasp. "Please, Hiram," she pleaded.

The anguish in the woman's voice sliced through Lee like a scalpel.

"Esther, we're leaving."

The woman hesitated, visibly torn. Giving in to tears, she covered her mouth with the back of her hand. She stepped in front of Linc, who still clutched his pup, and dropped to her knees on the dried-up grass. She pulled the boy to her, hugging him fiercely as though he were about to be snatched from her.

"Esther," her husband insisted.

Lee fought the urge to confront Huff, the hard-hearted jackass. Lee's hands curled into fists.

With a smothered sob, Jessie's mother tore herself away from Linc. She rushed past her husband. When she reached her sons, she took each by his hand and hurried them into the house. Without a backward glance, Huff marched after her. From her place on the porch, Miss Wright huffed her displeasure and turned away too.

Lee burned with outrage for Jessie. She was worth a hundred Huffs. Lee pictured himself catching up to Huff, turning him by the shoulder. Lee could almost feel the satisfaction of his right fist connecting with the holier-than-thou hypocrite's jaw.

"Mrs. Wagstaff," Reverend Mitchell said, "we didn't mean to cause a separation between you and your mother—"

"You didn't." Jessie lifted her chin. "She made her choice years ago when she married Hiram Huff."

Then she smiled, a plainly tight, pitiful smile. "Frankly, Reverend, I prefer your company. Come, Susan, bring your grandmother up into the shade of the porch."

Touched by Jessie's brave front, Lee stood with his hand on Linc's shoulder. As Jessie passed him, she asked, "Are you staying then, Mr. Smith?"

Lee made his voice match hers in bravado, "Ma'am, at the mere thought of Susan's fried chicken, my mouth waters."

"Dr. Gooden?" She paused in front of him.

The doctor bowed slightly. "I can only echo Mr. Smith."

She smiled at both of them. "Come. I'll need your help." The three of them walked toward the porch.

CHAPTER 7

"Mother, why doesn't step-grandfather like us?" Linc struggled, but his puppy finally wiggled out of his grasp.

Jessie bent and kissed her son's forehead. "It isn't our fault, son. He doesn't like very many people."

And I imagine very few really like him, Lee commented inwardly.

"Mother can I . . . *may* I," Linc amended, "go get out of my Sunday clothes?"

"Lincoln, just because we won't be eating in the dining . . ." She stopped. "I'm sorry, Linc. Of course, you can . . . *may.*"

Linc ran to the house with a "Whoopee!"

She explained to Lee and Dr. Gooden in an aside, "I hate it when I start to sound like *that man.*"

"Your stepfather is of a strong temperament. It is hard to overlook." Dr. Gooden smiled wryly.

Jessie grinned. "How perceptive. And you just met him."

"I'd say he's a man who's easy to know and hard to avoid," Lee added.

This forced a chuckle from her.

Pleased, Lee followed her up onto the porch.

She called out, "Caleb, Ben, will you come in and carry out the kitchen table. There's no reason to delay. Dinner is ready."

A flurry of activity ensued. Lee along with the other men brought out the kitchen table, chairs, napkins, plates, and silver. His appetite awoke as women arranged bowls of creamy mashed potatoes, yellow corn bread, and platters of golden fried chicken on the long table with its white oilcloth. The fragrance of butter and the chicken made his mouth water. Throughout the bustle, the pup he'd given Linc yapped excitedly, nipping at the men's black pant legs and racing back and forth under the women's wide skirts of navy or black.

When all was in place, Reverend Mitchell took off his hat and bowed his head. Lee noticed Susan reach for her grandmother's hand, and something deep inside him ached for a similar touch. His eyes automatically sought out Jessie. Their eyes met over Linc's blonde head. When Dr. Gooden edged closer to Jessie, Lee felt a grinding inside.

The pastor cleared his throat. "Father, we thank Thee that Thou hast brought Susan and Ruby together again. We know it was Thee who brought these two, our sisters, together once more. And bless this house, O Lord. Give Mrs. Wagstaff and her son back the kindness that they show us each day, pressed down and overflowing in abundance. Thank Thee for Lincoln on this day of his birth and thank Thee for this dinner and the hands that lovingly prepared it. In Christ's name, Amen."

Immediately, excited chatter and laughter broke out as the buffet line formed, but everyone stood back waiting for someone to go first. "Please, Susan, you and your grandmother go first," Jessie invited.

"No, Mrs. Wagstaff, you go first." Susan took another step back. Before Jessie could continue this genteel dispute, Linc, pulling Lee along with him, started the buffet with spontaneous glee. This brought a full smile to Lee's face and chuckles from many others. When Jessie shook her head at the boy, Lee held his hands out in a gesture of helplessness.

"It is the boy's birthday, Mrs. Wagstaff," Dr. Gooden said.

Then Lee offered Jessie a delicate china plate and gently urged her to follow her son. For once, she did not balk at a suggestion of his. But when she drew Dr. Gooden with her in line, Lee averted his gaze. That grinding feeling twisted inside him again. He pushed the sensation aside and joined the doctor.

When Lee made a substantial hill of mashed potatoes on his plate, he complimented Susan who stood behind him, "You've outdone yourself."

Susan smiled. "I didn't know when I was cookin' I was cookin' for my grandma." She wiped away fresh tears.

Soon the black picnickers, except for the elderly who had accepted kitchen chairs, were sitting on the grass in the slender shade cast by the shed and porch. Though Jessie had invited Susan and Ruby to sit on the porch, they observed a decorous separation of races by positioning their chairs on the lawn, just inside the shadow of the porch. Jessie, Linc, Lee, and the doctor were the only ones who sat on chairs on the porch.

Lee wondered if Jessie realized that her black friends did this to protect her. Did she realize the backlash she might reap if she continued to flout the standard separation between the races?

After dinner, Lee joined in the enthusiastic celebration. Linc blew out the candles. Jessie and Susan cut and served the cake. Lee, like everyone else, settled back comfortably, sipping iced coffee and enjoying delicious bites of the yellow birthday cake with white fluffy frosting. Lee relaxed. A contentment he hadn't known for years filled him.

When her son went back to the remains of the cake for a third helping, Jessie objected, *"Linc."*

"This one's for Butch, Mother."

Lee chuckled and tilted his head back, locking up into the clear, blue sky. *Life is good again,* his heart whispered. He replayed once more and savored Jessie's words to Huff: "This is my home. You are not the master here." How delightful to witness Jessie's routing of such a blatant hypocrite! Smiling, he took a deep breath and turned to watch her.

The doctor was speaking close to Jessie's ear, and she was smiling. The grinding feeling rushed through Lee once more. This time he identified it—jealousy. *What's happening to me? I can't be jealous of Jessie and the good doctor. He's just the kind who'd make her a good husband.* Lee squirmed at the thought.

Ruby spoke up, "This surely be da best day of my life. 'Til I find my girl, my onliest girl, I never enjoy freedom. Now I can die happy." Ruby leaned over and kissed Susan's cheek.

Susan gave way to tears again and hugged Ruby's shoulders. "Grandma Ruby, don't talk 'bout dyin'. We just found each other."

Lee noticed Jessie dab her eyes. He edged his chair closer to her, leaned forward, and whispered, "I wish your mother could be here."

"My stepfather has always forced her to choose him over me," she whispered back.

"A shame."

She turned away from him, raising her voice, "He's a shame to all Christians."

"His thinking isn't uncommon," Dr. Gooden commented.

Lee nodded. On the issue of how to treat newly freed slaves in the North, his Aunt Hester would be of one mind with Huff about "keeping up appearances"—even though it flew in the face of Christian principles. Lee admitted to himself grudgingly that he admired Jessie Wagstaff. She might be bossy, but when an issue of right and wrong was concerned, she was unmoved by criticism.

Unfortunately, this might put her in harm's way.

Did she really think she could change the wicked and unfair world they inhabited? He and Jessie, though each had been raised in families a thousand miles apart, had been affected by self-righteous hypocrites. Since the war, she had become more determined to fight for her ideals while he had deserted his altogether. His good humor ebbed.

Spontaneously, a few, and then more, of Susan's friends began to hum and sing, "O, happy day when Jesus washed my sins away. O, happy day. . . ."

After his years in the South, Lee was familiar with this spiritual. Sitting with his legs casually crossed, he found himself subtly swinging his crossed leg to its infectious rhythm. When he realized what he was doing, he stilled himself, then grimaced at his response. Ten years after his Aunt Hester's death, she still had the power to bully him. The song continued and he relaxed, letting the music move him again. He watched Jessie and Linc tapping to the tune also.

"O, happy day when Jesus washed my sins away . . ."

He hummed along, feeling the joy the words expressed, letting their balm pour through him like the bright, hot sunshine that shown around them all. Then the tune changed to "I'm Gonna Lay Down My Heavy Load."

"Yes, Lord, I done laid my burden down," Ruby sang and raised her hands upward to heaven. A look of purest joy settled onto her dark features. Lee felt suddenly as though he, an infidel, had stepped up to an altar where the woman prayed. Until he could reel in his unexpected emotions, he turned his head and looked away.

Glancing toward Jessie, he saw her lean closer to Dr. Gooden again. Lee strained to hear her words.

"Doctor, I want to make one more request. I know you've refused to take these people as patients, but if it were a matter of life or death, would you come—if I needed your help?"

Lee eyed the other man, wondering how he would refuse this request.

Dr. Gooden looked around him solemnly, then nodded. "If it is life or death, I will come."

Lee sat back in surprise. Dr. Gooden had unexpected depths.

As the song ended, Ruby sighed loudly. "Rev'rund, I wants to hear da song we couldn't sing. Can anyone sing dat for me?"

Without hesitation, Caleb stood up, tall and straight, his dark, handsome face fiercely proud. "I was born free, but I sing this song for the day when we all will *really* be free."

The way Caleb Mitchell, who appeared to match Lee in years, said the words "really free" made Lee certain the man wasn't alluding to heaven. Lee knew the song to which Ruby referred. Only one spiritual had been forbidden in the South before the war.

As Caleb began to sing, Lee found himself mesmerized by the man's deep bass voice and by the power he gave the simple words.

"When Israel was in Egypt's land, Let my people go! Oppressed so hard they could not stand. Let my people go!"

Other voices, full and true, harmonized on the chorus, "Go down, Moses, way down in Egypt's land and tell old Pharaoh to let my people go."

The low tones of Caleb's voice vibrated through Lee's bones and sinew, and the stark longing in them sobered him.

"No more in bondage shall they toil, Let my people go! Let them come out with Egypt's spoil, Let my people go!"

As Susan's rich soprano lifted above Caleb's voice in exaltation, a shiver sliced through Lee. Her voice proclaimed, "Thus saith the Lord, bold Moses said, Let my people go! If not, I'll smite your firstborn dead, Let my people go!"

As the people around Lee joined in the final chorus, long repressed sadness, longing, and defeat surged through Lee. "When Israel was in Egypt's land, Let my people go! Oppressed so hard they could not stand. Let my people go!"

The final notes, Caleb's and Susan's, reverberated in total silence. Lee felt himself near tears and couldn't think why. Slavery had ended. The war was in the past.

Having drawn close to Lee, Linc leaned back against Lee's leg as though seeking comfort. Lee reached down and ruffled Linc's hair.

"Mrs. Wagstaff!"

At the sound of a strident female voice with a thick German accent, Lee rose without thinking, but fell back to let the short, plump, gray-haired woman march past him to Jessie.

"Mrs. Braun," Jessie replied, but remained seated.

"Mrs. Wagstaff, I *cannot* put up with dis noise anymore."

"What noise?" Jessie asked in a deceptively mild tone that Lee recognized as dangerous.

The woman waved her arms toward the black congregation.

"Susan—" Jessie began to explain.

With her hands indignantly on her hips, the woman cut Jessie off, "Dis is a respectable neighborhood—"

"And these are all respectable people," Jessie finished.

CHAPTER 7

Lee had read about geysers, hot springs that periodically spurted skyward. In the throes of overwhelming outrage, the plump woman seemed to be about to "blow" in a similar fashion. He couldn't keep a wicked grin from sneaking onto his face. At the last possible second—instead of bursting—the woman executed a complete "about-face" and marched away.

As Lee sat down, he glanced at Jessie. Her face was flushed and her eyes snapped with irritation.

"Mrs. Wagstaff," Dr. Gooden said, "perhaps it would be best—"

The old, black preacher, who had stood also, cleared his throat. "I think I know what the good doctor is about to suggest. It's time we were going, Mrs. Wagstaff."

Jessie walked toward him. "Oh, please don't. It's Linc's birthday. Stay."

"Oh-oh," Linc murmured a warning.

Lee followed the direction of the lad's gaze, then Lee felt a similar sinking feeling. A tall, angular woman came from the house on the other side of Jessie's home.

This time Jessie rose and went to meet her neighbor. "Mrs. O'Toole, how nice. You're just in time for a piece of birthday cake."

"It's not for the cake I'm here," the woman snapped. "You send these people home. They don't belong here." She crossed her arms over her meager bosom.

Lee knew Jessie would never back down, foolish though it be.

Jessie stood straight. "These people are *my* guests on *my* property. It is not for you to dictate whom I may invite to my home—"

"This is outrageous. 'Tis bad enough you've hired a black girl instead of an honest Irish girl like my niece—"

"Mrs. O'Toole, I think it's time you went home."

Lee shivered at Jessie's tone. He had heard captured Rebel soldiers reply to Union officers in warmer tones. The tall woman audibly ground her teeth, giving a hideous twist to her mouth. She turned and stalked away.

Lee glanced at Linc and watched him whispering in Butch's ear. Linc let the pup go. Butch charged after the woman yapping and growling at the intruder. Linc paused a moment, then chased after the dog. The boy snatched the dog up in his arms just as Butch was about to follow Mrs. O'Toole through her gate, then ran back to his mother.

When the dog quieted, Dr. Gooden cleared his throat. "I must leave now. I am on duty at the charity hospital this evening." He patted Linc on the shoulder. "Happy birthday again. Here is my gift to you." He pressed a silver dollar into the boy's hand.

Linc shouted, "Thank you, sir!"

"You are very welcome. I will show myself out, Mrs. Wagstaff. Stay with your guests."

Lee had to be honest with himself that the doctor had surprised him by staying this long.

"Thank you for coming," Jessie said as the doctor bowed over her hand in farewell. Both Susan and Ruby dropped curtseys. The doctor nodded to Lee and walked toward the front of the house.

The doctor's departure seemed to signal an end of the celebration. Lee felt it himself, but decided he'd stay after everyone else had left.

After a moment, the black congregation began to rouse themselves. The men pulled on their black hats. The women shook our their full skirts and straightened their hat pins.

"Please don't go," Jessie implored. "I—" Her words were cut off by the arrival of three mounted police. She gasped.

Protectively, Lee stepped forward to meet them for her. "Good afternoon, gentlemen. What can we do for you?"

The oldest of the three officers swung down from his saddle. "We received a report of a black mob—"

"Mob?" Jessie repeated the word incredulously. "Does this look like a mob?"

Shaking his head at her to be still, Lee stepped closer to the officer to do what he could to calm the situation. "It seems you received a false alarm."

"Appears so, but—"

The black preacher came to where Lee stood. "Begging your pardon, officer, but did you mention a black mob?"

Lee felt as uneasy about this as the black pastor sounded.

The policeman nodded. "Yes."

"Are there others concerned about a mob?" the Reverend asked.

"I'm afraid so," the policeman replied. He gave the preacher a meaningful look. "You know how rumors start."

"And spread," Lee finished.

"Would you escort us home, officer?" the black pastor asked.

"No!" Jessie objected. "You are my guests."

"Jessie," Lee stopped her by resting his hand on her arm. "You don't understand."

His face stormy, Caleb spoke up, "Mrs. Wagstaff, what he means is if a rumor about a black mob has started, our people could be in danger."

Reverend Mitchell intervened, "But if these policemen will give us escort home, the rumor will be blunted."

Jessie appealed silently to Lee.

Lee didn't like the situation any more than she did, but this was reality. "He's right, Jessie. Matters could get out of hand in no time. You don't want people hurt." Memories from the past flared inside him. He'd seen what evil men were capable of.

After a significant pause, she reluctantly agreed, "Very well."

Susan was at her elbow. "Mrs. Wagstaff, can I see my grand-ma home?"

"No, Susan." Jessie turned and took both Ruby's hands in hers. "I'd like Ruby to stay with us."

Lee felt love flow from Jessie in this simple gesture.

115

Susan protested, "But Mrs. Wagstaff, we don't have room."

Lee fought slipping into this sentiment. *Jessie, the confirmed idealist.*

"We'll make room. Now take Ruby up on the porch into the shade. She shouldn't be standing here in the sun."

"But—" Susan tried once more, "what 'bout da neighbors?"

Yes, Jessie, what about your formidable neighbors?

"She stays, Susan." Jessie looked to Lee. "Are you deserting us, too, Mr. Smith?"

Challenged, Lee found he couldn't disappoint the appeal in Jessie's imploring gaze, especially when Linc also looked up at him hopefully. "I think I'll walk the Reverend's congregation home." The phrase came out before he could hold it back.

Jessie reached for his hand. "Thank you, Lee." Her unexpected touch took Lee by surprise. She'd called him by his given name for the first time since he arrived on her back porch. He gripped her hand in his, drawing from it unexpected warmth and pleasure.

A fierce protectiveness stirred in him for this woman and her son. Words from deep inside him bubbled up, "Don't worry, Jess. I'll come back after seeing them safely home. Everything will be all right."

CHAPTER 8

June 17, 1871

Jessie snapped off the stems from a handful of string beans and dropped them into a large pot in her lap. From her garden, she'd picked and washed a colander of green beans that now sat in front of her on the kitchen table. Along with the delicate scent of the beans, she inhaled the clean fragrance of fresh starch.

Standing at the ironing board by the stove, Susan put the cooled iron down on the stove grate with a resounding *chink,* picked up the hot one off the stove, then licked her finger and tested the iron's heat with it. The iron sizzled. She began pressing Linc's white Sunday shirt. The black iron hissed as it touched the damp fabric. Susan asked again, "Are you certain-sure?"

"Your grandmother stays." Jessie punctuated her sentence by snapping off the ends of two beans. *Snap. Snap.*

"But the neighbors—"

"My hiring a cook is none of their business." Though Jessie had opened all the windows and doors, the cloying heat and quiet of the afternoon wrapped around her. Even the flies buzzed sluggishly. She paused to dab away the perspiration at her temples with the hem of her apron. "Susan, are you sure you should be ironing in this heat?"

"I used to pick cotton on hotter days. Don't be trying to turn me. Are you sure it best to have Grandma Ruby live here?"

"Your grandmother stays." *Snap. Snap.* The long beans fell into the pot.

"But we ain't got enough room," Susan protested.

"Leave that to me."

Susan set the cool iron on the stove and hung the shirt on its hanger. Bending over a round wicker basket, she unrolled the mound of dampened clothing wrapped in a tablecloth. Lifting out a black blouse of Jessie's, she slid it onto the board, then began to press the collar. "When are you gonna get out of mourning?"

"Don't *you* try to turn *me*." Jessie pointed a string bean at Susan.

Susan grinned. "I can find a place for Grandma Ruby." She began to iron the collar.

"My mind is made up." *Snap.*

"And you ain't changing it." Susan shook her head.

"Ruby's staying."

Susan paused, holding the iron in the air. "You're too good for you' own good."

"You mean stubborn, don't you?" Jessie grinned.

Susan snorted and bent to press around the placket of buttons down the front. "I wish everybody stubborn like you."

Jessie snorted in turn.

In the overpowering heat, the two of them fell silent. To the homey sounds of the beat of the iron as Susan lifted and pressed it down, the hiss of the steam, and the snapping of the beans, Jessie's mind drifted.

Her memory brought back the sound of Margaret's singing hymns softly as she ironed. As though catching Jessie's thought, Susan began to hum, "I'm gonna lay down my burdens, down by the riverside . . ." This hopeful tune comforted Jessie, but her longing for Margaret remained.

Her mother's betrayal—siding with her husband against Jessie on Linc's birthday—still stung. Not ever Susan's nearness prevented a stunning loneliness from sweeping through her. *If only I could have Margaret here with me again. My stepfather never changes. He always made certain I always came last with my mother, and I always will.* Setting the pot of beans on the table, she stood up before she gave way to tears. "I have to go tell Miss Wright—"

"Tell me what?" the old woman, drooping over her cane, asked from the kitchen doorway.

Jessie, wiping her hands on her apron, walked to Miss Wright. "Let's go into the parlor. It should be cooler on the east side of the house by now."

The spinster scowled, but she allowed Jessie to draw her into the parlor. Jessie helped the older woman to sit down on the rose-sprigged sofa by the front window. The damask curtains fluttered slightly with the breeze. Jessie pressed her hankie to her perspiring face. "There's going to be a change. I am going to move you downstairs—"

"Downstairs? Where?"

"Here." Jessie waved her hand, indicating the parlor.

"Here? I would lose all my privacy. Why anyone can walk in or look in from the entryway."

"I'll keep the pocket door to the foyer closed from now on."

"Why are you doing this? It's because of that girl's grand-mother, isn't it? You're going to take in another colored servant."

Jessie opened her mouth to speak.

But the old woman would not give in. "How can I make you understand? You're making a mistake. Susan's people don't belong here. They belong in Africa where God put them. Some of them are smart enough to be willing to go back where they belong."

Jessie had anticipated Miss Wright's objections. But just as the miasma of the day's heat and humidity had depleted her, these successive waves of confrontation had worn her down. Why did everyone have to argue with her?

Jessie tried to sound patient. "How can I send Ruby to live apart from Susan? I know I would give anything to have Margaret here again. No one could keep me from having her with me."

"I'm not saying you should send the woman far—"

Jessie lost her forbearance. Couldn't this old woman see right from wrong? "Ruby isn't the only reason I'm making this change. I'm doing this to help you. The fact is, soon you won't be able to get up and down the steps and you know it."

Miss Wright flushed red at Jessie's blunt words. "If Margaret were here—"

"You know if Margaret were here she would do just as I am doing. She would never turn Ruby or anyone else away if they needed help." *Margaret didn't turn you away.*

The elderly spinster blinked back tears.

Jessie regretted upsetting her. *But what must be said must be said.*

Miss Wright looked away while dabbing a handkerchief at her eyes. "You didn't know Margaret as long or as well as I did."

"You're right. I didn't grow up with her, but I loved her just as much as you did. Every time I do something *you* don't want me to do, you use Margaret against me."

"I'm trying to make you see reason." The spinster's voice was thick with unshed tears.

Jessie couldn't keep the anger from her voice. "Why am I the one who must see reason? Is it reasonable for my neighbors to call out the police merely because my guests have dark skin?"

"You don't seem to understand the boundaries of accepted conduct—"

Jessie's temper pushed her to say more. "Is it reasonable for doctors to refuse patients merely because of the color of their skin? If these things are reasonable, then I'm glad to be thought unreasonable."

Miss Wright crimped her lips and said in a tight, little voice, "I see you won't listen to me." She halted abruptly. "What will you use for a parlor then?"

"The dining room. It's warmer in the winter and I think I can fit a few of these chairs at one end."

Suddenly aware of the tension in her neck, Jessie rotated her head to loosen the taut muscles. "I will help you move your things down as soon as I have the curtain sewn and Ben to help me move the furniture."

"What curtain? You already have curtains on the windows."

"It will be a privacy curtain, dividing the parlor into two rooms."

"*Who* is going to share this room with me?" Miss Wright's shoulders drooped.

"Linc and I."

"Why?"

Jessie took a deep breath. "Ruby can't climb two flights of steps to the attic, so Susan will give her grandmother her own little room off the pantry and Susan will take my attic room. Linc and I will move into the other half of the parlor with you. I need to rent out your room. Linc is getting older and I need more money. I don't want him to have to leave school early to go out to work."

"And if I don't want to share the parlor with you and Linc? My wishes mean nothing, I suppose?"

Jessie sighed. She'd prefer a larger house with room for everyone, but that wasn't possible. She had to be practical for them all, and that meant moving Miss Wright in with Linc and her downstairs. It was necessary they all make sacrifices.

"Moving you downstairs will be better for you." Their eyes met and held. The painful words *It will make it easier to care for you when you can no longer walk at all* were left unsaid, but Miss Wright appeared to tacitly understand.

As Miss Wright stood up, she grunted with pain. In a weary voice, she said, "I'll go and sit on the porch."

Impulsively, Jessie stood up and reached out to touch the old woman, but stopped just shy of her sleeve. Hands at her sides, Jessie watched the old woman shuffle out of the room.

Jessie folded her arms over her breast and bent her head as though weighed down. *I'll keep my promise to Margaret. I'll take care of Miss Wright for the rest of her life. But why was Margaret the one taken, Lord? I'm sorry, Father, I wouldn't want anything to happen to Miss Wright. But I miss Margaret so. Why can't Miss Wright remember how kind Margaret was? They grew up like sisters. How is it that one turned out gentle and the other one so cold? She has forgotten Margaret, the real Margaret.*

"But I never will." Jessie breathed out a sigh that quivered through her. On the wall hung two samplers her mother-in-law had cross-stitched. They read: "God Is Love" and "Do unto others as you would have them do unto you."

"I will, Margaret, God willing. I will live the life you taught me to live, regardless of what others think, especially Hiram Huff."

June 25, 1871

The bright Saturday sunshine made Lee pull the brim of his hat farther forward as he walked along the side of Jessie's house.

"You're a liar!" a childish voice shouted from the backyard.

"Am not!" Linc insisted.

"Are too!"

"Am not!"

Linc's pup began barking, and the unmistakable grunts of boyish fisticuffs made Lee hurry into the backyard. *"Lincoln!"*

CHAPTER 8

Startled, the boys parted, but the acrimony between them blazed on their sweat-and-dirt-smudged faces.

"Explain yourselves." Lee's stern tone allowed no delay.

"He said I lied," Linc declared, his expression stormy.

Jessie stepped out the back door, then stopped on the top step.

Lee nodded to her, but spoke to the other boy. "Who are you, young man?"

When the lad didn't answer, Jessie said, "He's Tom Braun. He lives next door."

"Well, Tom, out with it. What do you think Linc was lying about?"

"He said you played ball with the Knickerbockers."

"Yes, I did get to play an inning of a practice game with that famous team. I was visiting friends in New York at the time." Lee had to keep from grinning. He didn't want to antagonize the boy any further, but the way Tom eyed him left no doubt that he didn't believe Lee either.

Lee continued, "Tom, I'm from the East originally. That's why I got the chance. I wouldn't lie to you or Linc."

Yes, I would, and I did. Lee had to close his lips firmly to hold back these words from pouring forth. The more time he spent with Linc, the harder it became to conceal the truth from the boy. He forced himself to go on, "Now, you two shake hands like gentlemen."

Reluctantly, the boys shook once. Tom dug his hands into his pockets and turned to leave.

"Hold on, Tom." Lee suggested nonchalantly, "Why don't you stay, and we'll toss the ball a while? Linc and I have some time before we leave for the game later."

"You mean it?" Tom's face glowed.

"Sure. Come on. Let's see what you can do." *Perhaps I can't tell the truth, but I can do some things right.* He glanced up at Jessie, who nodded and turned back toward the kitchen.

123

The events of the Sunday before still lingered vividly in Lee's mind. He hadn't wanted to end up helping Jessie's "cause." But he helped anyway by escorting the black congregation home. He wouldn't let anything like it happen again though. Jessie's crusade would stay hers alone. *I want no part of it. That wasn't in the bargain Will and I struck.*

⁂ ⁂ ⁂ ⁂ ⁂

Inside the kitchen, Susan smiled at Jessie. "That man come at just da right time."

"Yes." Deep in thought, Jessie picked up the dishcloth and began drying a plate.

As Susan scrubbed a skillet, she hummed to herself. When she set the pan on the stove to dry, she dried her hands. "Jessie, I'm going to do the shoppin' now."

"Thank you. I'm afraid I just don't have the energy today." Jessie dried the last dish and set it on the shelf. With a weary sigh, she took off her damp apron and hung it on its peg. She smoothed her hair, lifting the tendrils off her neck and brow.

She walked out onto the back porch and sat down on the rocker to watch the three-way game of catch. Before long, a disgruntled Tom was called home. Lee and Linc continued tossing the ball back and forth. Butch scampered back and forth also, yipping cheerfully.

Outwardly calm, Jessie rocked and fanned herself with a reed fan Susan had woven for her. Because of the day's unrelenting heat and her rampant emotions, Jessie felt like a pot simmering on the stove. Her confusion over Lee's place in their lives bubbled and rolled inside her.

In the weeks since early April, Mr. Smith hadn't yet tired of spending time with Linc as she had expected. And with his gift of a pup, he'd taken Linc's heart completely. So far nothing the man had done was wrong, but some sixth sense or intuition told her there was something about him that didn't ring true. But what? Was it just his cynical streak, or something more?

Linc ran toward his mother with Butch yapping at his heels. "It's time to go, Mother!" The look of joy on her son's face meant more to her than a gold nugget straight from the West. Denying Mr. Smith to her son would not be easy now or ever. Linc quickly tied Butch to the porch railing near the doghouse.

Jessie stood up and walked down the steps to Linc, brushing her hand over her son's head. "Have a good time at your ball game."

Mr. Smith strolled up behind Linc. "I'll have him home before supper."

Jessie nodded and smiled. "Thank you, Mr. Smith."

"I thought you dropped the 'mister' last Sunday, Jess." He smiled a wicked, teasing smile at her.

She folded her hands together and made no reply.

With Linc chattering at his side, Lee sauntered away, fuming at himself. *Why do I always have to tease her? Why can't I just ignore that "oh-so-proper" way she has about her? I am not interested in the Widow Wagstaff.*

❋ ❋ ❋ ❋ ❋

That evening, sitting on the back porch, Jessie threaded her needle and began to sew a button on Linc's blue shirt. The golden glow of twilight still provided enough light to mend by. The heat of the day had not released its hold, however, so she rocked, creating her own breeze. Cicadas screeched in rising crescendos, and laughter from a nearby house floated to Jessie on the heavy, summer air.

Mrs. Redding, another widow, sat in the rocker next to Jessie's. "Are you sure you won't join Mrs. Bolt and me? So many people are joining the temperance movement."

Keeping her eyes on her sewing, Jessie nodded, but didn't answer.

"We begin by singing. Then Miss Willard reads us letters from other cities. It is so good to hear the news of every victory—even small ones. Drinking spirits can be so ruinous for families."

"I'm sure you're right." Though Jessie agreed with Mrs. Redding's passion for the cause of temperance, it was difficult to work up much enthusiasm for the local temperance union—since Mrs. Redding kept letting her gaze shift to the backyard. Jessie surmised that the woman was not avidly awaiting Mrs. Bolt, but was anticipating Mr. Smith's return from the ballpark.

One corner of her mouth twisted ruefully. Mrs. Bolt was not the only widow pursuing Mr. Smith. Other neighbor ladies—from as far as five or six blocks away—just "happened" to drop in or stroll by just when Mr. Smith arrived each evening to play catch with Linc.

As though reading her mind, the woman went on, "You are so fortunate Mr. Smith takes such an interest in your son. You lost your husband in the war, too, didn't you? Where did he fall?"

"Outside of Petersburg, Virginia, during the last days of the siege."

"My husband was killed at Antietam."

"That was a horrible battle." Dark memories of those years of fear and waiting drew a shade over Jessie's heart.

Mrs. Redding gripped the arms of her rocking chair. "I will never forget reading the Antietam casualty lists—seeing my husband's name. For days afterwards his printed name on that awful page would appear before my eyes. I couldn't rid myself of the image."

Jessie's needle stilled. Those awful, those terrifying casualty lists. How many times had her hands shaken as she'd scanned the small type, searching, but hoping not to find, "Wm. Wagstaff" on the row after row of neatly printed names of those who would never come home. Tears moistened her eyes. She reached out and grasped the other widow's hand. For a moment they clung to each other, united by the horror they'd both lived.

CHAPTER 8

Mrs. Redding broke the silence. "I hope you don't mind my coming early in the evenings to escort Mrs. Bolt to our meetings." She lowered her voice, "You see, I delivered a still-born son six months after Antietam. When I see Mr. Smith and your son together—I don't know—somehow it fills an empty place inside me."

The poor woman's double loss burned through Jessie like molten steel. She nearly winced in pain. Finally she swallowed with difficulty. "You're welcome anytime. Perhaps I will come to a meeting with you some evening."

"You'd be very welcome." Mrs. Redding gave her a slight smile filled with gentle sweetness. "And I've heard of your work on behalf of the freed slaves here. I would like to give this to you for medicine." She handed Jessie a folded dollar bill.

"Oh, that isn't necessary." Jessie knew Mrs. Redding, a seamstress who lived and sewed in two rented rooms, was even poorer than she.

"Please, I want to. It would mean a great deal to me."

Jessie thought of the "widow's mite." "Thank you."

Mrs. Bolt stepped through the back door. "I'm ready then, Constance."

Mrs. Redding stood up. "Thank you for your hospitality, Mrs. Wagstaff."

"You're welcome anytime," Jessie murmured sincerely.

Mrs. Bolt cooed, "Good-bye." The two widows walked away. Mrs. Redding glanced once over her shoulder at Jessie. Jessie managed a smile. But when the two were out of sight, she pulled out a handkerchief and let tears over memories fall freely. *Dear God, thank you, thank you for my son. Keep watch over him by day and by night.*

※ ※ ※ ※ ※

Jessie sat back and closed her eyes. Mr. Smith had brought Linc home from the ballpark, then left. After supper, Susan had put Linc to sleep and helped Miss Wright, then her own grand-mother, to bed before going to her own room. Alone on the back porch, Jessie knew she should go up to bed, but the heat made her languid, reluctant to move. Rocking gently, she let herself relax. Summer sounds—the rattle of an occasional wagon on the street, voices of children calling to one another as they caught fireflies, the chorus of crickets—soothed her as she rocked. She began nodding.

"Mrs. Wagstaff!"

Jessie sat up. "Ben? What? Not the baby again?"

"No, ma'am. Caleb sent me to fetch you. The Reverend can hardly breathe."

Jessie stood up. "It's his heart." She hurried inside and gath-ered up the basket of herbs she took nursing. Before donning her hat and gloves, she wrote a quick note to Susan and left it on the table. Ben and she set off briskly. They covered the three miles to Reverend Mitchell's modest home in good time.

Jessie stepped inside. Though the sky had been darkening steadily, her eyes needed a few moments to adjust to the low light of one feeble lamp on the table. Before she saw Reverend Mitchell in the dark room, she heard his labored breathing. She felt a sinking sensation in her stomach. *He's much worse this time.*

"Good evening," she spoke calmly, set her basket on the table, and began removing her hat and gloves. Margaret had taught her that a soothing tone and quiet motions reassured the ailing. "Are you experiencing pain in your chest again?"

"And in his arm," Caleb answered.

When she came close to the narrow bed, Jessie recognized the clear signs of dropsy. The thin man's feet and abdomen were swollen. She'd often come when the Reverend had one of these "spells." "Caleb, do you have a kettle on the fire? We'll try a stronger dose of Margaret's heart tea." Caleb lifted a kettle off a hook over the fire and met her at the table.

In the low light, the dark faces around her nearly disap-peared. As she brewed the tea, she felt like a pale wraith in a murky netherworld. The soft sigh of Ruth's praying and the hard-won, hissing breaths of the pastor added to the unnatural aura around her. This time, would she be able to bring the old man relief?

Soon, with Caleb supporting his father in his arms, Jessie lifted the cup to the old man's grayish white lips. She shuddered with fear. He looked so haggard, so beaten down. She had trouble getting any of the tea down his throat. His whole body strained at the intake of each breath.

Suddenly his labored breathing stopped.

The tea cup fell from Jessie's hands and shattered at her feet.

"Oh, Lord, no!" Caleb cried out.

Twisting her hands, Jessie cried out silently, *Margaret, I can't remember! What should I do? Oh, dear God, tell me what to do!*

Then she remembered, Margaret's voice a whisper in her mind. "Caleb, turn him onto his left side. Press his nostrils closed. Take a breath and blow into his mouth—hard! *Now!*"

Caleb followed her instructions intently repeating them over and over. Seconds ticked by. Jessie could hardly breath.

Finally the old man gasped, choked. He took a shallow breath. Jessie let herself inhale too.

Caleb wiped perspiration off his forehead with the back of his hand. "It's bad this time. What are we going to do?"

The alarm in his voice deepened Jessie's own fear, but she now knew what action to take. Turning, she spoke, "Ben, I want you to go to the hotel where Dr. Gooden lives. Tell him it's a matter of life or death. If he isn't there, ask where he is. Tell them you're asking on my behalf. Ben, don't come back without him."

Without answering, Ben pulled on his cap, kissed Ruth on the cheek and rushed out the door.

Caleb's eyes gazed at Jessie in the night gloom. "Do you think your doctor will come *here*?"

"He promised me he'd come if it were life or death."

Caleb grumbled something too low for her to understand.

"I didn't catch what you said." Then she realized he must have voiced some doubt about the doctor's coming. Until that moment, she hadn't doubted. *What will I do if he doesn't come, or can't?*

Suddenly she couldn't stand still. She paced back and forth between the table and the bed, the only furniture in the one-room house. She listened to each breath the old pastor drew. As each ended, she prayed he would take another. Time passed, measured breath by breath.

Ruth tried to get her to sit down for tea, but Jessie paced in time to the loud, wheezing breaths. Gasp in. Gasp out. Over and over.

Ruth, cradling her son in a blanket, finally fell asleep on the floor. The humid night breeze floated fitfully through the windows. Mosquitoes buzzed around Jessie's ears till she tied a handkerchief around her head. Though her weary feet felt as though they'd been coated with cast iron, she still paced.

Finally Caleb pulled her to a hard chair by the table and made her sit. Then he went back to hover over his father, fanning away mosquitoes. "He's not coming, you know," Caleb said bitterly. "Your doctor won't stop here, not at this door. You know it."

Jessie pressed her lips tightly together. She couldn't make any promises she couldn't keep, and she had no words of comfort for Caleb.

"Don't . . . argue . . . son." His father nearly strangled on the words.

Jessie expected Caleb to answer his father, but he merely slumped down on the floor within the faint glow of the hearth, then lowered his head into his hands.

Jessie sat, waiting. Competing with the old pastor's strained breathing was the sound of the boats moored on the nearby Chicago River bumping against the piers, the slap of waves hitting the pilings and boats, and the climbing shriek of cicadas that floated in through the open window and door.

CHAPTER 8

In spite of the advancing night, the stifling heat refused to relent. Jessie pressed her handkerchief to her temples until it became saturated. Discreetly she unbuttoned her collar and her cuffs, trying to release the heat that glowed from inside her. Finally she moved her chair into the doorway to catch any desultory breeze. She must have dozed off because she awoke suddenly.

"Jessie?"

The vestiges of sleep made her mind fumble at first in trying to recognize the man's voice. Then Dr. Gooden's face was in front of hers. "Doctor!" She stood up, nearly upsetting the chair. "You came!"

"*Ja,* I am sorry it took so long, but Ben had many places to go before he found me. I have worked a busy day."

Jessie let Ben lift her chair out of the doctor's path and Dr. Gooden stepped inside. He immediately crossed to the table and opened his black bag. "Reverend Mitchell, you are having a bad spell, I hear. I have brought a powder that should help you."

Jessie brought over the kettle and poured water into a cup and handed it to the doctor.

He opened a small white packet, measured out a few grains of powder, and stirred it by swirling the cup. "Caleb, would you support your father behind the shoulders?"

Caleb propped up his frail father and watched while the doctor helped his patient painstakingly sip the mixture. "How long will it be before this drug takes effect, Doctor?"

"Not long." The doctor looked at Jessie. "This is a new mixture of digitalis. I like this mixture for the heart because it is a purer one, and takes very little." The old man finally drained the cup.

Dr. Gooden motioned Jessie to sit in her chair by the door again. "We wait now." Drawing the only other chair next to hers, in the doorway he joined her in the meager breeze. Caleb hovered beside his father. Ben had collapsed on the floor beside his wife and was already sound asleep. Jessie heard rather than saw the doctor snap open his pocket watch.

His accented voice came to her in the darkness, "It is near midnight. We stay up together another time."

The tiredness in his voice made her feel guilty. She reached for his arm. "I'm sorry to call you out, but—"

He grasped her hand. "Don't apologize. I gave you my promise."

Emotion choked Jessie. The worry and the waiting released their hold on her. The relief of having someone capable, not just sympathetic, to turn to swept away her normal reserve. Under the cover of night, she lifted his hand and pressed its back to her cheek. She whispered brokenly, "I've fought alone for so long."

"Jessie," he murmured, "I'm here now."

She nodded, but didn't trust herself to speak. In the darkness, she lowered his hand to her lap, holding it there, drawing strength from him. Minutes passed. She dozed again.

"Hear it? Jessie?" His voice urged her awake once more. "Hear what?" She straightened stiffly.

"He breathes better."

"My father is sleeping easily." Caleb walked to the doorway. Faint moonlight silvered the strong features of his face. "I owe you, Doctor."

"Not much. I charge only fifty cents for a call. I leave you another packet of medicine. Tomorrow you must come to my office for more."

"I owe you more than money."

Dr. Gooden stood up and offered Caleb his hand. They shook.

Caleb turned to Jessie. "And thank you, Mrs. Wagstaff. You always come whenever you're needed."

She touched Caleb's arm. "You should sleep now. Will someone stay with your father tomorrow while you're at work?"

"Ruth stays with him during the day."

Jessie nodded. As she gathered her bonnet, gloves, and basket, the doctor finished giving Caleb instructions.

She and the doctor left together. He led her to his gig. Soon they were making their way home through the nearly empty streets. A church bell struck one. The doctor didn't hurry his tired horse. Its hooves made a sad clip-clop on the wooden streets.

Almost without realizing it, Jessie leaned against the doctor's side. She knew she should draw away, but when he took her hand in his free one, she didn't pull away. Having someone to lean on, after standing alone for so long, just felt too good to deny.

Finally, the gig stopped in front of Jessie's house. She sat up, but when she tried to pull her hand from his, he prevented her.

"A moment. I ask a favor of you."

Jessie cleared the sleep from her voice. "What is it?"

"In a little over a week, I will attend a party at the Potter Palmer home."

"The Palmers?" Jessie was surprised. The Palmers were high society.

"Yes, I am invited by Mrs. Palmer. She toured Rush Hospital this week and was very interested in my ideas for better public health through cleaning up Chicago."

"Oh, that's wonderful."

"Yes, I think I begin to make the contacts I need for my future work. But for success I need one thing more."

"What?"

"You to go with me."

His words shocked her into silence.

"I need a woman like you on my arm. I need you to charm the men and speak with intelligence to the women. As Linc would say, I need to cover all of my bases. Will you help me, Jessie?"

So many thoughts rushed through her mind she couldn't speak at first. "I'm not the kind of woman you need. I'm just a poor widow."

"You are poor only in money. I will buy you a dress for the occasion."

"Oh, no! You can't!"

"Please. I need you. I count on you, Jessie."

If he'd said any other words, she could have refused. But how could she deny this good man her help?

She bowed her head. "If you think I'd be of help to you, I'll go."

Bending toward her, he kissed her hand.

Jessie felt a chill go through her when she realized he had kissed the palm of her hand, not the back.

CHAPTER 9

June 27, 1871

THE SHARP RAT-A-TAT ON THE front door caught Jessie on her hands and knees polishing the railing of the front staircase. Perturbed at the interruption, she sat back on her heels and pushed the damp tendrils up from her forehead. Before she stood up, she untied her apron.

Susan sailed by through the entryway to open the door. "Yes, may I help you?"

A young voice answered, "A delivery from Field and Leiter's for Mrs. Jessie Wagstaff."

With a small gasp, Jessie lost her balance and landed on her backside. *The dress. Not now! Oh, no!*

To Jessie's relief, Susan only half-opened the door in order to shield Jessie's disarray from view. Susan said formally, "Mrs.

Wagstaff, a delivery for you." Then Susan cocked an eye back at Jessie and, with her hand behind her back, she motioned Jessie to stand.

Taking a calming breath, Jessie pushed herself up, yanked off the apron, and hurried down the steps. Arriving beside Susan, she summoned up a smile for the young man in the blue uniform with brass buttons who held a large box with an invoice on top.

"Will you sign the receipt, ma'am?"

"Certainly." As Jessie signed, she felt Susan slip something into her side pocket. Susan stepped forward and took the package for her. Then Jessie reached into her pocket and pulled out a dime, which she pressed into the boy's palm. "For your trouble."

"Thank you, ma'am!" The boy left with a bounce to his step.

Jessie closed the door. "Thank heavens you remembered the tip."

"I got the shoppin' money in my pocket already." Susan nodded at the box in her arms. "Now, what's dis?"

Jessie experienced a painful twinge around her heart. The last time he'd visited she'd tried unsuccessfully to persuade Dr. Gooden to change his mind about purchasing an evening dress for her. All she accomplished was that he had promised to be discreet, but how had he been discreet? How had he protected her reputation? "I think . . ." her uncertain voice didn't even sound like her, "it's from Dr. Gooden."

"A package?" Miss Greenleigh called down.

Jessie looked up. The unusual occurrence of a department store delivery had garnered an instant audience—Miss Greenleigh on the landing above, flanked below by Miss Wright in the doorway to the parlor and Ruby in the dining room arch. Jessie wanted to shrink, then vanish. Why couldn't the delivery have come when everyone was out?

"What did that doctor send you?" Miss Wright glared.

CHAPTER 9

Ruby cleared her throat and admonished quietly, "Susan, when you open that, you be sure you be careful."

For just a second, Jessie longed to run up into the attic and hide. She'd hoped Dr. Gooden would reconsider his invitation. She almost convinced herself she'd imagined the whole conversation!

But she couldn't evade the reality of the situation or her audience. Ignoring the fluttering of her heart, she drew herself up and said calmly, "Dr. Gooden has invited me to accompany him to a dinner party this Saturday evening."

"A dinner party!" Miss Wright gasped.

"How exciting!" Miss Greenleigh ran lightly down the steps.

"Lord above!" Ruby raised her arms.

Within seconds, Jessie had been tugged and pushed into the open end of the dining room. There, all the women gathered in a circle around Susan, who knelt in front of the package. Susan carefully untied the string and lifted the cover from the box.

At the sight of the dress, Jessie involuntarily sighed, "Ahhh!" In fact, a similar sound came from all the women.

Jessie couldn't move. Miss Greenleigh tenderly lifted the folded dress by the shoulders and held it up for all to admire. "Oh, Mrs. Wagstaff, Jessie," the young woman enthused. "It's silk, amber silk."

Jessie's mouth opened wide. "I've never worn a silk dress." In spite of her protest, the sight of the gown sent a shiver of delight through her.

The gown was very discreet, but—being evening wear—the neckline dipped in a shallow V-neck. At the neckline, cream-colored lace draped like a shawl, topping the dress.

"It's charmin', just charmin'," Ruby put in. "Look at dat ivory lace at da top. Susan, don't it look just like da dresses Miss Charlotte wore to da cotillions and parties?"

Susan nodded her gaze locked on the gown.

Holding the dress to her waist, Miss Greenleigh dipped and twisted to and fro, making the skirt flare in a shimmer of gold and brown.

"It's so lovely," Jessie murmured.

"Lovely?" Miss Wright huffed, "What I want to know, Jessie Wagstaff, is why a man is buying you *clothing*? Even if you were engaged to him, this would be improper. As it is, it's scandalous! Why men buy dresses for their kept women, not for respectable widows!"

"I told him not to," Jessie said weakly. "I know it's improper. But he said he'd be perfectly discreet. What could I say? He's counting on me to go with him, and I certainly can't afford anything appropriate." Caught in the conflicting currents of temptation, respectability, and obligation, she sat down on the nearest chair and pressed her hands to her mouth.

"You'll send it back. That's what you'll do!" Miss Wright blustered. "You may be without male protection, but I will not allow your good name—*Margaret's* name—to be dragged into the gutter! Who knows who saw him buying you this dress and having it sent here!"

"Just a minute." Susan held up her hand. "Da tag here on da box don't say nothin' about Dr. Gooden. It say da dress from 'Mrs. C. Abbott'."

"Who dat?" Ruby put her hands on her wide hips.

"That's the matron of nurses at Rush Hospital," Jessie answered faintly. "She's very supportive of Dr. Gooden's plans. I don't understand."

"I do." Miss Greenleigh held the dress snugly to her as though protecting it. "It's obvious. Dr. Gooden knows better than to compromise Mrs. Wagstaff's name. He must have asked Mrs. Abbott to purchase a dress and have it delivered."

"Well," Miss Wright grumbled, "that shows he has some sense, but it's still improper. A decent woman cannot—"

CHAPTER 9

"Mrs. Wagstaff," Miss Greenleigh interrupted. "There's something special about this dinner party. This is an evening dress, isn't it?"

All of the women, even Miss Wright, gazed at Jessie.

Although she felt as though a brick had become wedged sideways in her throat, she took a deep breath and sat up straighter. How would they react to her news? "Mrs. Potter Palmer toured Rush Hospital last week. Dr. Gooden had the opportunity to explain some of the new concepts of better health through public sanitation—"

Miss Greenleigh squealed, "You've been invited to dinner at the Palmer mansion!" The young woman danced a little jig. "Oh! I can't wait to tell Mrs. Bolt. She'll turn absolutely pea green!"

"Potter Palmer?" Ruby quizzed Susan. "Who dat?"

Susan exclaimed, "One of the richest men in da city—that's who!"

"Lord above!" Ruby clapped her hands.

"I don't care who's giving the dinner party!" Miss Wright thundered. "You can't accept that dress!"

A moment of contrite silence followed. Jessie clutched her hands together and lowered her eyes.

"Maybe it not a gift," Susan began cautiously as she reached for the gown from Miss Greenleigh. "Maybe Mrs. Wagstaff gonna pay the doctor for it. Maybe he just sent it to save her the trouble of shoppin' for it. If the party only five days from now, we only got enough time to fit it to Mrs. Wagstaff."

"But, Susan, I can't afford a silk gown!" Jessie stared at her friend.

"Maybe you can't afford the whole price, but maybe I pay half?" Susan held the dress to her.

"Why would you pay half?" Jessie looked at Susan as though she were speaking a foreign language.

"I always wanted a silk dress for my weddin'."

Jessie stood up. "Susan!"

139

Miss Greenleigh clapped her hands. "Has that handsome Caleb proposed?"

"Not yet." Susan looked down demurely. "His pa so sick. We're waiting."

"That's proper," Ruby said with a nod.

Jessie touched Susan's arm affectionately. The dress wasn't the real issue here. "I truly would like you to have this dress, Susan, but how can I go to Potter Palmer's? No matter what I wear, I'm no one special. I—"

"You're the equal of any of those society women!" Miss Wright's adamant words halted everyone.

Jessie stepped forward. "But—"

Miss Wright held up her hand, then drew her bent body up as if to lecture them. "It is improper to accept such a gift from a man, but if you are paying for it, it isn't a gift. And I, for one, see clearly why Dr. Gooden wants you by his side."

"Then explain it to me." Jessie folded her arms over each other. "I don't understand what good I can do him."

"Dr. Gooden knows that the men he'll meet are all busy making and tending their fortunes. In the matters of charity, it's their wives who must be influenced. That's why he needs a woman like you, Jessie."

Miss Greenleigh continued Miss Wright's explanation, "I see. A single man like the doctor must tread warily around these married women. He mustn't give the wrong impression. But if he comes with a lovely, intelligent woman on his arm, he'll give just the right kind of impression."

Jessie's feelings of inadequacy nearly choked her. Why had the doctor chosen to ask her, of all people? "But I'm not lovely or intelligent."

"Stop that nonsense right now!" Miss Wright thumped her cane. "Your mother raised you for any occasion!"

"And you are attractive," Miss Greenleigh insisted. "Just look at your beautiful brown eyes! This dress will look gorgeous on you!"

CHAPTER 9

"Besides," Ruby urged, "if da doctor need you, you got to help him. He he'ped Reverend Mitchell and Little Ben."

"They're right. Besides, how many times in your life will you be invited to the Potter Palmer mansion anyway?" Miss Greenleigh motioned Susan to hand back the dress. "Susan, would you please get my sewing box from my room? We'll have this fitted to Jessie in two shakes."

After a flurry of activity around Jessie, there, in the midst of the four women in the dining room whose shades had been pulled low and whose pocket door had been shut tight, stood Jessie. Susan slipped the black dress off over Jessie's head, revealing Jessie's embroidered white corset cover and starched petticoats, then slid the silk dress over her in its place.

Again a spontaneous "Ahh" breathed through the ladies who surrounded Jessie on all sides. Jessie was too keyed up to do anything more than remember to breathe.

"Oh, it look just like da dress Miss Charlotte wore to dat fall Cotillion her daddy give in '59. Oh, yes. Oh, yes." Ruby rubbed her hands together.

From the elegantly carved wooden sewing box, Susan lifted out a round pink pincushion. "But, Grandma Ruby, dis is da height of style now. Look how da overskirt sweep up into dis bustle. Miss Charlotte's dress had a hoop."

"It does outline your tiny waistline perfectly, Jessie." Miss Greenleigh grinned.

"Very nice. Very nice." Miss Wright lowered herself onto a chair.

Jessie blushed at their compliments. Being the center of attention was a new experience—both thrilling and horrible. She had a hard time lifting her chin to face them, but she had to or the hemline would suffer. Besides, she had to be practical. She couldn't look at the Palmer's floor for a whole evening!

While Ruby hovered nearby in the doorway, Miss Greenleigh and Susan deftly lifted and adjusted the fit at the cap of the sleeve, then conferred about deepening the darts around

the waistline. Jessie took no part in the discussion and adjust-
ments.

"Ruby!" Miss Wright's sharp voice made Jessie and the
other three women jump. "You're too old to be standing. Sit
down in that chair." She pointed her cane to an extra dining
room chair positioned by the door.

"But . . ." Ruby looked at Susan hesitantly.

"Sit!" Miss Wright ordered her.

Ruby sat.

Jessie, Susan, and Miss Greenleigh exchanged covert glances,
which told Jessie they were just as surprised as she about Miss
Wright's concern for Ruby's comfort.

Miss Greenleigh and Susan continued tucking, consulting,
and pinning. Jessie felt like a dressmaker's form, not herself at all.
Finally the two "seamstresses" were agreed on the alterations to
be made. Miss Wright spoke up, "Now, you two young women
step back so I can see the effect."

The two obeyed the old woman. "Jessie, turn slowly so I can
see the dress on you."

Jessie did as she was told.

Miss Wright sighed. "Lovely. Elegant. Now remember what
I said, Jessie; you're the equal of any woman there. They're just
women who married men who made money. You were the wife
of Will Wagstaff. The Wagstaff name has been respected in
Chicago for over thirty years, and don't you forget it!"

Jessie still couldn't believe this was happening. *I'm not a society lady!* "But—"

"Mrs. Wagstaff," Miss Greenleigh suggested, "why don't you
come up to my room and look at yourself in my full-length mirror. If you only saw yourself, I'm sure—"

Jessie panicked. "Oh, no! I can't look at myself! Not in this
dress."

They all stared at her as she flushed, surprised at her own
vehemence.

Then Susan muttered, "One of these days I'm gonna burn every black dress in dis house."

"Amen," Ruby said.

June 30, 1871

"Doctor Jones, can't I say anything to change your mind?" Jessie, clutching her purse with both hands, tried to keep the quaver from her voice as she tried to persuade the fifth doctor she'd approached. The arrival of the silk dress had prompted Jessie to try to find another doctor for the Reverend's congregation. It wasn't that she doubted Dr. Gooden; she just hated feeling beholden.

The young man with a fair beard shook his head. "I'm sorry. What you suggest is impossible."

"But you've just opened your practice—"

"If I take in black patients, my practice will close even more quickly than it opened."

"But . . ." Jessie's mouth was so dry she couldn't finish her sentence.

A bell jingled.

"My next patient." Doctor Jones smiled with tight lips and showed her to the door.

Jessie departed without another word. A horse trolley passed her, raising dust from the unpaved street. She pressed a handkerchief to her nose and mouth to filter out the dust as she breathed.

She walked blindly for several blocks, trying to understand why everyone believed so differently than she did. Why couldn't they see the obvious? Susan's people needed medical help regardless of their dark skin. How could people just ignore such a glaring need? The mental burden made her hunch forward as though it were a physical weight she carried.

When she stopped thinking so deeply, she realized she was only about a half mile from her mother's home. It was unusual for Jessie to be away from her own house at this hour of the afternoon. By now, her twin half-brothers would be out playing ball and her stepfather would be at work. She hadn't seen her mother since Linc's birthday. The chance of a quiet visit alone with her mother was too inviting to be ignored. She strode down the familiar streets and turned up the alley.

Smiling, she ran lightly up the back steps to her mother's home. "Mother!"

"Jessie!" Esther threw open the back door and wrapped her arms around her daughter. "I saw you coming!"

Tears sprang to Jessie's eyes. Her mother's embrace was more than she had hoped for. How many times in the lonely years after losing Will and Margaret had she yearned to feel her mother's touch?

"I'm so glad you came," Esther murmured. "I was afraid after . . ." Her voice ebbed, then died.

"Let's not discuss him," Jessie replied, dabbing her eyes with a handkerchief.

Esther put her arm around her daughter's shoulders and drew her into the kitchen. Jessie sat down at the dark oak kitchen table. Glancing at the stark white walls, she felt a painful tug at her emotions. As long as she could remember, her mother had longed for a blue kitchen, but Hiram Huff decreed the extra charge for tinted paint was an unnecessary extravagance. After all, his mother's kitchen had been plain white—like a kitchen should be.

Jessie nudged these worrisome thoughts from her mind. She wouldn't let Hiram Huff spoil this rare, private visit with her mother. "How are the twins?"

Esther set two cups of coffee onto the table and pushed the creamer toward her daughter. "They're fine. Tim is working hard, preparing for the sixth-grade spelling bee this fall."

"That's nice." An uncomfortable pause began. Jessie wanted to ask for sympathy and encouragement in her effort to find a doctor for Susan's people, but knew—out of a sense of duty—

her mother would not voice any opinion that countered her husband's.

"Mr. Smith seemed like a very nice man," Esther said softly, then looked into her daughter's face.

"He's been very good to Linc. He comes every evening to play ball and takes him to Saturday games as often as he can." Avoiding her mother's glance, Jessie sipped her coffee.

Again an uneasy, unnatural reticence cropped up between them.

"How's Susan's grandmother?" Esther traced the rim of her cup.

Jessie looked up. "Fine."

"I was happy she found her granddaughter again."

"Yes." *As happy as I would be if I could be close to you, Mother, as I've always wanted to be.*

"It must have been a terrible thing to be separated from your only living relative like that."

"Yes." *I know how that feels.* Tears threatened Jessie again. She regretted coming. Sitting near her mother, trying to chat politely made Jessie's emotional separation from her mother feel more stark, more cruel than ever.

Esther took a deep breath. "I wish—" She broke off at the sound of heavy footsteps coming up the wooden back porch steps.

"Esther—" Hiram stepped into the kitchen and halted. "*You're* here?" Her stepfather wore his fire captain's uniform, now blackened with smoke.

"Yes." Jessie rose to face him. "I happened to be in the neighborhood."

"I didn't expect you home, Hiram," Esther said, also rising.

Jessie silently fumed. How did he manage to make them feel as though they had been caught doing something wrong?

"Didn't you hear the alarm bells all night?" he snapped. "My men are exhausted. I had to call the next shift in early." He pulled off his fire hat and raked soot-blackened hands through his hair.

Esther murmured, "I'm so sorry—"

"One small fire after another and *then* an abandoned warehouse down by the river. Someone's careless match destroyed it. We barely contained it. Water pressure was dangerously low."

He glared at his stepdaughter. "Evidently having a new cook gives you time to gad about, Missy."

Hot words frothed up inside her throat. She choked them back for her mother's sake. "Missy" was the childhood name he had used during his lectures on all her failings. He must know his using it would goad her. He nearly succeeded in making her say something indiscreet, but she wouldn't give him the pleasure of knowing he'd vexed her. "I do need to go," she said in a carefully colorless voice.

"Even a few of my men had heard about your *colored* party. Everyone in your neighborhood is outraged by your ridiculous display, Missy. You don't seem to have any sense about what is proper social behavior, or how it might affect us."

Jessie stood stock still. She felt her face warm with a deep flush. "Stepfather, I don't dignify gossip by regarding it—nor do I regard those who spread it." She would have continued, but out of the corner of her eye, she caught her mother's pained expression.

If she continued, her mother would suffer for it—not with blows, but with endless hectoring. Her eyes averted, Jessie walked past her stepfather. Without a wave or backward glance, she said, "Good day, Mother."

July 1, 1871

Tense and afraid to sit down and possibly wrinkle her dress, Jessie stood in the middle of her parlor. As she turned to walk to the window, the amber silk skirt and petticoats beneath flourished and rustled around her.

CHAPTER 9

"He's not here yet," Miss Wright announced. "The sun hasn't set, so we'll see the carriage through the lace curtains when it draws up."

As Jessie returned to a high-backed chair, she turned and her skirts whispered around her. Arranging her skirts with care, she perched gingerly on it.

"You will do fine," Miss Wright said gruffly.

Jessie looked askance at the old woman who kept watch with her. "I'm worried I will do something that may reflect poorly on Dr. Gooden."

"Keep your talk brief. Answer questions, but don't offer any extra information. Tell the truth, but don't explain."

"You mean such as the fact that we're as poor as church mice?" Jessie managed to smile.

"We're not poor, just thrifty. You carry yourself well. You speak well. This is America. Remember, you're the equal of any of the ladies you'll meet tonight."

"And I married Will." Her eyes strayed to his daguerreotype on the mantel. What would Will say to her in this silk dress? She knew. He'd say, "You look beautiful, Princess." A lump formed in her throat. Will would want her to enjoy this evening and do her best for the doctor.

The sound of the carriage brought both women's eyes forward. "He's here," Jessie croaked. She stood up and drew on the long gloves that she had laid on the table.

"Just remember, hold your head high," the old woman rumbled.

"I will."

Earlier, Miss Greenleigh had done Jessie's hair, buffed her nails, and creamed her hands and shoulders with rosewater and glycerine. She'd loaned Jessie a modest string of pearls, long gloves, and a gossamer shawl. Before that, Miss Wright had surprised Jessie by giving Susan the money to buy a pair of shoes of silk dyed the same color as Jessie's deep amber dress. Everyone had been so helpful, as though the dress bound them all together.

147

The knock at the door came. Susan walked sedately through the hallway to answer it. Jessie heard Susan greet the doctor, then held her breath as he walked toward her.

"Jessie, how lovely you look tonight!" He took both her hands and kissed them.

"Good evening, Doctor," Miss Wright called his attention to herself.

The doctor continued to hold Jessie's hands, but he turned and bowed to the old woman. "Miss Wright."

Jessie motioned toward the arm of the chair where the gauzy shawl Miss Greenleigh had loaned her lay, though Jessie really couldn't understand why she required it. The evening was uncomfortably warm as usual.

The doctor deftly arranged the shawl around the top of her bare shoulders. As his fingertips brushed the nape of her bare neck, she shivered involuntarily. The lace at the neck shone with a pearl-like glow against her pale shoulders.

"Shall we go?" The doctor offered her his arm.

Jessie nodded and tucked her hand into the crook of his elbow.

As they stepped into the hall, Mrs. Bolt called down to them from the landing. "Don't you two look charming!" she gushed.

Jessie cringed. She'd noticed that Miss Greenleigh had stayed discreetly upstairs in her room. Ruby and Susan had lingered in the dining room, while Miss Wright had stayed in the parlor to bolster Jessie's resolve. Her confederates had tactfully given her the privacy and support she needed to nerve herself to the task at hand.

But, of course, Mrs. Bolt had no tact.

"I hear you two are off to a special evening," the redhead said brashly. "Though how a poor widow can afford a silk dress, I'm sure I don't know." She finished with a trill of laughter.

Jessie squeezed the doctor's arm.

"I am sorry, ma'am. We do not have time to chat. Dinner is at 7:30. Good evening, ladies." The doctor swept Jessie through the hallway, where a grinning Susan held the door open for them.

With a jolt, Jessie saw Linc and Lee at the bottom of the front steps. Earlier Linc had left to go for a walk with Mr. Smith. She had told her son she was going to a party, but she had hoped to avoid seeing Mr. Smith. As he looked up the steps at her, she felt exposed, vulnerable.

"Mother! Where did you get that dress? It isn't black!" Her son spoke loud enough to alert everyone in the neighborhood.

More gossip! What story would be spread to her stepfather now?

"Hello, Linc," she said as calmly as she could. Dr. Gooden led her down the steps.

"Good evening, Mrs. Wagstaff." Mr. Smith swept off his hat and bowed low. He lowered his voice, "Or should I address you as 'my lady' this evening?"

The slight taunt in his voice made Jessie blush hotly while the doctor and Mr. Smith exchanged greetings.

"Mrs. Wagstaff has agreed to attend an important dinner party tonight," Dr. Gooden announced and drew out his watch. "I am sorry, but we cannot stay to chat or we will be late."

"I wouldn't want to make you late," Mr. Smith said wryly.

The man made her feel like a hypocrite. She wanted to scream at him, *Yes, I know I don't belong in this dress or going to this party, but I have to. Dr. Gooden has proved he's a fine man and he needs my help.* But, of course, she couldn't say anything in her own defense.

Avoiding Mr. Smith's mocking gaze, she looked down at her son. "Be good, Linc. I'll be home very late. Good night." She hurried past them.

Dr. Gooden helped her into the hired carriage and shut the door. In the dimness and privacy of the carriage, she diligently rolled back the waves of self-reproach that seeing Lee Smith had caused her. She simply had to remember she was here to help Dr. Gooden, and she needed a clear mind to do that. The driver "chucked" to the team and they started off, rolling down the street.

Jessie smiled at the doctor. Between the distractions of Mrs. Bolt and Mr. Smith, she hadn't noticed how nice he looked in his black dinner jacket. "You look like you were born to dress for dinner."

He smiled. "I think perhaps I fit better the doctor's dark coat."

Jessie smiled. This man did have a way of taking himself lightly.

"Now, Mrs. Wagstaff, I ask you a favor. We have not known each other long, but tonight I wish you will call me Henry."

"Henry?" She sat forward a bit. She remembered him calling her Jessie the night he'd invited her. How had their relationship moved so quickly? Was it the effect of the long nights they had spent together saving two lives?

"Yes, it is better that we seem to have a longer acquaintance."

Her mind went back to Miss Wright's explanation of why Henry wanted her to accompany him. "I see."

"Good. Now. Mrs. Palmer is our hostess. She and Mrs. Field, the wife of Mr. Marshall Field, are the two women most likely to help in my work. Both of them have begun to follow the example set by Eastern ladies in sponsoring charity work."

Jessie nodded, ignoring a sinking feeling in her tightly laced middle. She prayed for strength, for understanding and guidance. She'd need all that and more tonight. *Thank you, Father.*

By the time their carriage pulled up in front of the Palmer residence, Jessie felt queasy. Only a quick prayer for strength gave her legs the ability to step down onto the walk to the house. *House?* The Palmer mansion loomed above her like a castle of old, a castle alight with gas lamps. To Jessie it appeared more like a formidable fortress whose battlements she was about to breach.

CHAPTER 9

Clutching the doctor's arm like a lifeline, Jessie strolled up the red-carpeted steps and entered the massive double doors. Her pulse thrummed in her ears. But a childhood spent concealing all emotion from her stepfather came to her rescue. Inwardly she felt as stiff as the whalebone that pinched her waist.

Henry handed an engraved invitation to the butler.

"Ah, yes, Dr. Gooden," the man said dourly. "And the lady?"

"Mrs. Wagstaff." Henry patted her hand.

The butler inclined his head in greeting, then motioned to a footman liveried in navy and white. The young man led them to the drawing room.

As they stepped away from the butler, Jessie finally took a breath, a small one because Susan had tightened her stays a bit more than usual.

Henry whispered in her ear, "If I met the butler on the street, I would think he was a bishop—at least."

The joke took Jessie by surprise. She smothered a chuckle.

Down the thickly carpeted hall, they sauntered. Gaslight flames danced in their protective glass globes along the richly papered wall. Jessie, too keyed up, couldn't take in the decor piece by piece. She merely absorbed the surroundings in terms of rich color, spaciousness, and elegance.

They arrived at last at the drawing room door.

A tall woman, wearing a dress of silver brocade and a rope of silvery pearls, stood up and swept toward them. "Dr. Gooden, welcome to our home."

Henry stepped forward and kissed the woman's gloved hand.

"Mrs. Palmer, thank you again for the kind invitation. May I introduce you to my friend, Mrs. Jessie Wagstaff?"

Mrs. Palmer and Jessie curtseyed slightly to one another. Then the lady took both of them around the ornate gold and maroon room, which could have held the whole first floor of Jessie's house twice, to introduce them to her husband and eight other couples.

Mrs. Palmer ended by saying, "So you see, it's an intimate group really. I didn't want either you or the good doctor to feel overwhelmed."

Jessie felt overwhelmed, but she smiled and nodded. The only names and faces that had stuck in her mind were Mr. and Mrs. Palmer and Mr. and Mrs. Marshall Field because Henry had mentioned them. No one else had made an individual impression on her at all.

The women's gowns distracted her. They glittered, shimmered, frilled. Every woman—from their curled and pomaded hair to the ruffled hems of their skirts—put Jessie in mind of lavish German Christmas trees.

I must seem a sober red hen.

If only the ladies back at home could see how her own amber silk dress and simple pearls were overshadowed in this lavish setting!

The butler approached Mrs. Palmer. "Dinner is served, Madam."

Mr. and Mrs. Palmer led the way into the dining room. It dazzled Jessie. Glittering crystal, gleaming silver, flickering candles, glinting golden candlesticks, sparkling chandeliers. She blinked her eyes, trying to accustom them to the golden light—reflected and multiplied.

She saw name cards at each place. Dr. Gooden was already drawing Jessie to two seats side by side near the middle of the table. He pulled out her chair and seated her.

Glancing down, Jessie glimpsed a row of forks and a row of spoons flanking the gilt china setting. Her pulse awoke with a jerk. She closed her eyes, then opened them. The array of silverware stared back at her with a mocking gleam.

A footman stepped over and with a flourish placed a large white napkin in her lap. She swallowed a small gasp. The dinner began with soup. Jessie kept a half-smile on her face as she observed the footmen serving. She accepted only a modest amount of clear beef consommé.

CHAPTER 9

"I've kept the menu very light this evening," Mrs. Palmer's voice fluted over the genteel conversation. "I don't believe in heavy meals in this dreadful heat."

Jessie nodded politely. But eyeing sideboards laden with serving dishes covered in white linen, Jessie doubted Mrs. Palmer's concept of a light meal would agree with her own.

One of the footmen offered to fill Jessie's wine glass. She murmured, "Water please." He placed a small glass pitcher of water with lemon slices floating in it beside her place setting.

Jessie watched which spoon Mrs. Field, who sat across from her, chose, and then followed her lead. The consommé was salty and tasty. Unfortunately, Susan's extra tug on Jessie's corset strings would prevent her from doing any real eating tonight.

As soon as she laid down her spoon and touched her napkin to her lips, a footman whisked her bowl away.

Lobster and smoked lake perch followed the soup, then cold beef and roasted turkey, fresh corn, wilted spinach salad, pickled beets, steamed carrots, and more. Listening carefully to the discussion about the mechanics of changing the course of the Chicago River, Jessie ate tiny bites of only a few foods. It was all too much.

Without warning, Mr. Palmer addressed her, "Mrs. Wagstaff, yours is a name I know. You're related to Old Will Wagstaff?"

Jessie swallowed and steadied herself. "He was my husband's father."

"The man was an artist. He designed the sideboard behind you."

Jessie glanced at it. "Yes, that looks like his work."

"He was a master. Do you know a duke tried to buy that sideboard from me?"

At this sentence, every head at the table turned toward the sideboard.

"The duke told me to name my price. The one in his castle had been damaged in a fire. He said he hadn't seen such workmanship in years."

Several compliments followed this.

"After dinner I'll show you gentlemen the rolltop desk he made for my library." He turned his attention back to Jessie. "You were married to his son?"

"Yes."

"I heard he fell in the war. His death was an end of a family tradition. He had shown great promise as a wood craftsman, too, I believe. A sad loss."

Jessie nodded. Hearing the mention of Will and his father made sitting at this table even more unbelievable.

"Indeed the war left a sad harvest." Mrs. Palmer motioned the butler to begin the dessert course.

A woman whose name Jessie couldn't recall said, "Yes, how wonderful that he left you well provided for." From a footman, the woman accepted a dessert plate trimmed with a doily. "Some poor widows have even been reduced to taking in boarders."

Jessie stiffened. She sensed that Dr. Gooden had become completely still beside her.

She struggled with her feelings of outrage over this woman's easy condescension. Miss Wright, for once, had been correct. She was their equal, but some here might not think so. If she were here not for Dr. Gooden's benefit, she would have told them what she thought. But she would tell them nothing.

The footman served pink, orange, and green ices in fluted goblets.

Jessie forced herself to sample the frozen sweet. But the fruit syrup tasted bitter on her tongue.

CHAPTER 10

July 3, 1871   J ESSIE PRESSED THE BACK OF HER
hand to perspiration trickling down her forehead, then bent to
go on scrubbing on the washboard. The rippled surface of the
board vibrated her arms with each move—up and down. "How
can it be this hot this early? We started before sunrise."

"Da sun don't care how hot it get down here." Standing in
the shade of the back porch nearby, Susan stirred the simmering
pot of white laundry with a broom handle.

With a mug in each hand, Ruby waddled out. "I got coffee
for you."

"Thank goodness." Jessie straightened up, tossed Linc's soapy
shirt into Susan's laundry pot, then reached for one of the mugs.
"Are you sure you won't need help with breakfast?"

"Da day I can't fix a little breakfast . . . well, dat'll be da day!" Ruby handed the second cup to Susan. "'Sides, it be so hot. I think coffee 'n toast be all any of us feel like eatin'."

"Exactly." Miss Wright stumped out. She held a coffee cup in her hand. She put the cup on the porch railing, pulled over one of the rocking chairs, then sat down. "It's time you told us, Jessie, about that dinner party."

"Yes, that's just what I came out to say." Miss Greenleigh, dressed in a rose-pink light cotton wrapper, pulled up a chair beside Miss Wright. She also carried a cup of coffee. "Mrs. Bolt is still sound asleep, so this is the perfect time for you to tell us *everything!*"

Sitting down on the top step, Ruby nodded vigorously in agreement. "We waited all day yesterday for that woman to get gone. But she stuck like a burr."

Jessie sank onto a lower porch step and looked up at her audience uncertainly. She didn't want to talk about the dinner party. All the uncertainties that she had been dishonest to herself and God by going roiled around inside her like the soapy water bubbling and whirling in Susan's laundry kettle.

Susan joined Ruby on the top step. Taking a cup, she asked gently, "Did you have a bad time?"

Jessie leaned back against the porch railing. "It was a lovely evening." Speaking these words made the whirling inside her speed up. She felt nauseated.

"What was it like inside the Palmer mansion?" Miss Greenleigh leaned forward.

Jessie took a sip of coffee first. "It was luxurious. Gaslights all along the walls. Polished wood. Polished brass. Flocked wallpaper. Rich Persian carpets." Jessie tried to put enthusiasm into her voice, but failed. She paused to take another mouthful of coffee and tried to work up some liveliness.

"What were the ladies wearing?" Miss Greenleigh prompted.

"Mrs. Palmer wore a silver brocade dress with a rope of the most beautiful white pearls." (It could not be called a string; it fell to her waist besides being wrapped once around her throat.) "The other ladies wore satin dresses. Most of them in brilliant summer colors—royal blue, a soft green gold. They shimmered in the gaslight."

Jessie didn't mention how overshadowed her simple gown of amber silk had been. She owed a full report to these women who'd aided her in this adventure. Perhaps working as she talked might mask her lack of energy and interest. She put down her empty coffee cup and went back to the washboard.

"What dey serve?" Ruby asked.

Jessie picked up another shirt of Linc's, rubbed the inside of its collar with the yellow soap, then began to work it up and down the washboard. The harsh soap stung her fingers like a just punishment for her foray into pretension. "We had consommé for the first course, turkey and fish for the second. For dessert we had fresh fruit and Italian ices."

"Mmmm," Ruby voiced her approval. "Just 'bout right for a summer dinner."

"Who else attended?" Miss Greenleigh asked with a far-away look on her face.

Jessie scrubbed harder. "Mr. and Mrs. Field, and I think the Leiters attended. There were only about eight couples for dinner. Mrs. Palmer didn't want a very formal dinner."

Ruby asked, "But dey had a butler and all?"

"And several footmen." Jessie didn't mind reciting the simple facts of the function. *Just don't ask me how I felt about it!* "You wouldn't have believed all the silverware beside my plate! And the English china was gilded. We drank from crystal goblets. Everything tasted delicious."

Miss Greenleigh breathed out happily. "Oh, I wish we could have been mice watching from the corner!"

The image of the women near her shrunk to miniature with whiskers and tails made Jessie smile. "I don't think the Palmers have mice!"

The ladies all chuckled in response to her teasing.

Miss Greenleigh sighed. "Anyway, you were able to venture into a world we may never see—even from afar."

"*Will* never see," Miss Wright asserted.

Ruby began, "I 'member—"

Miss Wright interrupted Ruby, "Jessie, did you notice the sideboard in their dining room?"

Jessie straightened up, tossed the shirt into the pot, then picked up some soiled table napkins. So Miss Wright knew about that. "Yes, Will's father made it. Mr. Palmer made the family connection between me and Will's father. He said a British lord had tried to buy the sideboard from him."

"Really?" Miss Wright sounded pleased. "I'm glad to hear they hadn't gotten rid of it and bought something new."

"No, Mr. Palmer was quite complimentary about Will's father's skill and said he still had the desk he had also made for him."

Miss Wright said in a voice that shook slightly, "Margaret was always so proud of her husband. Her son would have been as fine a woodworker as his father if he had lived. He had the gift, the love of wood and fine detail."

The old spinster's words dampened the festive spirit on the porch. Miss Wright showing softer emotions gave Jessie pause and must have caught the other ladies by surprise as well.

Susan finished her coffee and walked back to the simmering pot to begin stirring again. She murmured, "You don' sound like you had a good time."

"In a way, I had a lovely evening," Jessie paused in her rubbing. She couldn't hold back her misgivings any longer. "But in another way, it was a difficult evening. I just didn't feel like I belonged there. I felt out of place."

Miss Greenleigh ventured, "Did someone say something cutting to you?"

Jessie recalled the careless remark one of the women had made about widows taking in boarders. "Not really." *After all, to be honest, the woman didn't know I was one of those widows. She did-n't say it on purpose. It was just an ignorant remark.*

"Dey still people," Ruby grumbled. "I cook my whole life in da big house. Don't you ever think fine clothes and gilt on dey china mean no sorrow or sin."

"Well said." Miss Wright glanced at Ruby approvingly.

These words freed Jessie from the last of her constraint. Her revulsion at being less than honest bubbled up from inside her. "I felt like an actress playing a part! I would never have gone if it hadn't been to help Dr. Gooden!"

"What about Dr. Gooden, Jessie?" Miss Wright demanded. "Is it your intention to remarry?"

As though she'd been struck a blow, the unforeseen words took the wind out of Jessie. She gasped for breath. "Marry?" she said weakly. "Marry the doctor?"

"Yes, do you plan to marry the doctor or do you intend to marry Mr. Smith?" The spinster stared at her with narrowed eyes.

Jessie's voice revealed her agitation. "I don't intend to marry anyone. I haven't encouraged either gentleman to think that."

"Is that what you think?" Miss Wright "humphed," then went on, "That's not what the neighbors think. What with both men hanging around this back porch practically every evening."

"She right." Ruby nodded. "Dey be your gentlemen callers. Everybody can see dat."

I will never marry again. Jessie pulled a petticoat from the laundry pile, swished it in the soaking tub, slapped it on the board, and began rubbing furiously. "Mr. Smith is Linc's friend, not mine. We can't be together for more than a few minutes without his trying my temper."

Miss Greenleigh said slyly, "Yes, I've noticed that myself."

Before Jessie could think how to answer this, Miss Wright said in a starched-up tone, "This avoiding the truth will not wash, Jessie. Dr. Gooden and Mr. Smith may not have said anything plainly, but no man comes every evening just to play ball or just to talk about medicine."

"You got dat right," Susan said under her breath so only Jessie could hear her.

"Must I be held accountable for how two men choose to spend their evenings?" Jessie scrubbed the petticoat vigorously.

"That's 'nough scrubbing on dat petticoat," Susan pointed out. "I hanker to wear one with no holes in it."

Jessie blushed hotly and threw the wet petticoat into the tub. Miss Wright continued her propriety lecture, "If you don't wish to encourage these gentlemen, you must let them know that their suit would not please you."

"But why shouldn't their suit please you?" Miss Greenleigh countered, wide-eyed. "Both of them are eligible. There's nothing wrong with a widow remarrying. You've been alone for more than six years now."

Jessie grumbled, "I am still not convinced that either of them is looking for a wife or looking at me as a prospective wife."

Miss Wright said pointedly, "I see how that doctor looks at you. That man has marriage on his mind. He isn't a frivolous person. You had better believe that he isn't here just for the pleasant company."

Jessie thought of all the times Miss Wright had ventured onto the porch and made very unpleasant company for the two men. Jessie wished they'd stop this conversation.

"She speak da truth," Ruby seconded. "He a busy man. If he ain't interested in you, he don' spend dat much time with you."

Miss Greenleigh offered, "He'd make an excellent stepfather for Linc."

As though pricked with a sharp needle, Jessie cried out, "Never! Linc will never be under a stepfather!" She faced the women ranged on the porch. "I made Linc that promise the day we held his father's memorial service!" She nearly choked on the last word. Gripping the top of the washboard, she felt waves of chill and heat wash through her. Her hands shook on the board.

The women looked back at her—obviously shocked at her outburst. Jessie willed herself to calm down. Finally she could speak again. "I will never marry again."

Miss Greenleigh crossed her arms over her breast and spoke in a militant tone, "Then you had better give both of these men a hint of your feelings. Just dressing in black has not dampened their interest."

Susan spoke up, "Why you think it would be so bad for Linc to have a stepfather? Not every man be as hard as your stepfather. Maybe Linc want a stepfather—especially if he be someone like Mr. Smith. Did you ask Linc?"

"I know what's best for my son." Jessie tightened her mouth and bent to the washboard.

July 4, 1871

In the twilight, another wave broke around Jessie's knees making her squeal as the cool water swirled about her.

"Mother!" Linc splashed through the shallows at the Oak Street Beach. "I found some more shells." He slid the tiny wet shells into her hand. "Save them with the rest."

Before she could add them to the sandy collection wrapped in a handkerchief in her pocket, Linc charged out to meet another white-capped wave. He shouted gleefully. The same wave of lake water broke over Jessie, and she squealed again.

Dr. Gooden waded over to her. "I have never seen such waves on this lake before."

"I still can't believe Mr. Smith coaxed me into the water," Jessie explained self-consciously. The beach was lined with people. Many men and children were enjoying the water, but most women sat on the shore beneath parasols. She had meant only to venture ankle deep, but once in the water, she couldn't resist going deeper. "You must think it's shocking of me to—"

"No, no! Who could expect you to sit on the sand so hot and uncomfortable while we enjoy the lake?"

"I could have resisted if it weren't for the east wind. An east wind brings the waves in so high and warm!" Another wave crested over her and surged higher, lifting her skirts. "Oh!" She pushed at the wet fabric floating waist high. "Doctor, you must stand behind me and shield me from the people on shore."

Without asking why, he swiftly stood behind her. Bending forward, she reached back and caught the rear hem of her skirt and petticoats, then she pulled them forward between her limbs and tucked the hems securely into her belt in front. "There. Thank you, doctor. For a moment, I feared my skirt might float immodestly high, but now it's in place. As long as I stay—" A wave crashed over them, cutting off her words. "Oh, how delightful!"

"Ja!" Standing beside her, the doctor looked at her with an expression of pleasure.

She halted. She must not lead this good man to think she might be interested in marrying him. *Maybe it's just all in Miss Wright's imagination.*

He took her elbow. "Now that your skirt is taken care of, let us go farther. We are wet already!"

"Come on out!" Mr. Smith called to them. "Linc and I are on a sandbar. It's shallow."

Jessie let the doctor pull her along. She plunged into the waves beside him, fighting to keep up but hampered by the water dragging at her soaked skirts. Giddy with the exertion, she finally gained the sandbar. She felt daring, but the sky was already darkening, and the night would soon hide her indiscreet behavior.

"Sit down, Mother!" Linc plodded onto the shallow water of the sandbar.

CHAPTER 10

"Oh, I can't Linc. I'd be completely wet then," Jessie objected.

Without warning, Mr. Smith stepped off the sandbar into deeper water and spun around. A swirl of water cascaded over her.

Sputtering, Jessie wiped the water from her eyes. "You!" She rushed forward and shoved full force against Mr. Smith's chest.

Caught off-guard, he fell backwards. The water opened, then closed over his head. He came up, spitting water. "Jessie Wagstaff!" He made a rush at her.

Dr. Gooden stepped between them. Flinging up one hand, he declaimed melodramatically, "Cur! Would you offer violence to a lady?" He put up his fists like a boxer.

Mr. Smith curled an imaginary mustache. "Curses! Foiled again."

Linc clapped his hands. "Bravo. Bravo! That's what you say, isn't it? My teacher said that's what you say at a theater."

Mr. Smith flung himself down next to Linc on the sandbar. "That's exactly right, sport."

Suddenly a blast of loud brass band music fluttered to them on the wind. "It must be nearly time for the fireworks," Jessie said.

"Will we really see them from here?" the doctor asked.

"Yes, they do them at the lakefront downtown." Jessie sank down on the sandbar and modestly arranged herself. A smile she couldn't quell shaped her face. "Oh, look at the sunset." She nodded toward the western sky.

Dr. Gooden settled beside her with his knees bent supporting his elbows. The fiery, watermelon-red sun slid behind the tall buildings of the city. The sky turned the color of polished brass. "Another hot day tomorrow. My mother always said a watermelon sun at the evening means another hot day," the doctor murmured.

"I can't recall when we've had such a hot, dry summer," Jessie replied, but the cooling water made her feel wonderfully

comfortable and relaxed. She leaned back, braced on her stiffened arms.

"Thanks for persuading us to come, sport," Mr. Smith said.

"It's the Fourth of July! We had to do something special,"
Linc pronounced.

"Yes, when I was a little girl, my mother brought me here
whenever the wind was right," Jessie murmured. She fell silent,
recalling the severe scoldings her stepfather had given her mother for going into the water with her. She brushed the memory
back into the recesses of her mind. Along with the others, she
watched the sun dip lower, it's rays growing fainter and fainter.

Linc leaned against her. The sky turned from brass to deep
violet to slate. Jessie enjoyed the sunset and the silent company
of friends. Friends? For so long, she'd only had Susan to share
her life with. Though she rejected the idea of them as suitors,
the two men who sat one on each side of her and Linc had
become part of her life in these few short months.

Dr. Gooden had saved Little Ben and Pastor Mitchell. He'd
added a silk dress to her wardrobe and had taken her to dinner
at the Palmer mansion. She knew she must make clear to the
good doctor she wasn't looking for a second husband. She tried
to deny it, but he must be interested. His kiss on the palm of her
hand the night when he'd invited her to the Palmers' dinner had
been an unmistakable sign of a desire for greater intimacy.

While Mr. Smith still irritated her with his care-for-nothing
attitude, how could she feel anything but gratitude to him? His
kindness to her fatherless son had put her deeply in his debt and
had won her reluctant approval. But she refused to believe Mr.
Smith was interested in her. Miss Wright was completely "off
base" in regards to Mr. Smith. She smiled over her own use of
the baseball term. Linc's passion for the game had infiltrated
their lives.

Night came. Without speaking, Jessie and the others turned
south, toward the carnival and waterfront. The warmth of the

day lessened, but the water did not chill her. The lake felt like a refreshing tepid bath.

Boom! The first fireworks exploded overhead with golden streamers. The pyrotechnic show proceeded quickly. Jessie lost herself in the dazzling colors, pounding explosions, and the cascade of "ooh's" and "ahh's" from the shore and water. She glanced at her son and took pleasure from the joy in his expression. Her eyes strayed and caught sight of Mr. Smith too. Everyone else's eyes were skyward, but Mr. Smith had buried his face in his hands.

The war. He must be remembering the dreadful thunder of cannons and red flares of the bombs overhead. Her lips trembled. If Will had come home, he would probably feel the same painful memories.

The fireworks ended with a fantastic series of explosions in gold, brilliant blue, crimson, and startling green. Then, remaining between the two men, Jessie turned her attention west once more as she watched the city's gaslights begin to twinkle against the charcoal sky. All around her, people began to wade back to shore. On the beach, mothers and fathers gathered sleepy children for the walk or trolley ride home. The voices were soothing, homey. An overtired child began crying, and his mother sang him a weary-sounding lullaby.

Soon few people were left. Jessie became aware that Linc had fallen asleep heavily against her. Still she didn't speak or move. She didn't want to break the companionable silence. Besides, Mr. Smith appeared to remain wrapped up in his inner turmoil. Jessie did not want to disturb him until he had come to terms with whatever tormented him. Finally he looked up. It wasn't lost on her that he sought Linc's face first. Her heart tightened with this token of his attachment to her son.

Around her, the cooling lake breeze stirred. Jessie shivered. She moved her tired limbs in the water. In the moonlight, the white-capped waves still rushed the sandy beach, crashing against the shore. The white edge of the waves reminded Jessie of the ruffled lace on a hem. At last, the passage of time made her move. "Gentlemen, Linc has fallen asleep. I think we need to get home."

Mr. Smith stood up, then bent down. "I'll carry him." He swung Linc up into his arms. The boy didn't waken. Dr. Gooden helped her to her feet. Still in the middle, Jessie trudged through the waves to the shore. On the sand by moonlight, Dr. Gooden helped her gather up Linc's pail and shovel and everyone's shoes. Jessie dropped them onto the old blanket, then gathered up its four corners. Dr. Gooden took it from her and slung it like a bag over his shoulder. He offered her his arm and the three of them walked to the edge of the sand. As soon as they left the beach, Jessie discreetly let down her skirts. While she did this, both gentlemen politely kept their eyes averted.

The three of them walked silently through the quiet streets. As they approached her house, she noticed Mrs. Braun's front curtain twitch. Jessie was being watched. Well, she'd given the gossips something real to talk about this time. She strolled home between two eligible bachelors, and with her wet dress as witness, she had been shamelessly cavorting at the beach. Jessie could hear the disapproving voices. She shook her head. *I don't care what they say, Lord. You didn't mind me wading in your beautiful lake.*

While she felt guiltless over this evening's jaunt, she decided with sudden conviction that she must and would speak to Dr. Gooden tonight. They walked up the back steps to her quiet house. No lights in the house had been lit. Jessie murmured, "Everyone else must be down for the night. Mr. Smith—"

"I can put Linc in bed," he said gruffly. "You stay out here. Your skirts are still dripping."

With a sigh she leaned back against a porch column. "Thank you."

Dr. Gooden held the door to the kitchen open for Mr. Smith. Then she and the doctor were alone. Settling on top of the porch railing, Jessie watched the doctor put on his shoes. When he'd finished, he brushed sand off himself and rolled down his sleeves and buttoned them.

I should say something to him now. Jessie cleared her suddenly dry throat.

Dr. Gooden took a step closer to her. "I've wished to tell you how grateful I am for your going with me to the Palmer's party. Mrs. Palmer visited me at the hospital this week. She has gotten me an appointment to go with her to see Mayor Mason next week."

"How wonderful!" Jessie exclaimed, "Do you think they might really give your ideas serious consideration?" Sliding off the railing, she took a step forward and clasped his hands in hers. Her going to the dinner had helped!

"I knew you would be as pleased as I am!" With one smooth motion, the doctor pulled her into his arms and kissed her.

The kiss stunned Jessie. Lips touching hers. Arms holding her. She froze. The pressure ceased.

He pulled away. "I forget myself." He bowed and kissed her hand. "I see in your eyes I have surprised you. I act too soon. It will not happen again." He bowed over her hand, touched it to his forehead and left her.

Jessie didn't move. She couldn't.

❊ ❊ ❊ ❊ ❊

From inside the kitchen, Lee watched the good doctor kiss Jessie. A white hot anger scalded through him. He walked out the door and confronted her—face-to-face. "So the good doctor decided to steal a kiss?"

She looked at him, confusion plain on her face.

"From your expression, I'd say he kisses like a plaster saint. Not like a man." Compelled by swirling emotions he couldn't sort out and couldn't control, he pulled Jessie to him and kissed her. At first, perhaps shock made her pliant in his arms, but then she pushed against him. He tightened his embrace. Then, in pain, he released her and stepped back to rub his shin. "You kicked me!" He straightened up.

She slapped his face. "Don't you ever do that again!" she declared. "I didn't want the doctor to kiss me, and I don't want you to either. Go home, and don't come back if you have ideas of repeating this insult."

"Don't worry. Once was enough." His cheek still stinging, he snagged his shoes and scuttled down the steps. *Why did I do that? Am I losing my mind?*

* * * * *

Jessie stood a long time on the porch. Her breathing finally quieted to normal. Miss Wright had been correct. Both men evidently were interested in her. She touched her fingers to her lips. She had never wanted any man to kiss her again. Will's kisses were the only ones she'd ever craved.

Mr. Smith's words came back to her, "He kisses like a plaster saint." It was true. The doctor's kiss had not affected her in the least—unless embarrassment counted. But Mr. Smith's kisses . . . Jessie burst into tears.

CHAPTER 11

August 30, 1871

JESSIE STOOD IN THE DOORWAY of Miss Greenleigh's room. The room that was normally so orderly and neat today was a riot of clothing and new tissue paper. The pretty, young blonde was sorting and carefully folding the multitude of her underthings: white cotton corsets; corset-covers in shades of ivory, white, and pale pink. fine-woven cotton chemises frilled with ruffles around their hems and flowered embroidery at their yokes. *So many pretty, dainty items.* Jessie suppressed a tiny nip of envy.

Many duties nagged Jessie's conscience, but she could not drag herself away from the cheerful chaos. Miss Greenleigh was going to have her chance at "happily ever after." Just as sun attracted the round yellow faces of daisies, Jessie had been drawn to be a part of it. Mrs. Bolt must have felt the allure too. She sat, facing Jessie, on the only chair in the room. Between the two widows, the bride-to-be knelt among her clothing in front of her trunk.

"Yes," Miss Greenleigh replied to Mrs. Bolt, "my fiancé is older than I am by fifteen years, but we're very much in love and I don't think that should make any difference—"

"You ought to be marrying a man nearer your own age," Mrs. Bolt interrupted. "I'm just trying to make you realize that some day you'll be a young widow."

"That may be, but no one can foretell the future. I could die before Matthew," the young woman replied calmly and continued her careful folding of underwear in the crisp white sheets of tissue paper. Jessie admired the particularly lacy, white chemise the young woman was adding to the trunk.

Mrs. Bolt persisted shrilly, "You're making a rash decision. Just because you're afraid of being left an old maid—"

"I have received another proposal of marriage in the past year," Miss Greenleigh said.

Jessie watched the red-headed widow's mouth open, shut, and crimp into a sour pucker.

Mrs. Bolt shoved herself up out of the chair. "*Well,* I see that my words of wisdom are wasted here." With a flushed face, Mrs. Bolt brushed past Jessie and clattered down the hall.

Ill at ease, Jessie turned to leave.

"Please don't go. Come in and close the door."

Jessie hesitated.

"Please." Miss Greenleigh beckoned Jessie with her hand.

Jessie came in and shut the door. Sitting down on the edge of the bed, she looked into Miss Greenleigh's upturned face.

The pretty blonde grinned. "I'm afraid I wasn't completely truthful with Mrs. Bolt."

Jessie raised her eyebrows.

"This is my *third* proposal in the past twelve months." A puckish grin accented the blonde's radiant face.

"Three? But we never saw anyone call."

"I met many gentlemen when I spent weekends with my sister—my match-making sister."

"Perhaps we could hire her for Mrs. Bolt." Shocked at her outspoken comment, Jessie clapped her hands over her mouth.

The other young woman whooped with laughter. "No, I don't think so. Some cases are just too . . ." She stopped and rested her hands on her folded clothing. "I wish I could give Mrs. Bolt some 'wise words' about her hoydenish behavior around bachelors. To my mind, her arch coyness toward Mr. Smith is as shocking as it is embarrassing. If she continues the way she is going, she will never marry again."

"I have thought the same thing myself more than once. It's made me wonder . . ."

"Wonder what?"

Jessie lowered her voice. "I wonder if she was happy in her first marriage. I don't think she was or she wouldn't be so overly eager." Jessie confided, "You know, I can't imagine being married to anyone but my Will. I hope you and Matthew will be as happy as Will and I were."

"Thank you. I think we will be." Miss Greenleigh paused. "Do you think, since I will no longer be living here, we could begin to address each other by our given names?"

Jessie tingled with a spurt of pleasure. She had often wished to speak to Miss Greenleigh personally, but she had stopped short because of their relationship of landlady and boarder. "I'd like that, Sarah."

"Jessie." Sarah held out her hand. Briefly Jessie held the slender hand. Then Sarah lifted another tissue-wrapped bundle into her trunk.

With the toe of her shoe, Jessie pensively traced the rose pattern on the small bedside rug. "I wonder if I could ask for your advice."

"Yes, of course."

"You were right—all of you."

"About Mr. Smith and the doctor?"

Jessie nodded.

"May I be honest?"

Jessie tilted her head to the side, asking for more.

"I don't understand why you don't plan to remarry."

"I can't—I loved Will with all my heart."

"I understand that. But you must think of the future—Linc's future. It isn't good to raise a lone boy in a household full of females."

Miss Greenleigh's softly spoken words dropped like bricks inside Jessie's heart. Could she deny their truth? Jessie said reluctantly, "I'll have to give that some thought." Then gathering her composure, she smiled at the young woman who had become a friend in the past few months. "Tell me about your Matthew."

For the next few minutes Jessie listened to Sarah's glowing description of her beloved's fine qualities and her wedding plans, then Jessie rose. "I should be in the kitchen now, helping Susan. Again, my very best wishes on your marriage, and please don't forget about us, Sarah. You and your Matthew will always be welcome here."

"I'd like to send you an invitation. I'd like you to be there."

"Of course, I'll look forward to it." Jessie clasped hands with Sarah. Then deep in thought, Jessie walked down to the kitchen.

"She done packin'?" Susan had her dark hands deep into a batch of bread dough which she was kneading mercilessly.

"No."

"She the nicest boarder we had. I hope we git lucky with the next one."

Jessie stepped to Susan's side. "She said Linc shouldn't be raised in a household of women."

"She's right. Why don't you rent Miss Greenleigh's room to Mr. Smith? Dat's what he come for in the first place."

"Linc need a man 'round here." Wheezing softly as always, Ruby walked in, her large body shifting from one unsteady foot to the other. "What you maulin', chile?"

172

"Six loaves a bread."

Jessie's worry dragged her mind away from the kitchen. *Yes, Linc needs a man in his life.* But would Mr. Smith be content to be there for Linc, and expect nothing from her? In the weeks since she'd slapped his face, he'd been a pattern card of a gentleman. But there was still something about himself he hadn't told her. Something.

※ ※ ※ ※ ※

After lunch Jessie carried a lapful of mending out into the shade behind the rose trellis on the back porch. The house was quiet. In the heat of the afternoon, Ruby and Miss Wright napped. After lunch Sarah Greenleigh had ridden away with her brother-in-law. This caused Jessie's already somber spirits to dip further. Jessie agreed with Susan. Sarah had been their nicest boarder.

So she could breathe in the hot dead air around her more easily, she began rocking the old rocker back and forth. Jessie sighed and threaded a needle.

"Jessie?"

She glanced up and saw her mother coming up the back-yard path. "Mother, how did you ever get away?"

"I had to come and see you. I don't care if Hiram does come home unexpectedly."

Heedless of the mending that fell to the floor, Jessie stood up to welcome her mother with open arms. Jessie hadn't seen her mother in weeks.

"Jessie," her mother gasped. For a few moments she could say no more. They clung to each other.

Jessie urged her mother into a nearby chair. "I'll get you some tea."

"No. No, I can only stay a few moments, but I had to come. I've felt so terrible ever since the morning you visited me."

Anger instantly dug its claws into Jessie's heart. "Why should *you* feel terrible? Hiram Huff should feel terrible. You don't have to tell me he's the reason you aren't shopping mornings anymore. He told you to not speak to me, didn't he?"

"Jessie, please. Your stepfather's a good man. No fire captain in Chicago is as conscientious as he is."

"No doubt you're right, but he has a way of seeing things in only one way—his way. He's always put himself up as the judge of the world. I can't forgive the things he said about Will—"

"What things?"

"Have you forgotten?" Jessie could only stare at her mother.

Esther colored. "Do you mean about Will volunteering for the medical corps as a nurse?"

"Yes, your husband had the gall to tell me—in front of Margaret—that a son's duty was to stay home and provide for his widowed mother—"

"That was true in a way," her mother said. "It would have been better, too, for you and Linc if Will hadn't volunteered—"

"I would never have asked Will to stay or to avoid the draft the way your husband did."

Esther hung her head.

"Have you forgotten that when the draft was put into law in '63, your husband hired a man to be his substitute for three hundred dollars? I have always wanted to ask Mr. Hiram Huff what it feels like to hire a man to *die* in your place?"

"Jessie, it does no good to stir up the past—"

Words rushed to Jessie's lips. "I've kept my peace too long as it is. There are so many things I've never said to him, to you. I can't seem to hold everything back anymore."

Jessie stood up and began pacing in front of her mother. "I don't think I'll ever forget the day when I was only twelve years old and he left me here on this porch. He didn't even wait until Margaret opened the door. I've never been so frightened in my life. He didn't even say good-bye. Mother, why didn't you, at least, come with me?"

"Hiram said I would cry and upset you—"

CHAPTER 11

"Hiram said," Jessie parroted. "My whole life whatever Hiram said was law." Jessie stopped and looked to her mother's face. She couldn't mask her true feelings one more moment. "Mother, why did you ever marry him?"

Fanning herself with her handkerchief, Esther flushed scarlet. "Jessie."

"He is a pompous, self-righteous—"

"Please don't say such things. I know he isn't perfect, but deep down he's a good man."

Jessie couldn't help herself. She felt her lips twist sourly. She didn't like the simultaneous twist she felt knot her emotions. "All my life—all I can remember—he has continually tried to separate me from you."

"No—"

"It's true and you know it." Jessie tried to make eye contact, but Esther glanced down at white cotton-gloved hands folded in her lap.

"He always made certain I knew he didn't want me. Because he was forced to tolerate me, he made sure you always had to obey him, which always meant you had to deny me."

Tears sprang to her mother's eyes. "No, Jessie. No. He is a hard man, but I never let him abuse you. I never let him use a switch—"

"Words and looks can sting deeper than any switch."

"Oh, Jessie, please. That day if he hadn't been so exhausted and worried about the drought and all the fires, he wouldn't have argued with you—"

"You still choose to defend him." Jessie clenched her hands. "I will never remarry. I will never put Linc through this."

"Jessie, please don't say that. You're so young. I was hoping . . . Mr. Smith . . . Linc loves him so much . . . I thought . . ."

Jessie let her mother ramble through this series of phrases. When Esther fell silent, Jessie shook her head in an emphatic "no." "Since I was three years old, Hiram Huff has cheated me of my mother's love—"

"No!"

"You know it's true! I grew up thinking you didn't love me. Margaret had to explain that you did love me, you just couldn't show it because of my stepfather. Every time I would reach for you, he would step between us, lecturing me, disciplining me, shoving me aside."

"But Hiram speaks highly of you now. He respects your hard work. He was especially pleased that you didn't rent to men. He says most widows are 'shameless'—"

"Mother, I can't hide my feelings toward your husband anymore. I will not be visiting my family—I mean, *his* family again."

"You can't mean that!"

"Mother, on his birthday Linc asked me why his step-grandfather didn't like him."

Esther moaned.

Jessie drew herself up and folded her arms. "You are always welcome here. But if I never see Hiram Huff again, it will be too soon."

"Jessie," her mother pleaded, "I know he has wronged you, said things that would have been better to have left unsaid, but you are a Christian. You must forgive. You must."

Jessie looked away, hardening her heart against the crushed expression on her mother's face. "I can't help how I feel. I won't lie anymore."

Esther rose slowly and left. Feeling close to tears herself, Jessie turned her back and went into the kitchen.

September 2, 1871

In the waning light of sundown, Jessie approached her home. She felt crumpled and moody, and the unusual heat of the autumn evening didn't help. Why couldn't the cool, sometimes rainy, fall days begin? Dry leaves dropped and shattered on the parched brown lawns and dusty wooden streets. The lingering drought and her own futility oppressed her.

CHAPTER 11

As Jessie walked up the sidewalk that wound around the side of her house, she passed by Mrs. O'Toole, who sat on her side porch. The woman turned her face away. None of Jessie's neighbors had spoken to her since the day Ruby had arrived to stay. *So be it.* She lifted her chin and marched around the corner of her house.

As she hastened up the steps, she tried to free herself from the pain of receiving another rejection by a physician, her seventh rejection. She had been certain this doctor would say yes. He had studied for the mission field at a seminary in the East, but the man's hypocrisy had staggered her. As long as he was miles away, on their soil, he did not mind treating "darkies," as he had called them. But for him to do so in Chicago was unthinkable.

From his doghouse on the porch, Butch welcomed her with a quick yip, and several voices coming from the kitchen drew her attention from the turmoil of her thoughts. One voice was Caleb's. She quickened her steps and called to him.

Caleb opened the door for her. "Mrs. Wagstaff, I'm so glad you've finally come home."

"What is it? You looked worried."

"My father . . . his heart . . ."

Jessie impulsively grasped one of his hands. Ruby and Ben stood in the background.

"The Rev'rund wants you to come," Susan added with a break in her voice. "We bin waitin' for you."

"Of course, I'll come. I'm sorry I've kept you waiting."

Lee entered through the kitchen curtain. "Linc's in bed." When he spotted Jessie, he halted. "Linc and I missed you tonight, Mrs. Wagstaff. Was your mission successful?"

"I don't have time to discuss my appointment now."

Lee surveyed the company gathered around Jessie. "Something's wrong."

"Caleb's father is bad again," Susan said.

177

"What are his symptoms?" Lee asked.

"This doesn't concern you." The tall black man folded his arms over his broad chest.

Ben spoke up, "Do you want me to go to the doctor again?"

"What are his symptoms, Caleb?" Jessie asked.

"He is experiencing chest pain and he can barely breathe. It's worse though than the last time."

"Heart failure." This medical pronouncement slipped out of Lee's mouth before he could prevent it.

Caleb stared at him.

"Ben, yes, go to the doctor's hotel. The Reverend needs him. And let us go quickly," Jessie urged. Though she'd kept Dr. Gooden at arm's length since the night he kissed her, she knew he'd come.

"I'm coming too," Lee announced.

"You're not . . . needed." Caleb glared at him now.

"I'm coming anyway and bringing a lantern along. It's nearly dark. Mrs. Wagstaff will need an escort home."

Caleb continued to stare as though he wished he could bar Lee from coming along. "Very well," he said at last.

Lee didn't want to go, but how could he let Linc's mother go out without an escort home? She seemed so sure the doctor would come, but Lee doubted it. He and Jessie walked down the backyard path side by side. Behind them came Susan and Caleb. Ruby, standing in the doorway, waved one last good-bye to them.

The few miles they covered brought them to a one-room house. In the encroaching darkness, Lee saw somber people hovering around the dwelling. That seemed ominous. He didn't believe the Reverend's flock would come unless they thought it was the end.

As they approached the door, Caleb moved ahead of Lee, opened the door, and showed them in. Only homemade candles clustered on the bedside table illumined the room. They cast flickering shadows on the unfinished walls. Lee looked away from the candles and the spent old man who lay on a narrow bed.

"Mrs. Wagstaff?" The old preacher's low voice sounded like sandpaper on rough wood.

Jessie went forward and began to kneel beside his bed. Several women made clucking or shooshing sounds and insisted she sit on the only bedside chair. Lee, feeling out of place, slipped to the rear of the people who surrounded the bed.

"Reverend." Jessie took the gaunt hand. "Shall I make you a cup of Margaret's heart tea?"

"I don't think . . . it will be of any . . . further help to me. Everyone's come. They know." As the old man labored to say these few words, he wheezed as though he had been running for miles.

Lee vicariously felt the effort each breath cost the preacher.

Jessie clung to the frail, black hand. "I've sent Ben for the doctor."

"God will bless you . . ." The old man gasped between phrases. "Stand firm . . . Let your light so shine . . . Whatever you have done for the least of these you have done for me."

"I don't deserve any praise. I haven't done anything anyone else couldn't do better."

"But who else does anything?" Caleb's voice came out, sounding harsh in the velvet cocoon of the dark room.

"Son, forgive. Forgive . . . Bitterness . . . will destroy you." His breathing worsened; it rustled like a rush of dry leaves swept over pavement.

Jessie looked helpless and frantic.

Unable to resist her silent appeal, Lee pushed forward and lifted the old man's featherlight upper body. "Bring more pillows or a bolster. He will breathe easier."

There was a momentary pause as everyone registered that he, Mrs. Wagstaff's escort, had spoken. Then several women hurried to find what had been requested. Finally a sack of potatoes

179

and a folded blanket were brought. Lee braced the old man with them.

"Thank you." The old preacher's voice thinned to an insubstantial gasp.

Lee pictured the worn-out heart and lungs laboring and failing. The man was literally drowning from within, fluid and blood pooling in his chest and compressing his lungs. Lee felt a sympathetic pressure on his own chest.

"Music," Reverend Mitchell whispered. "Sing."

A momentary silence greeted this. Then a woman started humming; another sang softly, "My Lord, what a mourning. My Lord, what a mourning. My Lord, what a mourning when the stars began to fall." More women joined in, reverently humming and singing the chant.

The melody took Lee back to war days in Mississippi and, later, Virginia. In this solemn setting, the rhythm and genuine feeling invested in each word opened him to emotions long buried.

Jessie walked to the door and looked out as though expecting the doctor.

Lee grimaced. *Don't get your hopes up, Jessie. The good doctor will disappoint you sometimes. Maybe tonight.*

Without pause, the next spiritual began: "Soon I will be done with the trouble of this world." An almost physical longing crystallized within Lee. If only one could be done with the trouble of this world. "Soon I will be done with the trouble of this world. Goin' to live with God." He drew a painful breath. The penetrating grief weighed him down. He leaned back, letting the rough wall support him.

Song followed song. At times, everyone inside and outside the house except for Jessie and him sang in harmony. In the funereal glow of the candles, Lee could not take his eyes from the old man. Though struggling for breath, the old man's face had slipped into a tender smile.

Jessie paced in front of the door, looking outside at the sounds of each passing wagon.

"O, Mary, don't you weep, don't you mourn. O, Mary, don't you weep, don't you mourn. Pharoah's army got drowned." The mood and voices lifted. "O, Mary, don't you weep, don't you mourn. Some of these mornings bright and fair." These voices sang not of mourning; they sang of victory. "I'll take my wings and cleave the air."

Jessie sat back down beside the old man.

Lee felt hard-earned barriers against remembering the war begin to crumble. He wanted to escape this room, his memories, but he couldn't disturb the death scene being acted out before him. The melody faded away. The doctor wasn't coming tonight. Lee didn't feel good at being proved right. But even if the doctor had come, there would have been little he could do.

"Son." The old man's raspy whisper sounded loud in the silent room.

Caleb stepped forward and knelt on one knee. Jessie stood up and stepped back. Caleb gripped his father's thin hand. "Father."

"Forgive, son. Forgive. Let go of your hate . . ."

Caleb did not reply, but he pressed two fingers against his closed eyes as though forcing back tears.

"You will . . . never know peace . . . forgive." The old man wheezed again. Speaking under the killing load of fluid and blood consumed his strength.

Once more Lee felt a phantom weight pressing down on his own chest.

Breaking the silence, one of the mourners intoned in a rich bass voice, "Swing low sweet chariot comin' for to carry me home. Swing low sweet chariot comin' for to carry me home." A crescendo of harmonies and emotions coursed through the grief-saturated room.

The old preacher raised one hand as though pointing to something. "The light, Caleb," the Reverend breathed. "See the light."

Lee saw Jessie respectfully move away from the father and son. She came to him. He held out his hand. She accepted it and took the place beside him. The touch of her hand in his strengthened him against the sorrow around him.

The old man tried to lift himself. "Praise God," he panted. "He comes to give life . . . " The dying man collapsed against the pillow. Silence descended. No one moved.

Lee waited until he realized that foreboding had immobilized everyone. He stepped close to the bed and pressed his hand to the man's throat, feeling for a pulse. "He's gone." Lee tenderly closed the old man's eyes.

A moan. A cry. A heartrending sob.

Lee felt his low spirits sink farther. In a flash, he was transported to the past. He stood at the edge of a battlefield at daybreak. The moans and shrieks of wounded men ripped and shredded the peaceful dawn. Lee began trembling. Before it could overtake him completely, he fled the house.

Heedless of her own tears, Jessie accepted and returned the embraces of the other mourners. Inside she felt scoured out, empty, aching with loss. In this moment, she recognized that Reverend Mitchell had been a spiritual father to her. His wisdom and kindness had fed her more than once. *Where are you, Dr. Gooden? Why didn't you come?*

After Susan released her from a fierce hug, Jessie searched the room for Lee. When she could not find him, she threaded her way through the mourners until she was able to reach the door and escape outside. In the blackness of nightfall, she spotted him by the glow of the lantern he held and hurried to him.

Before she could speak, he took her arm and began to rush her along the alley. She tried to keep up with him, but finally she pulled against him, arresting his progress.

Abruptly he swung back to her. Only then did she become aware of the trembling of his arm in her hand. "What is it?"

He groaned. The sound unnerved her, standing alone in the dark. Instinctively she moved closer to him, then closer. One more step brought her within inches of him. Drawn against her will, she leaned forward until her forehead rested on his chin. A drop of moisture, then another fell on her cheek. She looked up and realized the tears were not hers, but his. "What is it?"

He gripped her arms. "Will, those cannon are too close. We could be hit. Did they send up the men we asked for? Tell them to bring up the wagons. Hurry Will! They're dying. We have to get to them." He swallowed convulsively and his grasp intensified. "How many more nights like this can we take? Will—"

She shook him by the shoulders. She couldn't use his formal name at a time like this. *"Lee!"*

He moaned and pulled her to him. "Jess?"

The stark longing in his voice prompted her to wrap her arms around him, holding him close. She felt him quivering. As though soothing Linc when he was awakened by a nightmare, she stroked Lee's back and murmured sounds of comfort. His arms closed around her. One last harsh groan escaped him, and he was still.

She felt him lower his cheek to hers. This slight adjustment completely altered the tenor of their closeness. No longer were they mother, son. A man was holding her. His breath feathered the small curls at her temples. His nearness exerted a pull on her. She leaned closer.

"Jessie," he sighed her name. He lowered his face and brought his lips to hers. He exhaled, and she felt like she was drawing in his breath. He smelled of a rich spice and a natural scent that she recognized as distinctly male. He pulled her tighter against him. She did not resist him, but let her body mold to his hard, uncompromising frame. He kissed her, a demanding kiss.

Feeling weak, she gasped and he deepened his kiss. A yielding, errant cry filtered from her mouth. His embrace made her feel full, light-headed, small, feminine. Her breathing came quick and shallow. She knew she should pull away, but the same inexplicable magnetism she had experienced and resented that night on the porch compelled her to remain, resting against him.

When his eyelashes flickered against her face, she trembled with desire. Shocked at her own response, she forced herself to step back. Grudgingly, he let her go.

To fill the silence, she asked, "You were remembering the war?"

"Yes," he admitted curtly. He picked up the lantern and took her arm.

"Do you remember it often?" She walked faster to keep up with him.

"No."

"Why did you think about it now?"

"I don't want to talk about it, think about it. The war should never have happened." His pace became more brisk.

"Then Susan wouldn't be free." She tugged against him, forcing him to slow.

"If the South could have foreseen all the war would rob them of and all it would force them to endure, they would have let Susan's people go, and gladly."

"I doubt that."

"What do you know about it? I believed in freeing the slaves just as fervently as you said your husband did. We all joined to 'Save the Union' and 'Free the slaves.'" His voice became wilder and wilder. "On enlistment posters they don't say: 'Give us your youth,' 'Leave your wives widows and your sons orphans,' 'Die like dogs—worse than dogs.'"

He halted, faced her, taking hold of her wrists. "I have seen amputated legs stacked like cordwood. After winter battles, we had to chip men out of pools of their own frozen blood. Mortally wounded men at hospitals would arrange their clothing and limbs for burial so they wouldn't make extra work for us. The war was a *travesty. No cause justifies war.*"

The visions his words evoked terrified her, but a thought from her memory jarred her. She said in a dazed voice, "You said Will's name. You're Smith. You knew my husband. You drove an ambulance for the Sanitary Corps, didn't you?"

He looked shocked. His mouth opened and closed, but no words came out.

"You can tell me." She touched his arm. "I won't make you talk about it. But I need to know."

He closed his eyes as though drawing inner strength, then he nodded.

"I'm glad." She paused, searching for words to bolster him. "You and Will did what you had to do. Some things are worth dying for, but you have to go on."

He said at last, "Always the crusader."

Jessie did not speak, but she took his arm and began walking, leading him home. The night had exhausted both of them. Scenes from the deathbed she had just attended and the images Lee had described kept coming up before her eyes. She ached for Caleb in his loss. She ached for Lee, but she could not heal their pain. Only God could. And she doubted either man would seek God's healing. Why did it always seem that disaster piled on top of disaster? Lee's words tonight stirred her sympathy. He had suffered so much. He suffered with Will. He deserved peace now. Then her mind pulled up another painful thought. Dr. Gooden hadn't come. Why?

As they were parting at the top of her back steps, a thought came to her. She voiced it without letting herself ponder it, "Would you be interested in renting Miss Greenleigh's room?"

He eyed her as though trying to read her mind. "I thought you never rented to men."

"I've changed that," she stammered.

"Then I would like the room." By the lantern's glow, he looked her full in the face.

She avoided his eyes. "At the end of the week?"

"The end of the week."

Her gaze followed the swaying lantern light as he ambled away. It was done. She should have sent him away; instead, she had brought him closer to her, to Linc.

I let him kiss me. Her lips tingled with the memory. She touched them, fighting the warm tide that engulfed her. How did this man influence her to do things that did not jibe with her common sense or convictions?

What power drew her to him? Walking through her back door, she began humming plaintively, "My Lord, what a mourning when the stars began to fall."

★ ★ ★ ★ ★

The next night, the summer sky glowed between the frame houses along Jessie's street. Mr. Smith walked home with them from Reverend Mitchell's funeral.

He cleared his throat, "I'll bid you good night."

"Thank you for coming with us."

"Don't mention it."

Linc spoke up, "Good night, Mr. Smith."

Mr. Smith ruffled the boy's hair. "Good night, sport."

Linc walked him to the end of the block, then came back to his mother. "I can't wait till Mr. Smith moves into our house!"

Jessie nodded wearily, weighed down by her grief. Inside the kitchen they performed the nightly ritual of a sponge bath for the tired eight-year-old.

Though their room was warm, the strong lake breeze was blowing through the windows, swelling the sheers. The white privacy shades lifted and fell with each gust. Very soon the sky would be dark and this coolness from the lake would soothe them all. Jessie pulled the crisp, white sheet up to her son's chin and patted both his cheek and the soft, patchwork horse with the tangled mane of red yarn that he had slept with since birth. "Good night, Son. God bless you."

Yesterday had been laundry day, and in spite of Susan and Ruth's help, her back ached from bending over the washboard. She knew she should kneel beside her son's bed and pray with him at bedtime, but most nights she felt if she got down on her knees, she would merely lie down on the wooden floor and go to sleep.

If only Will had come back from the war, there would be someone with strong hands to rub her back. She could easily picture Will humming softly as he worked the tenseness out of her tired muscles. Sitting down on the chair at the foot of Linc's narrow bed, she sighed wearily.

Pressing a hand on either side of her head, she forced herself to stop this downward spiral into self-pity. Will had loved her, had given her a son, and left her a house with which she could support herself and their son. Many women were in much worse circumstances. Slowly she unhooked the buttons of her shoes, one by one, then she slid down her garters and black cotton hose. The first breath of air on her legs was refreshing, and the bare floor felt cool to the bottoms of her feet.

The sun set and the full moon rose, flooding the room with its silvery light. Linc's breathing became regular, telling her he was deeply asleep. Miss Wright snored evenly on the other side of the curtain. As soon as she could, she would advertise for another boarder for Miss Wright's old room upstairs now that they had both moved into the parlor. She still needed to paint it first. She sighed at the thought of more work.

She pressed down the images from the funeral tonight. Susan and Ruby had decided to stay with Caleb tonight.

Beside her chair sat the old trunk that had been her mother-in-law's. Reaching over, she opened the lid, careful not to make a sound. Under her winter woolens lay the packet of letters from Will tied up with a faded blue ribbon. Keeping the ribbon in place, she let her fingers walk on top of the letters' edges.

How many times had she read and reread these letters in the past six years? But in the months since Mr. Smith had arrived on the scene, she hadn't had time or inclination to look at them. Now that she knew Mr. Smith had served with Will, she could reread these to find out more about him. Smith's knowing Will had explained why he had sought her out in April and why he had befriended her son.

In this private moment, she could not deny the unsettling truth. She looked forward to Mr. Smith's nightly visits as much as her son did. In light of this she must know more about this man who remained substantially a stranger. The remembrance of how he often looked in her backyard—his strong arms and hands as they flexed and tightened while playing catch with Linc—captivated her. She closed her eyes, willing the image away.

She had invited him to move into her house. Will's letters might tell her what she needed to know to understand this man. But she dreaded coping with the memories these letters could invoke. Biting her lower lip, she opened a letter from the middle of the packet.

"Dearest Jessie." Reading it in the moonlight, Will's greeting still had the power to move her six years after his death. Her eyes scanned the page and then more pages as she read Will's distinctive large script. Accounts of battles, bravery, deaths featured in each letter she read.

Then a notation jumped out at her. "March 3, 1864. Jess, bad news today. Smith, the driver, died last night. I am sorely grieved."

She pressed the letter to her breast. Her heart thudded beneath it. If Smith died March 3, 1864, and Dr. Smith died

CHAPTER 11

shortly after Will, who was the man who had mourned with her tonight at Reverend Mitchell's funeral?

CHAPTER 12

September 12, 1871   THE ORGAN PLAYED THE CLOSING
hymn, "Just As I Am, Without One Plea." At its end, Jessie, Linc,
and Dr. Gooden walked up the crowded church aisle. As he took
her arm, Jessie asked silently, "Why didn't you come?"

That morning, just as they were leaving for church, Dr.
Gooden had showed up to accompany them. There had been no
chance to talk. So Jessie had listened to the sermon and sang
hymns and counted the minutes until she could confront the
doctor.

Too much had happened in the past week in Jessie's life.
Miss Greenleigh had moved out. Mr. Smith had moved in. She'd
discovered Mr. Smith had lied to her. Reverend Mitchell had
died. This last event overshadowed all the rest. After he refused
to come the night Reverend Mitchell passed away, Dr. Gooden

hadn't been to visit. She had taken the doctor's absence since that night as an admission of guilt.

Now at the double church doors, he was here shaking hands and chatting with her pastor. She smiled farewell at the minister and led the doctor down the front steps to the sidewalk.

"Doctor, Mr. Smith moved in this week!" Linc blurted out the most important news in his young life.

"Is that so?" Dr. Gooden looked to Jessie.

"Yes, Miss Greenleigh left to plan her fall wedding, and Mr. Smith moved into her room." Jessie's tension level mounted. *Why didn't you come?*

Linc ran ahead and began kicking a stone.

The doctor stopped while she snapped open her white parasol. "I have been busy also. I had meetings with Mayor Mason about poor sanitation causing cholera and typhus. He wants to hear more about Pasteur."

"Really?" Jessie said. Her interest lifted in spite of herself.

"Yes." He looked around the street. They'd left the crowded church entrance behind them. "We are alone. Now, Jessie, you can tell me how angry you are."

Jessie stopped. Somehow his words threw her off her stride. "Why didn't you come?"

"I was with a sick little girl. Typhus. I couldn't leave her. She was critical."

"So was Reverend Mitchell!" The anguish of the awful night nearly choked her.

"I know. But, Jessie, the Reverend was old and so sick—"

"Does that mean he didn't need a doctor?" Her voice shook. She wasn't angry at this man alone, but at the forces that had left Reverend Mitchell to die without any medical treatment.

Dr. Gooden stopped and turned to her. "No, it means that the Reverend was going to die whether or not I came. Do you think it is easy for a doctor, for me, to make such decisions?"

With her black-gloved fingers, she wiped away an angry tear, then took his hand. She couldn't believe it. "He wouldn't have lived if you had come?"

"He had my digitalis. If that had ceased to help him . . . I had nothing else to give him."

The utter defeat in his tone and words made her recall the terrible sound of the old pastor gasping for breath, then the dreadful silence when he breathed no more.

Jessie couldn't move. "The little girl?"

"She lived."

"You had to choose?"

"That night I thought she was the one who had the better chance to live. I chose to stay with her." He gently took her hand in his. "Jessie, when I first became a doctor, I thought only of healing people. Then I found out, sometimes I must make these choices . . . And people die. I cannot stop death every time."

Tears trickled down Jessie's cheeks. What a terrible choice to be forced to make! She fought back her tears. "I'm glad she lived."

September 28, 1871

"Oh, Mr. Smith, are you leaving now too?"

Mrs. Bolt's coy, but shrill, voice froze Lee's insides. "Yes, but I didn't expect you to be up and out so early on a Saturday morning." He kept his voice absolutely devoid of emotion.

"I have a little shopping to do downtown. How nice we are going the same way. We can have a chat together on the horse trolley."

"I was planning to walk today." He fought his growing irritation.

"What an excellent idea!" As slick as an escaping cat, the redhead slipped her arm into his.

The urge to box the woman's ears nearly overwhelmed him, but he took a deep breath and nodded. The stroll to town began. The widow kept up an uninterrupted gush of meaning-less chatter.

Lee held his temper tightly. Women over thirty more prop-erly wore dove gray, lavender, or navy, but this brazen woman dressed in pink ruffles and lace like a young filly. Her inappro-priate dress and proprietary manner—as though she had some claim on him—made anger and discomfort flow through him in surges. *I don't know how much longer I can be polite to this woman.*

At the sight of the first office building they came to, he sup-pressed the desire to tell Mrs. Bolt he had to part from her there. But in the next block, in the front of the first three-story office building, he halted. "I must leave you here, ma'am." He discon-nected himself from her clinging gloved hand.

"Oh, could I see your office?" she cooed as she stared up at the sandstone edifice.

"So sorry. I'm due in a meeting immediately. Good day." He charged into the building and up the central flight of marble stairs. Standing near the second floor window, he watched until the redhead disappeared up the street.

Within minutes, he strode out the rear entrance and headed south—straight for the Workman's Rest. When he crossed the threshold of its alley door, he found Pearl waiting for him.

Wearing a dress of royal blue cotton, she gave him a sidelong glance. "You dress like a banker, but you don't work banker's hours, Mr. Smith."

"I was delayed by . . . ah . . . business."

Pearl gave him a provocative smile. "You could advance your position here, you know. How would you like to be proprietor?"

Lee's mouth went dry. *Why did I ever let a flirtation with my boss start?*

"Think it over." Letting her lacy, royal blue bustle sway, Pearl passed through the door into the main room.

Think it over? Lee groaned inwardly. He should never have—even subtly—encouraged his employer's first forays into flirtation. Instead, amused by it, he had let it go on. He had mis-led her and for that he felt guilty.

"Are you going to marry my ma?" Pearl's twelve-year-old son eyed him.

"No, young man. Are you done mopping in the main room?"

"No, I gotta dump the spittoons first."

"Better you than me." He softened his words by shaking the boy's shoulder playfully.

Looking glum, the boy walked out the back door.

Lee removed and hung up his coat and hat. He tied on his white apron and tucked a clean towel in its band.

I'm surrounded. Pearl at work. The redhead at Wagstaff House.

Jessie's face appeared in his mind. *Jessie.* He felt her lips against his, her soft body pressed to him. *Jessie.* Holding her had been bliss. But the comfort in her caring touch had meant more to him than any passion he had felt.

Jessie continued to clothe herself in black and gray, trying to conceal her natural comeliness. To the world, she presented a stern-widow mask. It no longer fooled Lee. Jessie was a tender-hearted, loving woman.

He felt unprepared for this turn of events. His years in the army and his life after the war had kept him immune to affairs of the heart. He had only the remembrance of a few infatuations in his salad days to judge by.

Had he fallen in love with Jessie? He rubbed his forehead, wishing he could reach inside, smooth out his thoughts, and make sense of this. He took the broom and walked out to sweep the sidewalk in front of the saloon.

He swished the broom back and forth. This pointless action suited his mental confusion. An exasperating combination of softness and fortitude, Jessie would help Susan and her people or die trying. She insisted on taking care of Miss Wright, an old witch anyone else would show to the door. She brushed aside his attempts to give her money to help with expenses, even for Linc. Jessie was absolutely genuine. She would never play him false.

And I lied to her.

Her crusade to find a physician for Susan's people made it impossible for him to reveal his true name now. With shame, he recalled how she'd returned home, looking crushed, after each rejection. Each doctor had subjected her to hostility and bigotry. What if she ever found out the truth about him?

If she finds out, she'll never forgive me.

October 3, 1871

"Missy, we need to have a talk."

Recognizing her stepfather's harsh voice, Jessie paused in mid-swing with the snowshoelike rug beater in both hands. The rag and woven rugs from the bedrooms hung over the clothes-line on the side of the house. "Why are you here?" She finished her swing, forcing a puff of dust to appear.

"I see you no longer make any attempt at common polite-ness."

"Why should I show you common politeness?" She contin-ued swatting a rug with an even rhythm. "You've never shown any politeness to me—that was more than a paper-thin mask." Out of the corner of her eye, she saw his lips crimp up in dis-approval.

"I might have expected you would act this way. I am here for your own good. The way you have been behaving has reached my ears once more, Missy."

"Don't call me Missy."

"I have always called you that when you behave incor-rectly."

Jessie burned to say, *What do people call you when you behave incorrectly?*, but she still couldn't speak rudely to the man whom she had been raised to obey.

CHAPTER 12

Instead, she tried to avert the gathering storm. "I am not interested in anything you have to say. For my mother's sake, please leave."

He drew himself up. "I'm not leaving 'til I've said what I've come to say."

"Suit yourself." She went on swinging the beater, feeling each impact through her arms and back.

"Put that rug beater down. I think we should go in so we won't be overheard."

Looking at the rug, Jessie did not miss a stroke as she moved ahead to beat the next rug. The stale scent of dust hovered around them.

"Do you really want others to overhear what I have to say to you?"

"I've told you *I* don't want to hear what you have to say and I've asked you to leave."

"As your father, I have a responsibility—"

"You are not my father. You have never treated me as though you were my father—"

"I provided for you for nine years—"

Jessie moved to the next rug and swung at it, matching each swing to the beat of her words: "*And* I'm *sure* you have *written* down in your household ledger *every* penny you were *ever* forced to *spend* on me. *But* since you made me *work* off each *penny,* I feel *no* obligation to *you.*"

"You're attitude is totally unacceptable."

"Thank you." She moved on to a rose-patterned rug and attacked it.

"Enough of this." Huff hurried forward. "When are you going to stop this foolishness about finding a doctor for blacks?"

"When I find one." Jessie kept the clothesline dancing rhythmically. With each movement, her irritation expanded, growing into anger.

"This morning, one of the other fire captains asked me if my stepdaughter's married name was Wagstaff. He proceeded to tell me about an embarrassing visit you made to his brother, a doctor—"

"His brother should be embarrassed." Jessie spoke through gritted teeth. "Indeed, he should be ashamed for not helping people who need him."

"No one elected you his judge. 'Judge ye not, lest ye be judged.'"

Jessie stopped in midswing, her anger blazing white hot. "How dare you quote Scripture to me—you hard-hearted, mean-fisted hypocrite! Have you ever heard 'Love one another even as I have loved you'? When have you ever loved anyone but yourself?"

He spluttered with outrage.

Jessie felt herself lose control. Scalding words long held back poured forth, "I have never forgotten how you criticized Will when he enlisted. You couldn't stand that he cared about slaves. But how could you understand his love for strangers—when you don't even love the people you *do* know."

With a hand upraised, Hiram crowded close to her. Automatically Jessie took a batter's stance, gripping the rug beater like a baseball bat.

Hiram stopped. "You'll never see your mother again," he hissed. He turned and marched away.

Jessie felt light-headed, her head throbbing. *He was going to strike me.*

✳ ✳ ✳ ✳ ✳

Esther was polishing silver when her husband walked in, slamming the door behind him. She dropped the spoon she held. It clattered to the floor. "Hiram, what has happened?"

"That daughter of yours!" he thundered and started pacing up and down the small room. "I went to her house to confront her about the way she's been disgracing us all over town. Captain Phelps described your daughter's outrageous attempt to persuade his brother to take on her black friends as patients."

"But those people do need a doctor," Esther said softly.

"That is no business of your daughter's!"

Her heart sped up. Esther pressed her hand to the high neck of her plain, navy blouse. "It is an act of charity. Perhaps God wants Jessie to do this."

"Nonsense! God wants no such thing!"

"Do you speak for God, Hiram?"

Silence. Hiram stopped pacing.

"Esther, you have never spoken to me like this before."

Esther clutched the edge of the table, her knuckles white. "You have never spoken for God before. I know it's your nature to feel things strongly and to express yourself strongly—"

"I forbid you to say any more."

"I'm sorry, but as a Christian, I feel compelled to speak."

"A Christian wife does not contradict her husband."

Her voice remained soft, but she stood up, facing him. "Even when he is wrong?"

"I'm not wrong! Your daughter—"

"Again, do you speak for God?"

He stared at her as though he doubted his ears.

She looked at him, a frown forming a crease between her brows. "I have been doing a lot of thinking over the past few weeks. We have been married for twenty-three years. In that whole time, Hiram, I have never once said what I was truly thinking. That's a long time to keep silent."

"Thinking?" he sputtered.

"I know it has probably never occurred to you, but I have my own thoughts and feelings. Last week Jessie told me that when she was a child, she thought I didn't love her." Her voice cracked. "Can you imagine how that wounded my heart?"

"That has nothing to do with this—"

"It has *everything* to do with this. Do you remember what you promised me about Jessie before we married?"

"I told you I would treat her as my own child."

"Yes, that's what you said." A sob formed deep inside her, but she held it in. "How was I to know what a rigorous and unloving father you meant to be?"

"What?" His face registered disbelief.

"You browbeat our sons with your rigid rules and cold discipline. You never show them love or even common kindness." Esther looked down at the floor, ashamed of her words.

"You're losing your mind." He sounded resentful, accusing.

She faced him. "No, I am *speaking* my mind for the first time."

"You will stop this immediately." He stepped up to her. "It's your daughter's rebellion we have to thank for this attitude. But I will tolerate no more of this from either of you." He took hold of her arms, gripping her painfully. "You will not speak to her again 'til she apologizes to me."

"No."

He squeezed her arms. "You will not—"

She wrenched away from him. An icy sensation radiated through her limbs. "You have always wanted to separate me from my daughter."

"You're not making sense."

Feeling as brittle as the first thin sheet of ice over a winter pond, she turned to leave the room.

"Esther, I forbid you to speak to your daughter until she apologizes to me, You will obey me."

"No, Hiram, I will not obey you in this."

He lunged forward, grasped her arms once more, and jerked her toward him, hurting her. "You will obey me. It is your duty as my wife. You promised to love, honor, and obey me. If you defy me, you will be breaking your wedding vows."

Esther ignored his agitation and the pain in her arms. "Hiram, you promised to love, honor, and cherish me. You have never kept even one of your vows to me. Let God judge between us."

His angry face, just inches from her, burned red. He raised his hand so quickly Esther didn't have time to dodge his blow. Her head swam and she couldn't get her breath. Trying to speak, she felt herself losing consciousness.

※ ※ ※ ※ ※

Mrs. Bolt held herself upright, making the most of her five foot four inches. She marched at the front of a dozen or more of her compatriots in the Temperance Union. Everyone around her chattered with excitement. Their common zeal had finally prompted them to take action against the drinking of liquor. A thrilling combination of trepidation and ardor carried Mrs. Bolt up to the swinging doors of the first "gin house" where she would crusade this evening.

Ever since childhood, she had crossed to the other side of the street when passing any saloon. This was her first chance to peer over swinging doors. A striking blonde woman, standing at the bar in the long, narrow room, caught Mrs. Bolt's eye. *A fallen woman!* Mrs. Bolt avidly absorbed every detail of the woman's costume. Though somewhat disappointed by the modesty of the apparel, she gloated that no decent woman would wear all that showy lace at the throat and atop the flaring blue bustle.

Mrs. Bolt chanted along with the others while she observed the woman flirting in a common and obvious fashion. The fallen woman laughed and tapped the arm of the man standing beside her. Mrs. Bolt caught the end of the hussy's sally. "I should pay the most charming bartender in Chicago more." The blonde counted four dollars into the open palm of . . .

When Mrs. Bolt recognized the face of the man, she smothered a faint shriek.

※ ※ ※ ※ ※

Sighing with fatigue, Jessie sat at the head of the dining room table. *Another day nearly over.* As she slipped a handkerchief from her pocket and surreptitiously wiped away the perspiration at her temples, she wished summer would finally end and the cool days of fall would begin. Her confrontation with her step-father in the backyard that afternoon had shaken her. She had felt tired but restless the rest of the day.

"That was a delicious meal, Mrs. Wagstaff."

"Thank you, Mr. Chaney."

Mr. Chaney, a young carpenter journeyman, had rented Miss Wright's former room yesterday. The extra three dollars a week would be helpful now that Ruby had been added to their household. And Ruby had advised her that Mr. Smith would feel more comfortable if he were not "the only rooster in da hen house."

"My condolences on the loss of your husband," the young man said.

"What?" Jessie looked up.

"You're still in mourning. I realized I didn't mention it yes-terday. Please excuse me."

From across the table, Miss Wright addressed the young man. "Her husband has been gone for over six years now." She turned to Jessie, "It's time you put mourning clothes behind you, Jessie."

Before Jessie could think of what to say to this, Miss Wright went on, "Now, I had a Tom Chaney in my classes some thirty years ago."

"Did he have white blonde hair and a lisp?"

"He did."

"That was my father, ma'am."

"He was a good student." Miss Wright gave one of her rare smiles. "What was your mother's maiden name?"

"Bliss, ma'am." He grinned. "My father always says he's got 'wedded bliss.'"

Linc looked at the young man as though puzzled by the teasing tone and why the others had smiled at Chaney's words.

"Linc," Jessie explained, "people call marriage wedded bliss."

"Oh." Linc appeared to study this. "I get it now."

Lee ruffled the boy's hair. "Go get the checkers and board."

Jessie kept trying to figure out why Mr. Smith had lied to her. Had he just wanted to be connected to her and Linc? Had he just been upset that night and not understood her?

"Please, couldn't we practice batting?"

Jessie opened her mouth, but was cut off.

Lee shook his head. "After eating such a delicious meal, my stomach needs a game or two of checkers."

Mr. Chaney said in a wondering voice, "I've never seen a stomach play checkers before, have you, Linc?"

Linc grinned. "I get it."

"Go get it," Lee said.

Jessie silently enjoyed the banter. Mr. Chaney was fitting in nicely. Hopefully Mrs. Bolt wouldn't make his life miserable with her flirting. The fact that the young man was more than ten years younger than the redhead probably wouldn't deter the woman.

Chuckling, Linc went to a low drawer in the sideboard and brought out the game in a tattered cardboard box. The boy and Lee set up the checkers on their board. Mr. Chaney said something to Linc that made the boy chuckle, and he turned to share the laugh with Lee.

Jessie heard a new voice in the kitchen. She stood up as Susan came through the kitchen curtain.

"Mrs. Wagstaff, you' mother is here."

Jessie quietly followed Susan back into the kitchen. Ruby was hovering over Esther where she sat at the kitchen table.

"What . . ." Jessie faltered. At the sight of her mother's bruised and swollen face, she rushed to her. "Mother!"

"Dat man hit her!" Ruby declared fiercely.

Susan clenched her fists. "I'd like to git a hold a him."

Jessie knelt in front of her mother, taking her hands. "It's because of me. This is all my fault—"

"No, Jessie," Esther whispered. "This is his fault. After he went back to work, I . . . I left the twins with our neighbor. I can't go back—"

The slamming of the front door and a strident female voice shouting grabbed the attention of the four women.

"Mother, come quick!" Linc stood in the middle of the parted curtain. "Now!"

"Go!" Esther pushed her daughter by the shoulders. "Your son needs you."

"Now what?" Jessie got up and hurried to her son. He caught her hand and pulled her into the dining room with him. She saw that everyone except Miss Wright had risen to face Mrs. Bolt, who stood in the doorway from the foyer. Jessie halted.

"Don't try to deny it!" Mrs. Bolt pointed her finger at Lee. "I saw you with that painted woman!"

"What are you talking about?" Jessie demanded.

"Vile deceiver!" The redhead's voice became thick with outrage.

"What are you talking about?" Jessie repeated.

"Mr. Smith is a bartender!" the redhead shouted.

"You work at a saloon?" Jessie felt the strain of two shocks within seconds of each other. *What's happening!*

"I am a bartender." Chagrin and shame combined in Lee's voice. Linc dropped his mother's hand and went to stand beside Lee.

Mrs. Bolt's face turned scarlet. "He isn't fit to sit at the table with decent people. Out of loyalty to you, Mrs. Wagstaff, I have endured painful criticism for living here despite your outrageous behavior. My forebearance is repaid like this."

Esther came through the curtain with Ruby and Susan hovering behind her. The sight of Esther's face made Miss Wright gasp. "Esther, what has happened to you?"

"Oh, Miss Wright," Esther sobbed and covered her face with her hands.

CHAPTER 12

"Why isn't anyone paying attention to me?" Mrs. Bolt, with hands on her hips, demanded.

"Because you wore out your welcome here months ago, you tedious ninny," snapped Miss Wright. "Pack your things. Mr. Smith isn't going to propose to you. A blind nitwit could see he's sweet on Jessie. You've stayed here for nothing."

"Well!" The redhead colored to a hideous red. Her voice shook. "Is this true, Mrs. Wagstaff?"

Jessie spoke quietly without taking her eyes from Lee's face. "He's sweet on Jessie" echoed in her mind. "I will be needing your room for my mother, and I do think you will be happier elsewhere."

Mrs. Bolt burst into tears and rushed from the room.

CHAPTER 13

October 4, 1871

At midnight, Jessie finally gave up trying to sleep. Slipping her thin cotton wrapper over her long chemise, she crept from her half of the parlor bedroom out to the refuge of the clematis vine-sheltered back porch. Butch, sleeping in his doghouse on the corner of the porch, opened his eyes, but closed them when she murmured his name.

The wood floor felt cool under her bare feet. She had been too troubled to braid her hair for the night. Now she lifted her unbound hair off the back of her neck and pushed it onto her shoulder, letting the refreshing breeze brush her neck. Massaging her temples, she paced up and down the rough floorboards. In her mind, Mrs. Bolt's spiteful voice repeated over and over, "Vile deceiver!" Unbidden, Linc's small voice at bedtime came to mind, entreating her, "Mama, say you won't make Mr. Smith go away. Please, Mama."

What a dreadful scene. What a dreadful evening.

After a continuous tirade of venom and recriminations, Mrs. Bolt had departed. Then Jessie had done her best to soothe Linc and help her silent mother get settled in Mrs. Bolt's former room. Her mother had gone through the motions of dressing for bed like a woman walking in her sleep.

What am I going to do? Twice now Lee has deceived me. Twice that I am aware. What else might he have lied about?

When did I start thinking of him as Lee, not Mr. Smith? And what does it matter? Neither name is really his. And why haven't I asked, no, demanded he tell me the truth? She arched her neck backward as a wave of tension rippled through her.

She moaned in exasperation. "I'm doing it on my own again, Margaret." She took in a deep breath and let it out gradually. She heard Margaret's voice, "When a mist clouds your spiritual vision, only God's light will help you see clearly." Jessie knelt beside the porch railing. Through the cotton, the old floorboards bit into her knees. "Dear Lord, I don't understand. Help me."

On her knees and bending her head against the railing, Jessie waited for God's light. She let the muted sounds of crickets and cicadas wash over her. Her thoughts roamed. She repeated, "Father, send your light." Soon the painful pressure on her knees prompted her to lift herself to sit on the railing.

Her heart slowed to its normal pace. The throbbing in her head ebbed and disappeared. Her stomach settled and bothered her no more. Sighing, she eased herself back against the corner beam of the railing, enjoying the cooling lake breeze swirling around her ankles.

She whispered, "Spirit of God, open my eyes. Help me understand why I haven't been able to confront this man?"

A wave of physical passion rocked her. She felt warm, alive, feminine. In her imagination, she felt strong arms surrounding her, Lee's arms. She leaped to her feet, her heart pounding.

CHAPTER 13

"Jessie?"

She whirled around. "Lee?" Her attraction to this man surged to full tide and swamped her. Floundering in its lush currents, she couldn't speak.

"I'm sorry . . . I couldn't sleep. I didn't . . . I had no idea anyone would be out here."

Barefoot and clad only in her thin gown and robe, she felt stripped of the everyday barriers between men and women. She stepped back into the deeper shadows close to the house while her awareness of him burned its way through her senses. His chestnut hair was tousled. Though he still wore his dark slacks, he was shirtless. His bare skin in the scant moonlight made her hands tremble. She imagined it as satin under her fingertips.

Her prayer for understanding had been answered. She had not confronted him because she was attracted to him. Why hadn't she gauged her spiraling desire? Was she so blind to her own weakness?

"I'll go back in," he mumbled.

"No." She held up her hand as though reaching for him.

He turned toward her, but stopped when she folded her arms over her breast.

"I think we need to talk." She swallowed, trying to relieve the dryness of her mouth. Her mind whirled. She could keep silent no longer, but she had to protect herself from her forbidden attraction to him. "Sit on the steps with your back to me."

Hesitating, Lee tried to think of something to say, but then gingerly obeyed. His face toward the alley, he rubbed his moist palms on the tops of his thighs. "I'm sorry about all this—about my job. That blasted redhead." In agonized uncertainty, he waited for her response. "Would you like me to change my line of work?"

"That isn't important now." Jessie's voice shook. "I want you to tell me what your real name is."

The words shimmered in the air around Lee's head. Pinpricks tingled up and down his spine. He couldn't form a word, not one word.

"I know Lee Smith died in '64."

Mrs. Bolt's words reverberated once again through his head, "Vile deceiver!" When that redhead had voiced this accusation, he had thought for a few seconds she had discovered he was living under an assumed identity. *But Jessie already knew. How could she? Why hadn't she confronted him before?* He almost choked on words, explanations, lies as they caught in his throat.

"I've known since just a few days after Reverend Mitchell's death that you'd given me a false name."

He stood up and spun toward her. "That long? You've known that long!"

She retreated from him, farther into the shadows of the trellis.

"I can't believe you've known, but said nothing."

"Who are you? I must know." Her voice was cool, demanding.

The warm, responsive woman he had held only days before had vanished. "I can't tell you."

"Why not? Is there a warrant out for you? Do you owe money?"

"Nothing like that!"

"Then what is it? You've taken a dead man's name, and I have to know why—"

He started pacing. "The war. I spent five years trying to forget the war, running from the past. Finally I couldn't run anymore. I came here to start over." He halted. They were only a few steps apart now.

"Who are you?" Her tone was implacable.

She was Jessie. She was Nemesis. He couldn't tell her the truth. He had to stall her. It was his only defense. "I need time. I'll tell you, but I need time."

"Time? How will time change the truth?"

He laughed without humor. "Oh, Jessie, Jessie. You're so . . . Jessie."

"What does that mean?" she asked indignantly.

"It means I know you. I know that once you decide something is right and must be achieved, you will pursue it to the ends of the earth."

"*I* am not the issue here. Who are you?"

He groaned and raked his fingers through his hair. He couldn't let her know who he was. She hadn't connected him with Dr. Smith. He couldn't take the chance of telling her the whole truth. The blessed sanity of his first sober year in decades was too dear. He couldn't chance a final descent into drink and delirium tremors. And that would be the price of practicing medicine again.

"Who are you?" Jessie, relentless Jessie, prompted him.

He couldn't tell her the whole truth. It would destroy him, destroy their chance together. How much of the truth could he tell her without revealing that he was a doctor? "The war . . . I still haven't been able to let some of it go," he stammered. "It's still with me."

"Do you mean you have fears from the war?"

"In a way, yes. I hate the cliché, but I couldn't run away from my past. Maybe no one can."

"But you must still be running away from the war if it keeps you from telling me the truth."

He flinched. She had jabbed a needle right in the center of his wounded soul. He knew she would never be able to understand why he could never again risk making the life and death decisions a doctor must always be prepared to make. "Do you think it's easy to face the ugly truth?"

"The truth will set you free."

"Don't quote Scripture to me."

"I cannot have a man who tells lies around my son. Don't you see? I cannot allow Linc to be in danger of heartbreak. If you are hiding something that—in the end—will force you to abandon him . . . or shatter his trust in you . . ."

He groped madly for an explanation to offer, some distraction. More and more he had become aware of her nearness, of the fragrance of lavender that clung to her, of the impression of her dark hair swept to one side of her head, its waves, a cascade down one of her slim shoulders.

He took a step closer. "Nothing I've ever been or have ever done can harm Linc. That's the truth."

"The truth? You've lied to me. How can I believe you?"

"I can show you why you should believe me," he said persuasively.

"How?"

He slid forward, tucking her into his arms. She gasped, but resisted only a moment. He sensed her acquiescence and breathed in the scent of her, exulting in this intimacy. "Oh, Jessie, you are the most irritating woman, the most determined, the most giving." Gently he began to rock her side to side. "And you don't know how irresistible you are."

Jessie struggled with herself. His touch was fire and it was all she craved and more. But moments ago she had stepped away from him, torn by unanswered questions. What was wrong with her? Her body and mind wrestled for control. As he began to stroke her back through the thin cotton, she gave up trying to think and shivered with his touch.

"Jessie," he whispered, "can't we let the dead past bury itself? Jessie, the truth is I want to kiss you." Not waiting for permission, his lips sought hers.

She turned her face as though to avoid his, but her lips wouldn't obey her. They wanted Lee's kiss. And his kiss was full and sweet and lifted Jessie to a height she had not known nor could recall. His lips brushed and teased hers.

She trembled with passion as she had just moments before he'd joined her. Though caught in this sensual undertow, her conscience fought to the surface. She pushed herself out of his embrace. "No."

With arms suddenly empty, he stumbled a step forward and then halted.

"I wanted you to kiss me, but I can't let that sway me. I must know the truth." She stepped another step backward and folded her arms in front of her, warning him away.

"I'll tell you everything," he pleaded, "when the time is right."

"When will that be?"

"I can't say." He reached out to her.

She turned her back to him.

"Don't go. Jessie, I can't lose you."

She bent her chin to her breast, pondering. Then she lifted her head, though she continued to face away from him. "A month. I'll give you one more month. April to November is six months. If you can't be honest with me after we've known each other half a year, then it's better we part." She turned to confront him. Her voice was emotionless. "If you can't tell the truth by then, you'll have to make some excuse to Linc for leaving town, and go."

One month and then I lose her and Linc. He felt icy fingers of despair clutch his heart.

October 5, 1871

Lee stood outside staring up at the three-story brick building's sign: Field and Leiter's Department Store. Glancing at his reflection in the gleaming store window, he straightened his tie. His leave-taking from The Workman's Rest had been a delicate operation. He honestly liked Pearl Flesher and felt he had led her on with his teasing encouragement of her flirtation. Therefore, he had employed all his tact and finesse with aplomb to leave her employment without wounding her with the truth. All for naught. As he had turned to leave her Pearl had asked, "So what's her name, handsome?"

He shouldn't have been surprised. Pearl was nobody's fool. "Jessie."

She had nodded. "Good for you. Let us know how you get on, okay?"

Thus, Pearl had shown herself a lady, despite Mrs. Bolt's snap judgment of her.

Now, gathering his resolve, Lee walked into the store and headed to the desk at the rear of the first floor. In this short distance, he became impressed by the display tables of embroidered handkerchiefs and ladies' gloves, the fine wood paneling, the marble columns, and floors that shone with polish.

After two preliminary interviews with floor managers, Lee, ushered into a commodious office, introduced himself to Mr. Field.

"Mr. Smith, do you have a background in retailing?"

"No, sir, I don't. I am eager to learn, however."

"Good. Good. Tell me about yourself."

Lee rapidly chose from his past and present those details he wanted to reveal. The interview ended with a handshake and an offer to begin the next day to train as a salesman in the Gentlemen's Finer Attire Department. Lee accepted. Working at Mr. Field's department store would certainly be a contrast to bartending at the Workman's Rest. Lee counted on Jessie's considering it a good example to Linc. Since he couldn't tell her the truth about his past, he had decided to convince her the past was dead and gone, that his future was all she need be concerned about.

Outside, Lee tipped his hat to a fashionable lady approaching the store entrance. He felt like tipping his hat to the world. Striding up and down the uneven wood sidewalks, Lee whistled as he planned the best way to tell Jessie about his change in employment.

On his way home, he passed Drexel Park. A young woman walked by him pushing a honey-colored wicker buggy. He glimpsed the rosy bundle inside. Suddenly he pictured Jessie strolling with their child. The image was electrifying. A family of their own. He stopped. *Jessie and he. Mother and father. Wife and husband.* He had not consciously contemplated marriage before. Now the desire to marry Jessie rushed through him, nearly taking his breath away.

❋ ❋ ❋ ❋ ❋

Jessie and her mother sat at the kitchen table. Both women wore full, white aprons and each had a lapful of potatoes. Jessie was peeling one potato after the other with deft, swift strokes while Esther still held the same potato she had selected when they first sat down.

"All those years . . . wasted. All those years we could have been together. I'm so sorry, Jessie."

"We were together, Mother."

"No, you were right. Hiram always pushed you and me apart."

"Your eyes always looked so sad when he was scolding me." Jessie dropped the potato she had finished peeling into the pot of cool water and reached for another.

"I never meant to neglect you. When Hiram courted me, he was so polite to you. He said he would treat you as his own."

"He's not much kinder to the twins."

"I know, but when we were courting, he showed me such courtesy, such respect."

"Is that why you married him? It wasn't love, was it?"

Closing her eyes, Esther sighed sorrowfully. "No, I've never loved Hiram, not the way I loved your father. Maybe a woman only loves that way once. Your father died so young, and neither of us had much family to fall back on. Times were hard. By the time Hiram proposed to me, I was nearly desperate."

"So you married him?"

"Yes, he was a decent Christian man, and he was the only one who wanted me." Her voice cracked on the last word.

"Mother." Jessie wiped her hand on her apron, then touched her mother's hand.

"I've prayed and prayed, but he never changes. I don't blame God. How can God change a man who thinks there's no need to change since he's about as perfect as a mortal can be? He gives no room for God at all, not really. He attends church. He reads his Bible, but nothing touches him. Sometimes I have felt that I married a man made of brick and iron."

Jessie had always thought that herself, but had never guessed her mother felt the same way. She kept her eyes on the potato she was peeling, embarrassed to see pain in her mother's eyes.

"Every harsh word he ever said to you broke a bit of my heart. A change in Hiram's heart—I have prayed for that for twenty-three years. I would give anything to change his heart, to fill it with God's healing love."

"I think he would have to grow a heart first. I don't think he has one."

"Please, daughter. Don't let what happened to me make you bitter. Hatred destroys people. You and Will were so happy with each other, and Mr. Smith is so good with Linc."

The scene from the night before—Lee holding her in his arms—swooped into Jessie's mind. The passion she'd felt in his arms sluiced through her senses, undiluted by the passing of the night. How glad she was she'd stepped away. She had been playing with fire last night. But never again.

As Jessie spoke, her voice shook. "I will never take the chance you did. I knew when I lost Will, I would raise Linc alone. My son can't have his father, but he will have me—all of me. I will never remarry." *Lee, there will be no more interludes in the dark.*

"Jessie, please don't say that. Please."

Susan stepped inside the kitchen curtain. "Jessie, Dr. Gooden is waitin' for you on da front porch."

Jessie's hands stilled. She cleared her lap, then stood, putting down the paring knife. "Tell him, Susan . . . Please tell him I'll join him in a moment."

Susan nodded, then withdrew. Jessie took off her apron, washed her hands, then smoothed her hair. She walked to the doorway.

Esther's voice stopped her. "Daughter, I've made my mistakes. Don't make decisions for your life based on mine. God has given you a life different from mine. You are very different from me. You have more fire and spirit."

Jessie turned and looked at her mother. "The doctor's waiting. I'll be back."

She didn't quite understand what her mother meant. What was true was true. She knew clearly that all she had ever wanted was to be the wife of Will Wagstaff, and nothing had changed.

When Susan saw Jessie, she nodded and withdrew inside.

"Dr. Gooden." Jessie offered him her hand.

He took it, bowed over it.

"Please sit down." She sat on the wicker chair beside the matching love seat.

He sat on the end of the love seat closest to her. "I make bold to call on you. I have a moment to tell you of good news."

"How did your interview with Mayor Mason go?"

"He listened very carefully. He is very interested in improving health conditions in the city."

"Will he actually make any changes, the ones you think would stop cholera?"

"I do not look for a miracle." The doctor smiled. "If he will just listen, that is a fine start."

She nodded.

"The same with you," he said gazing at her. "If you will just listen to me, get to know me better . . . Jessie, I wish to court you."

Her gaze fell to her lap, but she felt her face burn with a hot blush. This was what she had feared. Dr. Gooden had let his discreet interest in her show before now. She should have discouraged him.

She cleared her throat. "You have just paid me the highest compliment a man can pay a woman—"

"Jessie, I can wait. We have known each other so little a time—"

"No." She looked him straight in the eye. "Time won't make a difference. I am not the wife you need."

"But—"

She went on, "Doctor, you need a wife who is at ease in society, not me."

"But at the Palmers—"

"I felt completely out of place. The outing was glorious, but only as a onetime event. I couldn't do it again."

He looked at her. "I do not believe that. You do not know what you are truly capable of."

Jessie shook her head.

"Is there someone else? Smith?"

"No, no one. I don't intend to marry again."

He glanced at his pocket watch and frowned. "I must go. I am needed at the hospital."

Jessie stood. "I understand."

He kissed her hand. "I do not give up so easy."

She shook her head and withdrew her hand. "I won't change my mind."

The doctor hurried out to his carriage. With a wave, he set off.

Jessie sighed. *God, please bring this good man the wife he really needs—soon.*

※ ※ ※ ※ ※

Linc held up his small slate board. "Mother, look. Mr. Smith helped me with my long division. See? I understand it now."

Jessie sat at the end of the dining table, knitting another pair of socks for Linc this winter. In the heat of the room, she

wondered if the cooling winds of fall would ever come, bringing relief. She paused in her knitting and sighed. Winter would
come eventually, and the socks would be needed. She began
knitting the blue wool again.

"That's good, Linc." She smiled mechanically. *Linc shouldn't
be allowed to become any closer to Mr. Smith.* "Now why don't you
go out and do your last division problems, sitting by Butch?
There should be enough daylight left." When Linc passed near
her, Jessie kissed his forehead, then sent him on with a loving
push.

Jessie let the steady clicking of the needles soothe her emotions. Miss Wright dozed in a rocking chair by the door to the
foyer. By the window Mr. Chaney was reading an evening
paper while Esther read her Bible. Mr. Chaney, well mannered
and sociable, had fit into the household without any fuss. Jessie
smiled as she recalled how easily he had taken to Linc. She had
not realized how irritating Mrs. Bolt had been until they were
free of her. Miss Greenleigh had been correct in her advice. The
circle of people around the table provided more of what a
growing boy needed.

A loud knock rattled the front door. Susan entered through
the kitchen curtain and slipped around the table to go answer it.

"I'm here to get my wife." Hiram's strident voice shattered
the tranquil mood of the room. Jessie dropped her knitting.
Esther hopped up and started for the kitchen.

"Don't run away, Mrs. Huff," Lee said quietly. He rose. Mr.
Chaney, folding his paper, also stood up, alert. Jessie took
strength from their presence. Hiram stalked in with Susan right
behind him.

"Good evening. Mr. Huff," Lee said.

Hiram ignored Lee and tried to push past him. Lee's arm
shot out, checking the other man. "I said good evening, Mr.
Huff."

Jessie felt her pulse begin to race.

"I've heard about you, bartender. Stay out of my business."

"I'm not a bartender anymore."

At this Hiram shifted his attention to Lee. "I don't care what you are. I'm here to take my wife home where she belongs."

Jessie opened her mouth, but was cut off.

"At the moment, Mrs. Huff's home is here." Lee stood firm, blocking the other man's path.

"This has"—Hiram jabbed his finger into Lee's shirt front with each syllable—"no-thing-to-do-with-you."

Jessie stood up and Esther took a few steps back, closer to Mr. Chaney.

"Hiram Huff, you are just like your mother." Miss Wright's strident voice amazed them all. "Your mother moved here in fourth grade and she was an officious little brat even then."

Jessie couldn't believe her ears.

At first, even Hiram's shocked response stuck and garbled in his throat, then he declared, "This has nothing to do with my mother!"

"It has everything to do with why you have lost one of the sweetest wives in Chicago. Esther is a saint, because only a saint could have stayed married to you for more than twenty years."

Hiram's face turned a bright vermilion. "Esther, pack your things. I'm taking you home tonight."

Jessie couldn't think of what to say, what to do to stop him.

The man's audacity silenced the others too. But Esther drew herself up and faced him. "Hiram, when you decide to keep your vows to me, I will come home."

"How dare you say that to me?" Pushing Lee aside, Hiram started forward again, but halted when Mr. Chaney moved between Hiram and his wife. "Woman, I have never been faithless to you."

"You know that is not what I mean. I want your love, Hiram, and not only for me, but for my three children too."

"Your children! Hah! A lot you cared for your children. Leaving them alone while I went to work. I can't believe you abandoned them like that."

Jessie was shaking. She prayed for calm resolve.

Esther said, "I would have brought them with me if I had the wherewithal to provide for them. But I couldn't expect my widowed daughter to take in two more mouths to feed."

"The twins are always welcome," Jessie said with all the dignity she could muster.

"Keep out of this, missy," Hiram growled. "This is all your fault. You're the one who drove a wedge between me and my wife."

"No, she isn't," Esther said.

"Esther, if you persist in this folly, I will make certain you never see your sons again!"

Esther blanched and covered her mouth with her hand.

"I think we've had enough of you tonight," Lee said, then took Hiram by the back of his collar and the seat of his pants and propelled him past Susan and out the front door.

Lee returned, dusting his hands. "I've wanted to do that ever since I met that man."

Jessie sighed with relief. Ruby stepped into the room. "Miss Esther, you come in da kitchen. I makes you a cup a tea."

Esther, wiping away tears, agreed and followed Ruby. Susan brought up the rear. Mr. Chaney bid them all a tactful good night and went upstairs.

Jessie heaved herself back into her chair. "I feel as though I have just run a mile."

"Strong emotion always takes its toll," Miss Wright said.

Lee rounded on her. "You, our dear Miss Wright, deserve an award. No one else could have said what you did and have gotten away with it."

Miss Wright let a momentary hint of a smile flutter over her features. "The man's a fool, but that doesn't help our dear Esther.

He will keep her from her boys, and he will make her as miserable away from him as she was with him."

"I'm afraid he is a top hand at making people miserable," Jessie said bleakly.

Miss Wright struggled to her feet. "Only God can melt a heart of stone like Hiram Huff's."

"But so far God hasn't seen fit to act." Jessie massaged her neck muscles with one hand.

Miss Wright turned to her. "If you start telling God what to do or if you let yourself hate Hiram Huff, you'll be no better than Hiram himself is. And I don't care what you think, that is what Margaret would say."

Jessie stared at the old woman in surprise.

Miss Wright grunted with pain and hobbled from the room, but tonight even her cane thumping was subdued.

"Are you all right, Jess?" Lee sat down in the chair beside her.

His closeness made her feel like a canary with a tomcat at its cage door. "I'm fine. I thought my stepfather would come sometime, and he'll come again." She stood up.

"Most likely. But you aren't alone. Mr. Chaney and I will be here." He stood up and stretched out his hand to take hers.

Jessie ignored this gesture. She didn't want to be alone with Mr. Smith. "I'm going to the kitchen to help Ruby and Susan comfort my mother."

Looking disconcerted, Lee shoved his hands into his pockets. "I'll go out and keep Linc and Butch company."

They both passed through to the kitchen. He went on out the back door while Jessie sat down in the chair next to her mother.

"Miss Jessie, you want some tea too?" Ruby asked. She stood by the kettle from which the thrumming sound of near boiling water came.

"No thank you, Ruby."

222

"Grandma, you come sit down," Susan said. "I'll make dat tea."

"You ironed all da day long," Ruby objected. "Sit. I'm too old to do much, but I kin still bile water."

Esther wiped her eyes with a lacy handkerchief. "I'm so sorry, Jessie. I don't know what poor Mr. Chaney thought of such a scene."

"Don't worry, Mother. He seemed to take it in stride."

"He a nice boy, dat's for sure." Ruby shuffled ponderously, carrying the steaming tea kettle to the table and setting it on a cast-iron trivet.

"I surely was glad he and Mr. Smith be here." Susan folded her arms over her breast. "But don' you fret. We'll make certain sure dat husband of yours don' fine you 'lone."

"Bes' he not fine her here atall," Ruby spoke up, surprising Jessie.

"Grandma!" Susan scolded.

"I don' mean what you thinkin'. I mean dat this purty lady should shake dat man up good. Let him know she ain't gonna put up with his orneriness no more."

"What do you mean, Ruby?" Esther dried the last of her tears.

"I mean he think you dependin' on him 'lone. He think he just need to talk and talk and get mad and finally you come home."

"Yes," Jessie encouraged.

Ruby pointed to Esther with her free hand. "You need to get you some new clothes and wear 'em where he kin see you. You need a new bonnet, new gloves. You need to make him see dat you ain't gonna just sit 'round cryin' over him."

"But how?" Esther asked.

"You gotta go get you a job." Ruby nodded with each of her words. "Not cookin' or cleanin'—somethin' at one of dem big stores I seen downtown. Dat'll make him worry." Ruby poured out the steaming water into the teacups while the other women around the table appeared to absorb this interesting new idea. Could Ruby be right? Jessie wondered. Ruby sat down and picked up her teacup.

"I'll do it," Esther said quietly.

"A job? Mother, you don't—"

Esther sat up straight. "Don't tell me what I can and can't do, Jessie. Hiram has done that for twenty-three years. Besides, I don't want to be dependent on you, and you don't need me with Susan and Ruby to help you around here—"

"Mother—"

"No, Hiram Huff thinks I'll come crawling back to him. If I take a job and begin making my own way in the world, maybe he'll take me seriously. In any event, it'll give me something more to do than cry all the time." She smiled at Ruby. "Thank you."

Lee and Linc came in. "Linc's homework is done. I'm going to walk him to his room."

"I'll come too." Jessie stood up. Maybe now would be a good time to tell Mr. Smith that she wanted him to begin distancing himself from her son—unless he'd decided to reveal the truth. The three of them walked through the dining room to the foyer. Linc submitted to having his hair ruffled by Lee and to being kissed by his mother. Then he went into their half of the curtain-divided parlor. Jessie slid the pocket door nearly shut. Then she found herself face-to-face with Lee.

As if reading her mind, he offered, "I'd like to talk to you privately."

"Very well." Jessie led him out onto the front porch.

Lee felt awkward. Maybe it was the way Jessie half-turned from him. Or maybe it was due to Hiram Huff's visit. Impetuously he took Jessie's shoulders and turned her toward him. "Mrs. Wagstaff, I don't know if you noticed, but I announced that I am no longer a bartender."

CHAPTER 13

"Oh, yes." *I don't care what you are now. What were you?*

"In fact, tomorrow I begin training at Field and Leiter's. I have a position in Gentlemen's Finer Attire."

"That's good."

"Jess." His right arm hooked the inside of her elbow and swept her into his arms. "Jess, I don't think you are giving me your attention."

She pushed herself out of his arms. "The neighbors," she whispered. She pressed her index finger to her pursed lips. She said in an everyday voice, "I need to stable the goat. Would you like to come with me?"

He nodded, understanding the ploy to keep their conversation private. They walked around the house to the backyard and untied the goat from her stake. In the alley, he propped open the shed door and Jessie led the goat in. The musky smell of goat surrounded them, and the chickens were already in their roost for the night. Jessie murmured soothing sounds to the nanny as she tied her rope to the ring in the whitewashed wall.

"Please listen, Jess. Today I turned over a new leaf. I've quit the saloon. I'm going to prove to you I'm worthy—"

"You don't have to prove anything to me. Just tell me the truth." Her eyes avoided his.

"The truth is I'm not the same man I was when I came to Chicago. The past doesn't matter to us—only the future, our future together." He tried to make his voice sound positive.

"We have no future together." Jessie scattered fresh straw over the floor.

"Don't say that. I . . . it's hard to put my feelings into words because I never thought I would ever say them to anyone. Jess, will you be my wife?"

Jessie stiffened as though he had struck her.

Lee stopped. "What is it?"

Jessie took a step back from him. "I don't intend to remarry."

"But we . . . I have fallen in love with you, Jessie. Doesn't that mean anything to you?"

"I'm sorry. I didn't mean to mislead you, but I won't marry again."

"That doesn't make any sense." He couldn't believe her words.

"It does. I'm sorry. I thought you realized. I never . . . I've always been careful never to—"

He began to feel frantic. "Jess, don't you understand? I feel . . . everything's changed." He rushed to explain what he'd experienced earlier. Certainly she'd understand. "Today I was walking by the park. A young woman was out walking her baby. Suddenly I wanted it to be *our baby*." He searched her expression for a softening and understanding of what he was trying to express.

Jessie avoided his eyes. "I will never remarry."

"You can't tell me you don't have feelings for me. I know you do. I am the man you were kissing last night—"

"I'm sorry if I misled you."

"Why are you doing this? We could have a good life together." Panic twisted his stomach.

"I do not want Linc to grow up under a stepfather—"

"Under a stepfather? I don't know what you're thinking! You can't mean you think I'm like Hiram Huff. I'm not some sanctimonious hypocrite!" His heart began to pound.

"No, of course not." She frowned uncertainly. The nanny goat settled down into its bed of straw, her bell clanged dully.

"Then you're not being logical. I would never treat Linc like your stepfather treated you."

"You wouldn't mean to—"

"You're not thinking straight." He tried to sound logical, though his fear was fully alive now. He reached out to take her hands.

She took a step back from him and came up against the back wall of the shed. "You're wrong. It does. Don't you see?"

"No, I don't." Her attitude was impossible to credit. "Explain to me how I'm like your stepfather." He couldn't keep the sarcasm out of his tone.

Jessie's face flushed. "You said it yourself. You said 'our baby.' Lincoln will never be 'our baby.'"

"What has that to do with anything?" he demanded.

"If we did marry, we would always have a divided home. There would always be *my* son and *your* children."

Lee flung up his hands. "You're not making sense! I love Linc!"

She drew herself up primly. "You're not making sense. I've never done anything to lead you to believe I would marry you. How could I marry a man who won't even tell me his name!"

Her last words left him silent and staring angrily into her stormy eyes.

Finally Jessie said in a taut voice, "I'll bid you good night." She pushed past Lee and left him standing alone in the deep twilight.

CHAPTER 14

October 6, 1871 FOR SEVERAL MINUTES LEE
couldn't think straight, then he hurried around to the front of
the house. Stepping just inside Jessie's front door, he yanked his
hat and jacket from hooks on the hall tree and scuttled down the
front steps. Raging against women's illogical thinking and
Hiram Huff's hypocrisy, Lee set out in headlong retreat.

Heedless of direction, he hurried down block after block.
Finally a faraway church clock tolling ten stopped him. Looking
around the night-shrouded street, he tried to get his bearings.
He found he was on the South Side near railroad tracks where
shabby dwellings huddled among warehouses. He heard the distant lapping of waves against unseen pylons. Lake Michigan or
the Chicago River couldn't have been far.

He rubbed his face with one hand as though trying to clear away the turmoil in his mind. *I should go home to bed. I have a new job in the morning.* He took his hat off, then resettled it on his head. Going home and meekly to bed—in the room above Jessie's—struck him as impossible. As impossible as convincing Jessie that his past was not important to them.

He began trudging the darkened streets again. *I can't expect her to understand what it was like, what it meant to live through the war as a surgeon. No one who didn't go through it could understand.* Lee knew he was right.

Suddenly he needed to hear someone agree with him. Mentally he went through the short list of men he had become acquainted with in the past months. The only other veteran he could recall having talked to was Caleb Mitchell, an unfriendly cuss. They hadn't talked really, just traded a few words.

Still, the idea appealed to Lee. He didn't want platitudes about duty or any other soothing pap. He needed a man who would be completely frank, a man who would understand the way the war had really been, not the way people were already beginning to romanticize it. Caleb would understand. Lee looked around and plotted how to reach the late Reverend's house.

The warm night still felt like summer. He heard the faint clanging of a fire bell. Small brush fires on vacant lots had become commonplace after a summer-long drought. His steps matched the pealing of the discordant bells. When Lee finally found the one-room house, no light shone in the window. Having no other destination in mind, Lee hesitated in the yard, thinking what to do.

"What are you doing here?"

Startled out of his thoughts, Lee whipped around. "Caleb."

The black man stopped in front of him, leaning forward belligerently. "I said what are you doing here?"

"I . . . I just came to talk." Lee knew it sounded lame as an explanation, but it was, after all, the truth.

CHAPTER 14

"Why?"

The black man's unconcealed hostility turned Lee's stomach sour. Still he went on, "I . . . you . . . you were in the Union Army. I need to talk to another veteran."

Caleb started to speak, then checked himself. "All right. Come in."

Caleb pushed past him. Lee followed, sorry he had come. While Caleb struck a match and lit a lamp on the table in the center of the room, Lee stood by the door. He remembered too clearly the Reverend's death in this house. Those poignant memories rolled through Lee, leaving him vulnerable. The circumstances of tonight's visit already rendered him uncomfortable. But now he couldn't look around the room without seeing it filled with phantom mourners and hear again the melodies they had sung. *My Lord, what a mournin' when the stars began to fall. My Lord, what—*"

"Sit."

Lee could recall hearing warmer welcomes from Southern women holding loaded rifles. He eased down on one of the three ladder-backed chairs alongside the square table lit by the pool of sputtering lamplight.

Caleb swung his chair around backward and sat down astride it; his powerful-looking arms draped over the chair back.

Lee spoke, "It's difficult not to think of your father—"

"You hardly knew him."

"I didn't have to know him long to respect him—just seeing him die, how he died. He was an exceptional man."

"Thank you." Caleb's tone was grudging. His face twisted as though in pain. "What did you come to talk about?"

Lee shifted in his seat. *How to start?* "What outfit were you in?"

"I was with the 54th Massachusetts Regiment. And you were with Mrs. Wagstaff's husband."

"Yes." *But I wasn't Smith, the ambulance driver.* Lee didn't know how to go on. Neither spoke while silent seconds ticked by.

At last, Caleb slapped a hand down on the tabletop. "Are you going to tell me why you're here or am I supposed to guess?"

The black man's sarcastic tone almost goaded a sharp rebuke from Lee, but he held it back. "I need to talk to someone, someone who went through the war, who will understand—"

"Understand what?" Caleb barked.

Lee grimaced. "I was with Will Wagstaff, but I'm not Lee Smith."

"You lied to Mrs. Wagstaff?"

"I had to—"

"Who are you?"

Caleb had Lee cornered, and it was all Lee's own fault. He had wanted to rid himself of the guilt he carried by telling someone his awful secret. He had wanted to be absolved, not challenged. But in a haze of half-baked emotion, he had gone to the wrong person. The Reverend's son would, of course, side with Jessie.

But Lee had come too far to turn back. He squirmed in his chair, propped his elbows on his knees, and buried his forehead into his hands. "Did you ever spend time in or near an army hospital in the field?"

"I carried a few comrades to them." Caleb's voice sounded wary.

"Did any of them live?"

"One did."

"What did he lose?" Lee asked grimly.

"An eye."

"A fortunate man." Lee exhaled and sat up. "I have nightmares of those awful days and nights. The screams and moans still have the power to wake me. The stench of the blood and sweat . . . You've been there. You know what I'm talking about."

CHAPTER 14

In the low lamplight, Caleb nodded reluctantly. "I know Mrs. Wagstaff's husband was a nurse in the Union Army. It sounds like you were too. What did you lie about?"

Lee took a deep breath. "I'm not Lee Smith. He was an ambulance driver who served with us till he died in '64. My name is Leland Granger Smith."

"So?"

"Will was my best friend. I'm *Doctor* Smith."

"Doctor? You're a doctor! You mean you stood by when my father died and you did nothing!" His fists clenched, Caleb reared up like a fighter coming into the ring.

Lee flung his hands up in surrender, protection. "No medicine can give an old man a new heart! I did what I could for your father!"

Caleb halted, breathing hard. For long moments his eyes fixed on Lee's face. Then he settled down again on his chair and ran his big hands over his forehead. "I guess you're right about that."

Lee lowered his own arms. "I would have helped your father if I could have. All I could do was make him more comfortable."

"And pronounce him dead."

Lee gave a dry, bitter laugh. "I had plenty of practice at that. I could do it in my sleep. I often did."

"I still don't get what your problem is. Just tell Mrs. Wagstaff. She'll understand. You've been good to her son."

"I want to marry her."

"So?"

Lee resented the question, but he had started this and he must finish it. "How can I tell her I'm a doctor when she has been looking for one all summer?"

"Just tell her the truth and offer your services."

"Well, now that's the rub," Lee said harshly. "I can't ever practice medicine again. I can't."

"Why not?"

Lee's face twisted into a mockery of a smile. "Doctoring? Practice real medicine? I wouldn't know how! I came straight out of medical school into the army. For five years all I did was dig out bullets, cut off shattered or gangrenous limbs, and stitch up sword and bayonet slashes. I'm no physician. I'm a butcher! Give me a slab of meat—not a human!"

Caleb didn't speak at first. "You could start over, learn."

"I can't. Can't you see? Just the thought of doctoring again makes me literally sick to my stomach. My hands shake just thinking of holding a scalpel. I hoped you'd understand! You were there. I can't explain it to Jess. She couldn't know what it was like."

"She's a good woman. You'd just have to take time—"

"No. I can't face it. I can't even talk to her about it. In the last two years of the war, Will and alcohol were the only things that kept me going. And after Will died, that left only whiskey."

"Susan told me you quit being a bartender, but she didn't tell me you drank."

"I don't drink anymore. But it's true, I don't think I was sober from the night Will died until early this year." Lee broke off and in spite of the stuffiness of the room, shivered sharply. "It's more than that. My family hushed it up, but I fell apart. The army sent me home under restraint. I was out of my mind with drink, with—" He fought the images of that last hellish night of surgery when he'd begun screaming and couldn't stop. Even when he was too hoarse to make a sound, he'd gone on. A cold sweat broke over Lee. He could feel himself shaking with the memory.

"What brought you to Chicago then? If you didn't want to face this, why come to your best friend's family?"

Lee clamped his legs together and clutched the sides of the chair. The trembling lessened. He cleared his thickened throat. "I promised Will I'd take care of Jessie and his son."

"I see." Caleb bent his elbow to the chair back and rested his chin on his fist. "You lied to Mrs. Wagstaff so she wouldn't have to know you were a doctor. Now you need to tell her the truth because you want to marry her." He looked up. "Why not just keep on lying?"

Distant fire bells started up again, sending their message of danger. They suited Lee's mood. Alarms within. Alarms without. "She knows. She read some of Will's letters and found out Lee Smith was dead. She's known since a few days after your father's death."

"That long? That's not like Mrs. Wagstaff. She doesn't stand for things for a minute. There's your answer. Susan was right."

"What's my answer?"

"Mrs. Wagstaff cares about you. She's not a woman to hide from the truth. She must have feelings for you or she would have had it out with you right then and there." Caleb sounded sincere.

"You think so?" Lee wanted to believe him.

"Tell her. She'll be upset when you tell her, but she can't make you practice medicine—on whites or blacks—if you don't want to."

"I'm afraid I'll lose her and Linc." Saying the words made Lee sick with dread.

"She'll be angry. She has a right to be. I don't like people lying to me—"

"I can't take that chance!" Lee's pulse raced. "Jessie and Linc mean everything to me! I can't take the chance of losing them!" *Without them, I don't have a life.* He couldn't say this out loud.

"She'll forgive you," Caleb said it almost kindly. "You have to trust her."

"I'm afraid I'll lose her."

"If you don't tell her, you *will* lose her." Caleb's words, though spoken quietly, hit and echoed through Lee like a hammer on an anvil.

※ ※ ※ ※ ※

October 7, 1871

"Here we are." Jessie and her mother stood looking at Field and Leiter's Department Store.

"Yes." Esther gave her a nervous smile. "It's a very imposing place, isn't it?"

"You don't have to do this, Mother. We'll manage——"

"No, Ruby is right. I must do this. I must help myself."

"Very well." Jessie led her mother through the door. Escorting her mother to the office, she waited with her until a gentleman asked Esther to his desk for an interview. Jessie squeezed her mother's hand. "I'll go browse, but I'll be back. I'll meet you here."

Esther nodded timorously, then went with the gentleman.

Jessie wandered through the aisles. With money so dear, she rarely let herself enter a store. Today, as a treat, she tarried at a display table and let herself touch soft, kid gloves with tiny mother-of-pearl buttons at the inside of the wrist.

In the millinery department, she slowed to admire the selection of fall and winter hats. One particular hat, fashioned like a wing, caught her attention and brought her to a complete stop. The hat, the shade of reddish-brown oak leaves, sported a pheasant tail feather at the crown; and in front, a delicate veil to draw across the face. Her fingers itched to lift it from the form and let it replace her old-fashioned, black bonnet.

"May I help?" A young, modish saleswoman approached.

"No, I . . . I was merely browsing." Jessie felt like she'd been caught stealing and felt the urge to run out of the store.

"Certainly, but wouldn't you like to try that on." The woman nodded toward the striking brown hat.

"No, I really shouldn't," Jessie stammered. "I was just looking."

The woman scanned the nearly empty department. She smiled and said conspiratorially. "Why not try it on—just for fun? I'm not busy. Come sit down."

Jessie objected feebly, but soon found herself sitting in front of an ornate vanity with mirrors on three sides. The young woman removed Jessie's worn bonnet and arranged the new hat on her crown, making sure it was secure with two matching hat pins.

The transformation in Jessie's appearance was so startling that for a few seconds she couldn't speak.

"An excellent choice," the saleslady murmured. "It brings out the warmth in your hair and eyes."

Jessie, unaccustomed to compliments, blushed a dusky pink. Disconcerted by the alteration in her reflection, she half rose and reached to remove the hat. The woman gently urged her back into her chair. "The effect isn't complete yet. Allow me." The woman reached into a drawer of the vanity and lifted out a large silk scarf of the same rich autumn red, which she draped over Jessie's shoulders and breast.

Before Jessie's dazzled eyes, her reflection as a staid widow vanished from the mirror. Looking back at her was the image of a comely, young woman with russet-tinged brown hair. She gasped, "It doesn't look like me."

"I've seen this happen many times. When a woman has been in mourning for a year or more, she forgets how she looked in colors. Have you been in mourning for more than a year?"

Jessie nodded. *Six years.*

"Out of respect for the loved one, it is difficult to leave off mourning clothes, but your loved one would want you to go on living. You are young and attractive. It's time you let it show again."

Like misty rain on a dry garden, the words sank into Jessie's mind and emotions. Inside, a tight clasp—which had held her spirit constricted—swung open. A thrill of pleasure shimmered through her. "How much is this?"

"Only one dollar and seventy-five cents. A bargain."

"Oh." Jessie's voice fell. "I don't have that much with me."

"We have an easy time-payment plan. Merely put down 50 percent now; then you make a few weekly payments and it's yours."

Jessie's conscience balked, but one glance at the reflection in the mirror silenced it. "I'll take it."

As she watched the saleslady wrap the hat delicately in tissue paper and tie it up in a charming mauve hatbox, striped with gold, she felt free, airy. In her whole adult life, this was her first extravagance. Not even signing a note to pay another ninety-five cents within three weeks daunted her. "Where is Gentlemen's Finer Attire?" she asked.

The saleslady handed her the ribbon-handle of the box. "Upstairs, immediately above."

"Thank you. I'll see you in a week."

"Very good, madam. I'm happy you found a hat that was so flattering to you. I hope you'll let me serve you again."

Jessie felt herself beaming. With quick, light steps she ascended the marble and mahogany staircase. When she topped the steps and scanned the second floor, she located the gentlemen's department easily, but she did not see Lee. She walked among the mannequins, displaying men's suits that fit the description of Gentlemen's Finer Attire. Then she saw Lee just beyond her in the aisle.

She paused behind two mannequins, trying to decide what she had come to tell him. She hadn't seen him since she left him the night before in the goat shed. When he hadn't come home by morning, she had worried in spite of herself. She wanted the truth, but—

Before Jessie could come out from behind the mannequins, a tall, elegantly dressed woman glided up to him. "Leland, is it really you?"

"Eugenia! Sister!" Lee exclaimed. "What are you doing here?"

"Well, I thought that Chicago might be where you had gone to start over. So when Mrs. Field invited me here to consult with her about charity work, I thought it would be the perfect opportunity to try to discover if I was right and to see how you were progressing."

"Charity work?"

Jessie echoed his question. Her mind frantically tried to make sense of what she was witnessing.

Eugenia continued, "If you had been paying any attention to your family in the last five years, you would have known I've made myself one of the foremost women in the nation——"

"Yes, yes, Eugenia, I'm sure you have. Did you really come looking for me?"

"Yes, but I never expected to find you without even trying. I had asked Mrs. Field about doctors here, trying . . . Good heavens, Leland, you don't *work* here, do you?"

Doctor! Jessie's heart pounded so hard her temples throbbed. *He couldn't be!*

"Yes, Sister dear, I am employed here as a salesman in Gentlemen's Finer Attire."

"Leland, with all your education! Couldn't you find something more appropriate?"

"I told you in Boston, I will never practice medicine again."

He is a doctor. Jessie clutched the hatbox ribbon with both hands.

"Oh, very well. Father, Aunt Hester, and I never understood why you wanted to be a doctor in the——"

"That is old news, sister."

Not to me, Jessie wanted to shout.

"So, how is dear Father?"

"I don't know why you never could get along with Father."

"Eugenia, do we have to go over ancient history? How long are you going to be in Chicago?"

"Just another few days. Tonight the Fields are hosting a soiree in my honor at the Hotel Tremont." A self-satisfied smile lifted Eugenia's long, plain face.

"Indeed?"

"Yes," Eugenia lowered her voice, "and I realized her invitation was not only motivated by an interest in charity causes. Mrs. Field also desires to advance socially. But I have found her to be not quite as gauche as I had thought she would be. And I've found Mr. Field to be quite droll."

"I thought so myself."

"Do you know him?" Eugenia eyes widened.

"He interviewed me for this job."

Eugenia put her hand to her forehead.

Jessie felt like screaming at the patronizing woman.

"Don't worry, Sis. I'm using the name Mister Lee Smith, not Dr. Leland Granger Smith."

"Oh, thank goodness!"

Jessie felt herself alternate between flashes of heat and cold. Dr. Leland Granger Smith had been her Will's best friend in the medical corps, but how could he be alive? She'd seen his name on the death lists just weeks after Will. It must have been a mistake. Giddy, she was afraid to move for fear she'd faint.

Lee chuckled. "And I'm afraid I will be unable to attend tonight's soiree. My evening clothes are still in Boston."

"Your regrettable sense of humor, Leland." She shook her head at him. "Well, what shall I tell Father about you?"

"Nothing or everything. Whatever you choose."

"I think I may choose nothing. But you should give me your address in case I ever need to get in touch with you."

"Send any letters here, to Lee Smith. I intend to keep this job. If I quit, I will leave a forwarding address with the office."

"Very well. Oh, did you locate your friend Will's widow?"

A silent gasp caught in Jessie's throat. *It was all true!*

"Yes, I did. I'm staying at her boardinghouse."

Looking over her brother's shoulder at a large, free-standing mirror, Eugenia adjusted her hat slightly. "And how about her poor little son?"

Jessie's face flamed.

"He's not a poor little boy. He's a great lad."

CHAPTER 14

"Of course. Of course." Eugenia glanced at the gold pendant watch that was pinned to her gray bodice. "I'm sure they are grateful for your help."

Lee spoke stiffly, "So far Mrs. Wagstaff won't accept any money from me."

"A charity case with foolish pride. Ah, there is Mrs. Field." Eugenia wagged one finger to another well-dressed lady and turned away from Lee. "Good-bye, Brother."

"Miss Smith," Jessie overheard the other lady say. The rest of her sentence was lost to Jessie in the welter of emotions she wrestled to control.

Now she knew who this man was. He was Will's unlikely best friend, Dr. Smith, son of a wealthy Boston banking family. Will's letters had told her how Dr. Smith had defied his family by taking up medicine, then by enlisting as an army surgeon. And this man's sister thought of her and Linc as just another "charity case." *Foolish pride!* Her face flaming with outrage and shame, Jessie whirled away down the steps and out of the store.

✳ ✳ ✳ ✳ ✳

The church bell two blocks away tolled six times. Though the sunlight was beginning to deepen into the amber shade of dusk, the heat of the long day was undiminished. Jessie, alone on her front porch, paced back and forth.

"Jessie, what is it?"

"Mother . . ." Jessie halted, wringing her hands. Her mother was finally returning from Field and Leiter's. "How did your interview go?"

"Fine. I'm glad you didn't wait for me. They needed a saleslady in Infant's Wear immediately. I started right away, and I love it!"

"That's wonderful, Mother."

"What is the matter, Jessie?" Esther came up the steps.

"Nothing—"

241

"Look at your hands!"

Jessie glanced downward and immediately let her hands drop to her sides. "I can't talk about matters now. Please go in. Tell Susan to go ahead and serve dinner without me."

"Jessie?"

"Please, Mother."

Though Esther went past Jessie, she paused at the front door to cast a worried glance at her daughter. With a shake of her head, she walked through the doorway.

Jessie could not stand still. Back and forth she paced with her hands knotted together and pressed to her mouth. She knew Lee would come back to Wagstaff House for his clothes, for the supper he had paid for. So she waited for him.

"Mama, why won't you come to supper?" Linc appeared beside her.

"Lincoln, go inside please."

"What's wrong?"

"Lincoln, it's nothing you need to be concerned about. Now go insi—"

Lee sauntered around the corner of the block, headed right for them. Jessie panicked. "Lincoln, you must go in *now*." She pushed him toward the door, but, seeing Lee approaching, Linc struggled against her.

Lee walked up the steps. "Lincoln, if your mother wants you to go in, do so immediately."

The boy ceased struggling and the door closed behind him. "What is it, Jess? I know you're upset with me, but—"

"Upset?" She forced her voice to stay low. "I'm not upset. I'm incensed! I found out who you really are today! Why didn't you tell me you were Will's friend, Dr. Smith?"

Lee's mouth opened in shock.

"You're a doctor and you knew how I needed one! How could you keep still?"

"How . . . how—"

"I saw you today at Field and Leiter's, and I saw your sister—and heard her. Foolish pride!" She could feel her face burning again. "Yes, I suppose I am only a charity case to you, but at least I know how to tell the truth."

"Jessie, listen to me—"

"I've packed your things. Your valise is here by the door and packed with it is the money you paid for next week. Don't come back." She spun away from him and sped through the front door, shutting it firmly behind her.

"Mama, no!" Linc's voice called through the door.

Lee heard the boy crying and calling his name. Lee stood, petrified. His mind went blank momentarily. He'd lost everything again. Slowly, slowly sanity returned. He became aware of the sounds around him.

As he stared at the closed door, Linc's frantic pleas echoed in his mind. From his memory, a deep voice spoke weakly, "Take care of them, Lee. They'll need you."

Lee whispered, "I've failed you again, Will."

CHAPTER 15

October 8, 1871   R ETURNING FROM SUNDAY
evening service at dusky sundown, Jessie and Esther, each with
a Bible cradled in her arm, mounted the front steps. "Won't this
summer heat ever end?" Jessie tugged loose the ribbons on her
bonnet and slipped it off. Strong currents of hot, arid wind
swirled around them, catching and faring the hems of their
skirts.

"The summer has officially ended. Someone just forgot to
tell the sun." Esther grinned.

"And the wind. Where did this hot wind come from?"

"The person who forgot to turn the sun's heat low turned
up the wind wheel and this gentle breeze"—Esther waved her
arm—"is the result." A sudden gust kicked Esther's bonnet forward so that it fell over her eyes.

"Oh, Mother!" Jessie pressed her hand over her mouth, suppressing a chuckle.

"Go ahead and laugh at your poor mother—and on the Sabbath too!" Esther righted her bonnet. They exchanged glances and dissolved into laughter until, both feeling weak, they collapsed onto the porch's wicker love seat.

"I had forgotten how wonderful it felt to laugh, to really laugh like that." Esther drew in a deep breath.

"Mother, I . . ." Jessie paused and stared, as though looking at something far away. When she spoke, her voice held a quality of wonder she couldn't hold back. "Cherries. Cherries on my head and all around me on the floor." She looked to her mother. "Cherries in my mouth and we were all laughing. What does it mean?"

Esther said with hushed awe in her voice, "I can't believe you remembered that. You were only a toddler. Your father, your real father, loved cherry pie. I had picked a pan of sour cherries from the neighbor's tree." Reaching over, she took Jessie's hand in hers.

"Your father came home and he called to me. I went out to him. When we came in, arm in arm, there you sat, the pan upside down on the floor and cherries all over you. You had so many cherries in your mouth that your cheeks bulged like a greedy chipmunk's. Your father and I laughed until we couldn't laugh any more." Esther wiped tears from her eyes. "Fancy you remembering that tonight."

"Mother, I love you."

Esther hugged Jessie to her. "Daughter, I love you too. These past few days have been difficult, but somehow special. They have given me the chance to be close to you once more and to Linc for the first time."

They embraced and kissed each other.

"Oh, Miss Jessie, Miss Esther, you back at las'." Ruby appeared at the door.

"What is it?" Jessie glanced up.

"Your boy fin'lly come in aftah you been gone jus' a little while. I give him supper and a good scold for missin' church and sent him to his bed like you tol' me."

"What has happened?" Esther asked.

Jessie stood, worried by Ruby's expression.

"Later I goes in to check on him; he gone and lef' dis paper on his pillow. What it say?" Ruby pulled a scrap of paper from her apron pocket.

Jessie read the scribbled message aloud, "'Mother, I'm going to find Mr. Smith. I want him back. Linc.'"

Esther got to her feet. "Oh my!"

Jessie felt herself reeling as though the floor under her feet had bucked and rocked. "Dear God!"

"Now, Jessie, boys do this," Esther spoke up briskly. "Get hold of yourself. We'll find him. Ruby, is Susan home yet?"

"No, ma'am."

"Well, then you stay here to tell her what has happened. Jessie, you go through the neighborhood. What was the name of that saloon where Mr. Smith worked—"

"Linc wouldn't go there!" Jessie objected.

"He might," Esther said. "Maybe Linc thinks someone there would know where Mr. Smith has taken up residence."

"The Workman's Res'," Ruby supplied. "I heard dat redhead yell it all da way in the kitchen."

"I'll be back as soon as I can," Esther said and hurried down the front steps.

"Mother!" Jessie called after her. "Be careful!"

The increasing wind carried her mother's response back to her. "Of course I will, dear."

Jessie rushed out onto the sidewalk. After pounding on Mrs. O'Toole's door, Jessie turned one way, then another, searching for sight of Linc.

Mrs. O'Toole opened the door. "What do you want?" Icicles dripped from each word.

"My boy—have you seen him this evening? I think he's run away—"

"I'm not surprised!"

"Oh, please, have you seen him?"

"No, I haven't—" While the woman continued her lecture, Jessie dashed down the steps. She heard Mrs. O'Toole slam her front door.

Calling Linc's name, Jessie ran through the extended neighborhood that comprised Linc's world. She stopped at every house of a friend or classmate of Linc's. Calling his name, she ran down every alley and every street within a square mile around Wagstaff House. By the light of a late rising moon, Jessie fretted on the edge of desperation. Near tears, she finally returned to her own back steps and burst into the kitchen. "Is Linc here?"

"No, Jessie, he isn't," Miss Wright answered from the doorway. She stood with her hands resting together on the head of her cane.

Jessie twisted in pain. Looking for guidance, she cast a glance to Ruby and Susan, who waited beside the cold stove. Susan spoke up, "I know he wasn't 'round Caleb's. We all sat outside singing till this wind sent us home."

Ruby shuffled forward and took Jessie's hand. "Nothin' bad gonna happen. Boys run away. Then they come home hungry. He'll be powerful hungry when he come home."

"I know I shouldn't be so upset." Jessie ran her hands over her disheveled hair. "But somehow I can't shake the feeling—"

A distant fire bell began to toll frantically. Gusts of wind brought the ominous jangling in a reverberating ebb and flow, over and over.

"Another fire," Miss Wright grumbled. "Those bells clanged most of last night. How are we supposed to sleep—"

Jessie interrupted, "I won't be sleeping tonight until Linc and Mother return home." She approached Miss Wright. "I'll help you get settled, and I'll make certain your window is shut."

CHAPTER 15

Outside, the wind tore a shutter loose on the side of the house and it banged wildly against the wooden siding.

"I'll go poun' dat back into place." Susan hurried out the back door.

Letting the older woman lean against her, Jessie escorted Miss Wright through the dining room and helped her prepare for bed—at least as much as the old woman would permit her.

"Would you like some warm milk to help you to sleep?" Jessie asked at last.

"Why bother? With Lincoln running off like a scapegrace and the fire bells, I won't sleep a wink."

Jessie tried to think of something to say to this, but nothing came to mind. "Good night, Miss Wright." She left. As she returned to the kitchen, she heard Susan pounding on the shutter.

"What a night," Ruby commented from the table by the window.

Jessie nodded once and sat down at the table too. The banging outside stopped and Susan rejoined them. A look of helplessness passed between the three women as they glanced at each other.

"I think it be time to pray," Ruby announced. She stood up and raised her hands. Jessie stood up beside Susan. "Oh, Lord, dis be a bad night. Da wind is blowing. Fires is burnin' and Jessie's chile done run away from home. Please bring him and Jessie's mama back safe. Nobody know more'n I do how bad it hurt to have your child took from you. Oh, Lord, da hear'break. You 'member how it was. More'n ten years I mourned and searched, mourned and searched. Fin'lly you bring me here, to my onliest chile. I thank you agin, Father. Now bring Jessie's boy home safe—and her mama—like you brung me to Susan. I thanks you, Lord. Amen."

Jessie sniffed back a tear. "Thank you, Ruby."

"He be in God's hand, Miss Jessie. God won' let you down."

249

"I know. I know with my head, but my heart is struggling to believe."

Ruby hugged her, then lowered herself ponderously to the kitchen chair. While Ruby sat stolidly keeping vigil, Jessie and Susan paced in and out of the kitchen to look alternately out the front and back doors.

After the moon rose to its zenith, they also walked out to scan the alley in both directions. By now, fire bells to the south pealed incessantly. When the two women ventured outside, the growing wind tossed their skirts as high as it pleased and plucked their hair from their hairpins.

Hours later, buffeted by the wind and emotionally exhausted, Jessie and Susan surrendered and slumped down at the table with Ruby. More time passed, and though they heard the alarms and rushing wind, they became almost deaf to them.

"I'll make us 'nother pot a coffee." Ruby struggled to her feet. Suddenly she exclaimed, "Look out da window! What dat red glowin'? It look like Judgment Day."

Jessie and Susan crowded around Ruby at the kitchen door. "It must be the fire," Jessie said. "Let's go outside."

Susan was already opening the back door. Jessie hastened out after her. Puffing with her customary shortness of breath, Ruby followed them but stayed near the back door.

When Jessie, followed by Susan, ventured away from the shelter of the porch, the wind slapped her in the face like an angry hand. Instinctively seeking protection, she joined hands with Susan and ran to the fence. The whole southern skyline was lit by an eerie red light. Neither woman voiced a word of fear, but they moved closer together. A sudden explosion, powerful even when muffled by distance, drew them closer still.

"What is it?" Jessie asked, holding her hand by her mouth to funnel her words into Susan's ear.

"It sound like the war all over agin," Susan called to her over the wind even though they were only inches apart. "Sometime the battle, it go on after nightfall. The cannons start fires and dey burn all night. No water to put 'em out."

"Susan, Mother should have been back hours ago."

Susan pulled Jessie closer and put her arm around Jessie's shoulder.

Jessie looked into her friend's dark face. "I'm frightened for her."

"She be all right. We put her and Linc in God's hands. We got to have faith—"

A rampant burst of air flew around the side of the small shed on the alley. It picked up Jessie and Susan like cotton fluff. Being thrown against the fence hard knocked the breath from Jessie.

"It can't be a tornado!" Jessie struggled to pull herself upright. "There isn't any rain!"

"I never feel a wind like dat." Fighting the wind, Susan turned and made her way back to Ruby. "Grandma, you get inside. You can't stan' 'gainst dis wind."

"Dere's more-a me to knock down than you two. Git up here on da porch. Miss Jessie, you come too."

Jessie, her gaze still to the south, strove against the wind to reach Ruby. She, along with Susan and her grandmother, huddled near the back door, each holding onto the railing. But they didn't go back inside; Jessie couldn't resist the fascination with the scarlet southern sky. Other neighbors, some clutching shawls around flapping nightgowns, also endured the violent currents of air to stand and stare at the hellish red sky to the south. Soon the ringing of the fire alarms echoed louder—closer.

A man, running up the alley, startled them all. Jessie, followed by Susan, raced to catch up with him. "What's happening?" she called, cupping her hands. "Where are you coming from?"

Gasping, the man stopped and bent over, pressing his hands to his knees. He swallowed with difficulty. "The whole downtown is on fire," he said hoarsely. "The fires are out of control. The wind fans the flames, and they jump from roof to roof."

"What were you doing downtown this late on a Sunday night?" Mrs. Braun shouted from her fence. "Have you been drinking?"

"Lady, I'm the night watchman at Klegg's Warehouse on DeKoven. Or I was. It's completely destroyed."

"A fine night watchman!" Mrs. O'Toole yelled to Mrs. Braun, standing beside her. "He watched while the warehouse burned."

As the man took off once more, Susan shouted, "Where you runnin'?"

"The fire's headed this way! I'm packing my stuff and heading west! You should too!"

Everyone in the alley had an opinion and gave it loudly, though the wind swished most of them away. Only Susan and Jessie remained silent. Another surge of savage wind slammed against them. With their heads bent into the gale, the two women, holding hands, trudged back up the path. When they reached Ruby on the porch, they hovered around her, trying to shield her.

"It don't sound vera good," Susan told her grandmother.

Jessie bit her lip and looked to the fiery sky. "Is it my imagination or does the sky look redder than before?"

"It do," Ruby replied.

"You think the fire gonna get dis far?" Susan asked.

"It never has before," Jessie said uncertainly.

"Has da sky ever look like dat befo'?" Ruby worried aloud.

"Never."

"Den it could happen." Ruby folded her hands over her large abdomen.

Jessie began pacing again. "I should have gone after my mother hours ago."

"That man didn't say nothin' about anybody gettin' hurt," Susan pointed out.

"If you hadda gone out, you woulda just missed her comin' home. It always dat way," Ruby added. "Your mama is a clever woman an' she know dis town better'n you. She be all right. 'Sides, we done prayed her into God's hand, along with your chile."

Jessie wanted to let her fear fly out, let herself scream hysterically, but she couldn't. Both Ruby and Susan were looking to her to take the lead. *Oh, God, what should I do?* She took a deep breath. "We better take action."

"Just tell me what to do," Susan replied.

Jessie surveyed her property. Having a fireman in the family had one advantage: she had taken precautions against the spread of fire. Her pile of cooking wood sat at the back of the lot away from any structure, and she'd had the winter coal stowed in the coal cellar.

"Get out the garden sprinkling can and wet down the wooden sidewalk in the front. Ruby, you go in and close all the downstairs windows. I'll do the upstairs ones. That will prevent sparks from flying in and igniting the curtains."

Gripping the railing against the wild wind, Susan hurried outside while Ruby and Jessie went inside.

When Jessie latched the attic windows, she was able to get a better view of the fires to the south. It was a chilling perspective. As she scurried down the staircase, Miss Wright called to her, "Jessie, is your mother back?"

Jessie halted in the doorway. "No, she isn't."

"Why are you closing all the windows?"

"A man returning from downtown said the fire is headed this way."

"Do you believe him?"

Jessie considered not worrying the woman, but decided against it. "I just looked out the attic and it looks threatening, but I can't believe it will advance this far. It's this awful wind. I closed the windows against sparks, and Susan's wetting the sidewalk in front. Nothing else flammable lies near the house. We'll drench as much of the siding and roof, too, as we can.

Then if this fire does come anywhere near, it should pass us by for easier targets."

"I'm getting up."

"All right, but don't come outside. A little while ago a gust actually knocked Susan and me off our feet."

"All right. All right. I'll come to the kitchen."

"Fine." Jessie hurried out the front door.

For the next hour or more Jessie and Susan worked frantically, taking turns filling and dousing, saturating the wood sidewalk as well as the front and back steps. The fevered radiance in the south flared and flared until the moon was eclipsed in brilliance.

As Jessie and Susan toiled, a trickle of refugees from the south started, increasing to a steady stream, then finally to a river at flood stage.

The refugees carried a peculiar assortment of items: lamps, portraits, skillets, blankets, hatboxes, and valises stuffed so full they couldn't be latched. Some pushed baby carriages filled with everything but the baby, whom they carried. Others pulled toy wagons or peddler carts. But all of them were fleeing north, away from danger.

"That won't work!" a stranger yelled at Jessie and Susan.

"The fire's too hot!" another shouted.

"Pack your things while you have time!"

"The fire's out of control!"

"Get out while you can!"

But in spite of the low water pressure, the two women continued to douse the house. As more people streamed past, the warnings called to Jessie and Susan became a rising litany of terror.

Trying to ignore the ever-expanding crimson glow to the south, Jessie and Susan met on the side of the house to confer. "Susan, I think if I could climb up into the oak tree, I might be able to wet the roof some."

CHAPTER 15

"You ain't getting in that tree. I'm stronger 'n you." Susan headed for the old oak on the side of the house with Jessie close behind her, still arguing she should do the climbing. Ignoring her, Susan quickly pulled herself up into the broad branches. "Go get 'nother bucketful!" she called down.

"What are you women doing?" A man dashed from the street to the oak tree. "Are you mad? Do you think you can fight a fiery, rampaging monster with a garden pail!" His hair blew in all directions in the tumult of air.

Jessie stared at his soot-blackened face. "We have to save our house," she shouted.

"Don't you think we felt that way?" he demanded, waving his hand at the last of the refugees hurrying up the street.

"I'm a widow. This boardinghouse supports us!" Watching a shower of sparks dancing over the church steeple two blocks away distracted Jessie.

"You're in danger; don't you understand? People are dying!" A jolt of terror shot through Jessie.

Susan jumped down from the limb she had straddled. "You go on! Nobody ask' you!"

As the man retreated to the street, he yelled back, "For God's sake, woman, get out while you can!"

Susan turned to Jessie. "Don't lose faith! Your ma is fine, and Linc too. We gotta make sure they have a home to come back to, you hear?"

Jessie came out of her fear-inspired trance. "All right. Let's try it. The fire may never reach us."

"That's right!" Susan climbed the tree quickly and reached down for the bucket.

Just as Jessie, fighting the blasts of wind, handed it up to Susan, another explosion rocked them. Screams shocked Jessie, and she turned to see who was screaming. It was Mrs. O'Toole from her attic window. "It's only two blocks away! Dear God, save us! Mother Mary, save us!"

Jessie looked up to Susan. "God provided this house for us, and he won't take it from us!"

"Pack your things!" Mrs. Crawford from the front walk shouted to them. "The fire is nearly here!"

Jessie hurried to her. "Did Mr. Smith return to board with you? Do you know where he is?"

"I haven't seen him in the last few days. Mrs. Wagstaff, you must come with me. You are in real danger."

"I can't leave. We'll lose everything!"

"Better to lose everything and save your lives. Don't delay much longer!" Mrs. Crawford began to run to catch up with her son and daughter. "The fire is burning along the wooden sidewalks and streets, and jumping from roof to—"

Her final words were blown away. The gust brought a shower of flaming sparks into Jessie's face. Susan screamed. Jessie raced back to her. "What!"

Susan slid down from the tree and pointed to the faucet. "The water stopped! The water stopped!"

Jessie felt as though a mallet were pounding her again and again. Linc running away. Her mother not returning. The fire advancing, advancing . . . She wanted to run inside and hide under her bed like a little girl. She put her head in her hands.

"Look!" Susan screamed.

A line of flames suddenly flashed up in the alley behind them. The leaping orange flames began gnawing at her small barn and her fence. *It can't have reached us! My God, forgive my stubbornness! Help us! We've waited too long!*

"Susan, get Ruby to the front," Jessie shouted. "I'll get Miss Wright!"

Jessie found Miss Wright, calmly waiting inside the front door. "I'm ready to go. Here's your shawl—"

"I must get—"

"I've gathered all your daguerreotypes and letters from Will in this satchel, but you'll have to be the one to carry it. I can't."

Jessie accepted the bag and opened it. "You even found my cash."

"I know where everything in this house is—or was." Both women glanced around the foyer as though memorizing it.

"Jessie!" Susan screeched from the front walk. "Come out! The back porch done caught fire!"

Jessie took Miss Wright's arm and helped her through the door, and the spinster put Jessie's fear into words, "I hope we haven't delayed too long."

The comment stabbed Jessie's conscience.

Jessie led them out into the now empty street. The glare from the burning alley, overwhelming the night's darkness, cast them in a terrifying radiance. Embers, sparks, and burning ash swirled around them in the blistering maelstrom. Repeatedly their clothing and hair caught fire. Jessie with Susan's help frantically smothered these outbreaks with their hands.

The two old women staggered between Jessie and Susan as the four of them tried to outrun the fire. After Jessie had managed to lead them a block northwest, the wind shifted and, under her horrified gaze, outflanked them, blocking the street in front of them.

"Dear God!" Jessie despaired, covering her mouth against the heat. "We're hemmed in on three sides."

"Our only refuge is the lake," Miss Wright pointed out, struggling to speak. "We must get there before we are surrounded and cut off. We must hurry. *Hurry!*"

Miss Wright resolutely increased her halting gait. Jessie took her arm to help her move more quickly while Susan assisted her grandmother.

The scorching fire, almost surrounding them, made Jessie flush and perspire. Its crackling din filled her ears. The acrid smell of burning wood crowded out all other scents. To Jessie, the fire was a giant hand reaching out to grab them and pull them into its death grip.

"I shouldn't have waited!" Jessie moaned. The smoky air she inhaled made her cough violently, but she didn't slacken their pace. They were running a race for their lives. *God help us. Forgive me for staying too long. Please, Lord, these women, they depended on me. Save us!*

Suddenly Ruby collapsed in a heap. "I can' . . . go . . . on." The smoke she swallowed in speaking pushed her into a coughing fit.

Great clouds of choking smoke rolled and roiled around them. Approaching them from behind, the inferno was steadily devouring the block between them. The front wall of a nearby house gave way and crashed into the street. Flaming debris cascaded over them like a shower of flaming darts. For a moment, Jessie hesitated, paralyzed.

Then Susan shrieked, "Grandma, get up! Da fire is right on us. Get up!" The young woman tried to pull Ruby up, but could not lift her. "Help me!" Jessie dropped Miss Wright's arm and hurried to Susan.

"I can' go on," Ruby gasped. "Leave me." But Jessie and Susan struggled to get the old woman back on her feet.

Miss Wright's cane slashed down right behind Ruby, jolting them all. "Get up right now," the old schoolteacher commanded, "Get up or we'll all die!"

"Leave me," Ruby implored.

A second time, the cane crashed down. "Get up! If you don't, you'll have killed us all. We won't go on without you!" The cane slammed down again. "Now!"

Ruby lunged to her feet. Jessie and Susan grabbed Ruby under her arms. Overpowering heat roared around them.

"Go!" Miss Wright ordered and prodded Ruby with the point of her cane. "Go! I'll stay right behind you!"

Ruby leaned heavily on Jessie and Susan as they dragged her along between them.

Booms of exploding barrels, expanded by the overwhelming heat; the roar of the fire; collapsing walls; crumbling chimneys—

CHAPTER 15

all merged into a horrific din. Searing heat scorched Jessie. She panted for air and choked in the fog of black smoke.

She struggled along with Susan to keep Ruby on her feet. Her back was breaking. Her lungs were about to explode. But Miss Wright's prodding cane urged them all forward relentlessly.

"The beach!" Jessie gasped. They all stumbled across the last wooden street and stepped onto the narrow sandy beach.

"Don't stop!" Miss Wright ordered. "The fire is right behind us. To the water!"

Jessie fought to cover the last twenty feet of the harrowing trek and waded into Lake Michigan. The contrast between her scorched body and the icy October waves made her shiver violently. She led the others out onto a shallow sandbar—as far away from the shore as it would take them. They turned back to view the city.

"Oh, Lord!" Ruby cried out.

The whole western skyline flamed in brilliant orange and scarlet. Above the remaining skeletons of buildings, huge billows of black smoke surged and coiled toward heaven.

The sight ripped the last of Jessie's self-control into shreds. "My son! Lincoln! Lincoln!" she screamed. Wrenching sobs shook her. "Mother! Lee!" she screamed again and again. "I've lost them all! No! No!"

Susan pulled Jessie to her and fiercely wrapped her arms around her friend. She began to shout, "Almighty God, you save dat boy and Esther and Lee. God, save my people too! Caleb, Lord, keep him safe. He a stubborn man. You freed us. You can't leave us without hope. You saved us! You be our hope and salvation. Cover us with your mighty hand!"

"That we should live to see such a sight," Miss Wright said to Ruby as they listened to Susan's pleas to heaven.

Ruby replied, "Lord, have mercy on us. Lord, have mercy."

Tears sprang to the old spinster's eyes and slid down her deeply lined and sooted cheeks. "I don't know if I can bear to lose Margaret's only grandchild."

"Da Lord will protect him," Ruby said, looking up at Miss Wright.

"He must. He must." Miss Wright stepped toward Ruby, putting her arms around the black woman's broad shoulders, and began to weep without restraint.

Ruby bent her own head, rested it on the white woman's breast and let her tears flow. "Lord, have mercy on us. Please, Lord, have mercy."

CHAPTER 16

October 10, 1871　　　　THE CROWDED CHURCH-TURNED-
hospital was momentarily peaceful. The afternoon sun sparkled
through the stained-glass windows in brilliant crimson, royal
blue, gilded amber. As Lee took solace from the glittering display, his vision blurred from fatigue. He blinked his eyes, trying
to clear them. Since the fire began Sunday evening, he had slept
only an hour or two. Everything he'd thought he'd forgotten
about medicine had come rushing back when faced with the
glut of burnt and broken patients over the past two days. His
eyes closed.

"Doctor?"

Yawning behind his hand, Lee bent his head to look at the
plump volunteer nurse at his elbow.

"Some women from Waukegan just arrived with a wagonload of bandages and medicines, including burn salve."

"Thank God," he said, relieved. "Have you set up the dispensary yet?"

"Yes, a tent outside has been organized."

"Excellent. We'll need a list of what is available. Distribute it to the other doctors."

"Certainly, Dr. Smith." The volunteer walked away purposefully.

"Doctor?" The familiar feminine voice was filled with surprise.

Lee spun around. "Pearl!" He gratefully folded her into his arms. "You're safe."

Pearl returned his embrace, then stepped back to look at him. "So you're not a bartender; you're a doctor?"

"I'm Dr. Leland Granger Smith. I'm sorry I misled you, Pearl." His attractive former employer was soot-covered and disheveled, but two days and nights of raging fire had left its mark on all of them. "Are you here looking for someone?"

"Yes, my father." Her voice hoarse, Pearl searched his face. "I've been looking for nearly two days. His block burned to the ground. I finally found a neighbor who said my father had been struck by a collapsing wall. This is the third makeshift hospital I've been to." Her hands knotted themselves together.

His own heart aching for Jessie and Linc, Lee rested his hand on her shoulder. "What's his name?"

"Lorenz Schiffer."

Lee guided her to a small table near the pulpit of the church. He felt her eyeing him intently as he flipped through the pages in a stack on the table.

"He's on my list."

Pearl pressed her hands to her heart. "He's here?" Her voice broke with emotion.

Lee put an arm around her shoulder to brace her. She trembled against him. He led her down the aisle, flanked by pews that

CHAPTER 16

now served as beds, back to the rows of corncob pallets on the floor of the entry to the church.

Surveying the tired, injured men lying there, Lee paused and motioned Pearl to a pallet where an old man lay, bandaged, but awake.

"Papa!" Pearl knelt beside her father and bent forward to hug him. "I've been so worried—"

Lee stepped back, not wanting to intrude on their reunion. He had witnessed many over the last two days. He was happy for the loved ones reunited, but his own fear that he had lost Jessie increased.

Now his thoughts took him back down the same tortured path he'd gone back and forth for the past two days.

Had Jessie, Linc, and everyone else at Wagstaff House come through the fire safely? Where were they? Did they need him?

At last, Pearl stood up. "Lee, I mean, Dr. Smith—"

"'Lee' is fine, Pearl."

"How long will my father have to stay here?" She dabbed her moist eyes with a smudged, torn hankie

"He's bruised and has cracked a few ribs, but all he really needs is good food and bed rest."

"You don't know . . . the worry . . ." Her voice trailed off as her body suddenly sagged. Lee caught her, holding her against him.

Her eyes fluttered open. "What happened? Did I faint? I never—"

"Over the past two days, we've all done things we normally don't do." Lee spoke soothingly, "You probably haven't eaten or slept normally, like the rest of us. It all takes its toll."

She nodded, her lips pursed. "How's your Jessie?"

Burning pain flashed through Lee. He shook his head. "No word."

"That's rough."

He drew in a deep breath. "It's early yet." He repeated the same words he'd used to comfort so many others in the past

263

hours. "The fires only stopped burning hours ago. That made it hard to get word. Did your children come through safely?"

"Yes, but the Workman's Rest is a total loss." She looked down at the toes of her muddy shoes.

"What will you do?"

She sighed deeply. "Right now, I'm just glad we're all alive." Lee nodded.

She smiled suddenly; her usual teasing manner returning. "Are you going to tell me why a doctor was bartending for me?"

Lee recognized and appreciated her attempt to rally him from gloom. He grinned for her. "Sometime."

"You really *are* a doctor?"

Lee said in a mock serious tone, "Harvard, Class of 1860."

She shook her head at him. "I always knew there was something different about you. You just didn't fit my idea of a barkeep."

"Pearl, you never fit my idea of a bar owner. You know you have . . . *had* the best nickel lunch in town. Why not build a restaurant instead of a new saloon?"

"You may be right, Doctor." Pearl gave him a quick hug. "How soon can I take my father home?"

"Make arrangements to transport him and we'll release him to you. But I will want to check on him daily for a week."

"That suits me."

Walking Pearl to the door, Lee asked her to leave an address with the nurse there. Then he bid Pearl an affectionate goodbye. As he watched her leave, he thought how none of them could have prepared for the ordeal they all had just experienced.

Death and desperation weren't strangers to him. He had gone through a bloody war. In the face of this tragic fire, he had responded the same way he had to President Lincoln's calling up of troops in '60. He had found himself on a street corner downtown, telling a police captain that he was a veteran army surgeon, new to Chicago. He had, in effect, enlisted in this fire battle, the best way he could.

CHAPTER 16

Immediately he had been dispatched to this church that two other doctors had secured as a temporary shelter for the injured and homeless. Here he had been welcomed with open arms. When he had revealed his experience in field medicine, they had unanimously promoted him to director of the shelter.

Though uneasy about assuming this responsibility, he had surprised himself by falling easily into remembered duties and procedures. The past two days had been a round of washing and bandaging burns and cuts, setting broken limbs, and delivering a baby who had insisted on being born in the midst of chaos.

During the fiery days and nights, he had searched the face of each refugee, hoping to see Jessie, Linc, Susan. But in vain. Now the awful terror of not knowing welled up in him. The thought of what his future might be without Jessie and Linc overwhelmed him.

Never to see Jessie again! Jessie in her crisp white apron in command of her kitchen. Or Jessie late in the afternoon when tendrils of her hair escaped from her tight bun and formed a light brown halo of curls around her face. The thought of losing her forever slid through him like honed steel, left him reeling. He'd lost Will. Not Jessie and Linc, too. He slumped onto a chair at the back of the church. Yearning for Jessie and Linc swirled through his heart. *Oh, God. I can't live without them.*

God, Will was right. I can't survive this on my own. Tears gathered in Lee's smoke-raw throat. He recalled Will's face as it had looked by campfire light on battlefield after battlefield. Will's low comforting voice came to him, "You must humble yourself. Every man must let God be God. We are not able to understand why God allows death. Such matters are too great for us to know."

"I know that now, Will," Lee whispered and slid to his knees. *God, you've brought me to my knees at last. You are God; I am not. I wandered away from you a long time ago. I blamed you for the war. I blamed you for Will's death. I have resisted you all my adult years.*

Now I see your hand in my life.

You fed my ambition to be a doctor and gave me the strength to defy my family. You led me into the war. I hated the war. But some men lived because Will and I were there.

Because of my war service, I was able to help people here who needed a doctor. But I lost my best friend, Will.

Lee looked up. *I lost myself, too, but now you've let me taste life with Linc and Jessie. I can't face life without them. I can't believe you would take them from me now, just when I know what I really want in life. I don't deserve them. But have mercy on me—a sinner.* He stifled a wrenching sob.

Suddenly something within him released—the cinched-in feeling that had gripped him more tightly the last few days, but which had been with him since Will died. He took a breath as though testing for it. Warmth radiated throughout his body. He felt free, stunningly liberated. He stood up.

"I thank you, God," he whispered. "I don't know if Jessie and Linc will be restored to me, but I know we are in your hands. Thank you for giving me life and forgiveness. I am unworthy. I promise from this day to give my life to you. I want to be the best man, the best doctor, you can help me to be."

"Smith!"

Lee looked up and exclaimed, "Huff, praise God! You're safe!" He took Hiram's hand and gripped it. The fire captain's uniform was torn, burned, and black with soot. The man's eyebrows and lashes had been singed away. His face was covered with blistered burns.

"Smith, they told me you were a doctor here. Is it really you?" Huff's voice sounded gritty from a smoke-burned throat.

"Yes, it's a long story, but I really am Dr. Smith. Come with me. I'll treat those burns on your face and hands."

Huff pulled back. "I'm not here for medicine. Have you seen Esther? Have you seen my wife?"

"No, do you have any news about Jessie's neighborhood?"

"Burned to the ground. The fire was so hot there even the chimneys were turned to ash."

Hearing this, Lee felt as though a fist had slammed into his gut.

Huff went on, obviously near breaking down. "That devil-wind swept the fire blocks ahead of us. We couldn't stop it. We couldn't keep up. There wasn't any way we could stop it!" He stopped, pain contorting his face.

"Come on. Let's get you some coffee and a sandwich."

"I've got to find her." Hiram shook with emotion.

"You will." Lee put his hand on Hiram's shoulder. "You're about to drop. Coffee and food will help you keep going."

"It's all my fault. If I hadn't argued with her, she would have been safe at home with the twins." Huff coughed into a black-ened handkerchief, then he could speak again. "Our neighbor-hood wasn't touched. It's all my fault."

Lee made sympathetic, soothing comments as he led Hiram out to the tent. Lee forced him to sit down on a rickety chair and take a cup of thick, black coffee. Motioning to one of the women volunteers, Lee murmured to her, "Make sure he eats something before you let him leave. He's near collapse." She nodded.

An older female volunteer approached him. "Dr. Smith, do you have a sister by the name of Eugenia?"

"Yes, is she here?"

"No, but Mayor Mason has sent a call out to locate you—"

"How is my sister? How did she know where to find me?"

The white-haired woman smiled. "She is safe. And she told the mayor she was certain you'd be found as a volunteer doctor at one of the shelters."

"She did?" Lee mused, relieved his sister had been spared. Evidently she knew more about him than he did himself.

"I will send the policeman back to the mayor to report your whereabouts." Lee nodded his thanks. "And, Dr. Smith, more injured have been brought in."

Overhearing her, Hiram jolted to his feet, spilling his coffee. "Any women?"

"No, I'm sorry. No women."

The chair creaked as Hiram let himself drop back into it.

Lee squeezed Hiram's shoulder. "I'll have to stay here until I'm no longer needed. Please let me hear immediately if you locate any of our loved ones."

Hiram nodded, his eyes nearly shut with fatigue. When he brought the tin coffee cup to his lips, his hand trembled.

Lee left him and joined the other two doctors in the area that had been set aside for sorting out the different injuries, assessing their severity, and deciding who could best treat each patient.

A dog barked.

"Butch!" Whirling around, Lee searched for the brown-and-white pup. Butch bounded up to Lee, yapping in agitation, leaping knee-high to him. "Butch, where's Linc? Where's Linc?"

Keeping up his avid barking, the pup surged away. Periodically glancing back to make certain Lee was still following him, the dog led Lee to a small boy huddled among battered and blackened men.

"Lincoln!" Lee swung the boy up into his arms. He couldn't speak. Tears fell from his eyes. Waves of gratitude and joy coursed through him. *Thank you, Father.*

Finally he asked, "Linc, where's your mother?"

"I don't know." Linc's voice vibrated with the force of his own tears. "I ran away from home. I was trying to find you."

Lee soothed the boy, stroking his hair and rocking him in his arms as he did a visual examination. Bruises and a few cuts appeared to be the only wounds Linc had sustained. Lee looked around.

Linc clutched him. "Don't leave me!"

"I won't leave you."

One of the other doctors was swabbing clean the burns of two men. The other was setting a dislocated shoulder. He said, "We can handle these, Smith."

"Thanks, Benson." Lee turned to one of the nurses. "A weak solution of laudanum please." Within minutes, Lee was coaxing

Linc to swallow the nasty-tasting medicine. Then Lee settled him onto a corncob pallet at the end of a pew. While the lad lay there already relaxing from the sedative, Lee gently examined the boy's arms, legs, and ribs.

"Linc, how did you get so bumped and bruised?"

"Everybody was running. I was on the bridge . . ." His small voice started to quaver with tears once more.

"Son, it's all over. You will be safe here. There's nothing to worry about anymore."

"But, my mother—"

"It's late. We'll find her together in the morning. Turn over. I'll rub your back until you fall asleep. Don't worry."

Linc rolled onto his side. "You won't let them take Butch away?"

"No, of course not."

"I ran away from the other place they took me to. They wanted to take Butch—"

"Don't worry. He'll stay right here with you."

The boy lost his anxious expression then. Lee stroked his back until Linc fell into an exhausted sleep. Butch settled down on the floor beside his master and panted happily.

Lee stood up. Soon he was engrossed in setting the wrist of a policeman. After that, nearly a complete company of firemen came in, led by the hand like blind men. It took the doctors more than an hour to bathe their swollen, red, smoke-burned eyes and treat all their burns, contusions, and lacerations.

Lee tied the last bandage on the final firefighter needing treatment. "It's a wonder you men were able to walk here at all."

"It was a long siege all right," one of the firemen said.

"We'd still be out there if it weren't for Milwaukee's sending practically their whole fire department by rail on Monday. I don't know how we could have finally doused everything."

"They've been as dry as we've been. Hope they get rain so they don't burn," another added.

"We sure could have used a shower—"

"A shower! We could-a used a downpour—"

"How about a gully washer?"

"How about two gully washers?"

The fire crew broke into loud guffaws. Lee marveled at their ability to laugh after fighting fires from Sunday night until Tuesday afternoon.

One of the volunteers came to lead the men away to a hot meal. They each put a hand on the shoulder of the man in front of them. They walked single file down the main aisle of the church.

Lee walked to the back of the church again. He stood over Linc, content just to watch him sleep. Butch had jumped up on the boy's lap to sleep. Now he opened his eyes to acknowledge Lee. Scratching the loyal dog behind his ears, Lee stood while the pup once again settled himself comfortably on his master's lap. Lee continued to gaze at the child he thought he had lost.

Thoughts of Jessie intruded, but he pushed them away, forcing himself to lay his troubles at the feet of Christ. Finally Lee's tired legs complained. His fatigued eyes began watering so heavily he couldn't see clearly. A nurse came up behind him with a chair and bullied him into sitting down. Settling himself into the roomy chair, he watched the gentle rise and fall of Linc's chest in slumber. Lee's head drooped.

* * * * *

Lee, still half-asleep, saw the pup raise his head, then stand up. Butch gave one soft bark.

Startled, Lee awoke fully to see Jessie stride into the candlelit room. Joy shot through him. He leaped out of the chair and rushed to her. "Jess!" He pulled her into his arms. At first, all he could do was hold her—feel the softness of her body against his, knowing she was real, not imagined. He buried his face in the crook of her neck, letting his cheek glory in the feel of her hair and skin against his face.

CHAPTER 16

"Jess." His arms drew her more tightly to him. He kissed her deeply. After minutes of holding her against him, his feeling of urgency finally unwound like a loosened watch spring. He released her so he could look down into her face. "Jess."

"Lee." Rising onto her toes, she gave him a tender kiss. Then she rested her hands on his arms and studied him as though memorizing him.

His words came out husky with emotion. "I was so worried."

She sighed and nodded wearily. "It has been the longest two days of my life." She ran her hands over the muscle and sinew of his arms again, as though making certain he was real. "I feared I had lost you."

"Never—as long as I have breath."

Butch gave a yap from where he guarded Linc.

Jessie glanced at the pup, then spun back to Lee. "Linc! He's here!"

"Yes. Come." He took her hand and led her to the pew where Linc slept peacefully.

Jessie dropped to her knees, pressing her prayer-folded hands to her lips. "My son." With an angel touch she examined his face, shoulders, arms, hands, chest, abdomen, and legs. She looked up, concern in her expression.

Lee dropped to one knee beside her and touched Linc's cheek. "He's a little bruised up and very tired. He said there was a stampede on one of the bridges when it caught fire."

Jessie moaned and lay her head on her son's chest. "It's all my fault—"

"No, I was the one who lied and caused Linc to run away."

"But if I hadn't—"

Lee placed his hands under her arms and lifted her to her feet. "None of us could have predicted a disaster like this would occur." Again he pulled her into his embrace. He had to hold her, had to know that she was really with him.

"Dr. Smith?" One of the other physicians cleared his throat.

"Yes?" Lee turned.

"The kitchen is just about out of food again. You haven't eaten since lunch, and we insist you go to supper, *now.*"

Lee was touched by the genuine concern in the other doctor's voice. "Thank you. Dr. Cooledge, this is my very dear friend, Mrs. Wagstaff. The boy is her son, Lincoln."

The doctor greeted Jessie, then urged her to go with Lee to the food tent.

"I don't want to leave Linc." Jessie hung back. "What if he awakes and I'm not here?"

"I gave him a sedative. He won't wake until morning," Lee assured her. "Besides, Butch is here to alert us. You'll keep watch, won't you, Butch?"

The little dog sat up and looked at Lee with serious eyes.

"See? Jess, come on. We need to talk." He led her by the hand. Outside, the day's light had waned to a faint glow over the bleak, "burned over" horizon.

"Every time I look to the west I can't believe what I'm seeing," Jessie murmured.

"It looks grim. It's still a miracle the fires are finally out. I have never experienced such wind in my life."

"It was horrible." Jessie's voice broke on the last word, and she began to tremble.

Lee put his arm around her shoulders and drew her to a chair and table beneath a canvas canopy. Soon he returned with two tin cups of soup and hunks of warm, fresh bread. He sat down beside her.

"The thought of food makes me sick. I haven't been able to eat anything." She clenched her hands in her lap.

"What is troubling you? Are Susan, Ruby—"

"They're all safe—thanks to Miss Wright."

"Miss Wright?"

"It's a dreadful story. I delayed leaving the house too late. We should have left long before we did. I couldn't believe the fire would reach us." She bowed her head.

"You weren't the only one who thought that." He lifted her chin with his hand.

"But it could have cost us all our lives. Susan, Ruby, Miss Wright were depending on *me*! I thought that I, by the strength of *my* will, could succeed where everyone else failed. What miserable pride. God sent warning after warning, but I wouldn't listen. I was going to save my house, no matter what!"

"Jess, stop blaming yourself. How could you know how devastating this fire would be?"

"I should have known." Her voice vibrated.

"That is pride, too, Jess."

She looked up, her eyes wide.

"We're only human. We don't, can't, know everything. You may think you failed God, but I doubt He would agree. You didn't abandon the women who trusted you—"

"*You* speaking of God?" She touched his hand.

He took her hand in both of his. "Yes. This fire burned away a lot of foolish guilt and pride from me too. Now He's brought you safely here—you and Linc. I told God I couldn't live without you." He drew her hand to his lips and kissed it. "I'm a new man, Jess. 'The old is passed away, all is new.'"

"Lee." She leaned forward and kissed his lips lightly, reverently. "Oh, Lee."

Gazing into each other's eyes, they sat a long time, knee to knee, hand in hand.

Finally Lee sat up straighter. "I insist you eat some of this before it's stone cold." He pushed the tin cup toward her and lifted his own. "Now, tell me how our dear Miss Wright saved Ruby."

"Oh." Jess picked up the mug and took a sip. "She was magnificent, Lee. When we finally left the house, the fire was right behind us. Ruby fell and wouldn't get up. Miss Wright pounded the ground behind Ruby with her cane and insisted if she didn't get up, we would all die because we wouldn't leave her."

Lee stopped in the act of taking another sip of the hot soup. "She said that!"

"Yes. Somehow it made Ruby get to her feet, and we reached safety—with only minutes to spare."

Lee took a sip of his soup, then frowned. "You must eat," he coaxed.

"I can't. Not until I find my mother."

"You became separated from her?"

Jessie nodded, tears beginning to fall. "She went to town to look for Linc. She thought he might try to find you at the Workman's Rest."

A groan filtered through Lee's lips. "Where have you looked?"

"Everywhere. Yesterday we were finally able to leave the beach. We had been marooned on a sandbar for hours—all through that damp night. Miss Wright and Ruby are suffering dreadful pain in their joints from it. When we left the beach, I found shelter for Susan, Ruby, and Miss Wright at a Lutheran church, but I've spent all today searching." She passed her hand over her forehead.

Lee looked up. "Your stepfather was here looking for her too. I had forgotten—seeing you pushed every other thought out of my mind."

"*That man!*" Jessie's voice surged with anger. "Their neighborhood wasn't touched! If *that man* hadn't driven her away, mother would have been safely at home! If anything has happened to mother, I'll . . . I'll—" Jessie's voice broke off.

Lee moved his chair closer and pulled Jessie to him until her cheek rested on his shoulder. Witnessing her heartbreak cut him. But knowing he could do nothing to ease it was worse. Minutes passed. Jessie finally was able to eat enough to satisfy Lee. The two of them went back to stand over Linc.

"Jessie!"

She looked up and saw Dr. Gooden in a group of well-dressed, though somewhat disheveled, men.

Chapter 16

"Dr. Gooden!" She hurried forward and took Dr. Gooden's outstretched hands. "You're safe."

"Thank God, you are safe also. I couldn't get away to come to your house. When I was told your neighborhood burnt, I—"

"I know. But we're all well and safe." She held back the news that her mother was still unaccounted for. She couldn't find the strength to voice her concern. "You are helping with the relief efforts, aren't you?"

He nodded. "I am here with Mayor Mason, Dr. Moody, and others. We are finding out—"

The group of men clustered around them. One came forward. "Dr. Smith?"

Lee, who had hung back to give Gooden a chance to talk to Jessie alone, moved to stand behind Jessie and rested his hands on her shoulders. "Yes?"

Dr. Gooden cast a surprised look at Jessie.

She blushed, but gazed directly at the men who were now questioning Lee.

For the next few minutes she listened to the group question Lee about what supplies he needed, what he thought the health risks to the general public might be, and how to prevent them. Many of the new ideas Dr. Gooden had discussed with her on her back porch were mentioned.

"Thank you, Dr. Smith." Dr. Gooden shook hands with Lee. As the others echoed their thanks, Dr. Gooden leaned close to Jessie's ear and whispered, "I hope you and your doctor will be very happy."

Surprised, Jessie couldn't think what to say.

Then they left.

Lee smiled down at her. "How about one more cup of coffee? Then you can sit the rest of the night beside your son." Lee walked her back to the food tent.

Jessie accepted coffee from the volunteer. Looking over Lee's shoulder, Jessie saw her stepfather approaching them. Rage shot through her like the thrust of a hot poker. The cup of coffee dropped from her hands. "You!"

Before she could say more, Hiram—for the first time in her life—wrapped his arms around her. Shock froze her.

"Jessie, Jessie." Shaking with emotion, Hiram tried to catch his breath.

Standing stiffly within his embrace, Jessie felt the tremors that coursed through his body. Sudden dread gripped her. "Mother. It's Mother, isn't it?"

"Yes," Hiram gasped. Releasing Jessie, he gripped the back of a chair as though bracing himself during a spasm of pain.

"What is it? Tell me." Jessie heard the shrillness in her plea. When Hiram continued to struggle for words, she fought the urge to shake them out of him.

He finally spoke, "The captain of the Coventry Company caught up with me at my station." He gasped again, drawing another ragged breath. "He saw Esther. He's sure it was Esther—"

"What happened? Is she at another hospital?" Jessie felt her control slipping. "Where is she!"

"We've lost her. Dear God, she's gone." He began to weep in strangling gasps.

"No!" Jessie shook him by one of his shoulders.

"She was helping a family get out of their burning house. She went back in. Coventry Company tried to stop her." He struggled for breath. "The roof collapsed. She never made it out." Dry rasping sobs wrenched his body.

Jessie staggered. "No, no. It's not true. You're lying. Your lying!"

Taking hold of her, Lee said her name repeatedly. The sound of his voice was a buzzing in her ear.

"I didn't deserve her," Hiram moaned. "If I hadn't argued with her, she would have been home safe with the twins."

White hot anger seethed inside Jessie. She pulled away from Lee. Her hands clenched and unclenched, as though reaching for a rod to beat her stepfather with. She wanted to beat him, see him bleeding and broken on the floor in front of her. She wanted to hear him scream with anguish.

Hiram dropped to his knees in front of Jessie. "Dear God, forgive me. Forgive me."

Jessie half-turned away from him, seeing his abject sorrow, but unwilling to let it sway her.

Huff, in his painful raspy voice, went on, "I've sinned against God and man. Esther, Esther, I'm sorry. I always had to have my own way in everything. Forgive me, Jessie. I was wrong." He buried his face in his hands.

Jessie took a step back from him.

"She said I had never loved her. Oh, God, it's true. I loved only myself. Forgive me, Jessie."

She wanted to refuse. But the stirring sorrow in his voice forced her to turn back to him. She fought the pity that reared up for him. She brought to mind all the times he had forced himself between her mother and her, all the times he drove a painful wedge between them. Then she pictured the day he had marched her to Margaret Wagstaff's back door and coldly left her there alone.

Margaret. She saw Margaret's sweet, lined face. But Margaret had taught her to love no matter what, no matter who. Then she recalled Reverend Mitchell's dying words, "Forgive. You'll never be free until you forgive." He had said the words to Caleb, but she had needed to hear them too.

She hated her stepfather.

In her mind, she heard Margaret's soft voice, "Forgive, Jessie, forgive." It was almost as though Will and Margaret stood one on each side of her. She felt bathed in their love for her; her love for them.

God didn't hate. He forgave.

Moments passed. Jessie closed her eyes. She heard people moving around them, speaking in quiet, troubled voices, near but apart. She fought the plea in Margaret's remembered voice.

She tried to harden her heart against it. She couldn't. She opened her eyes.

Feeling older than her years, she took Hiram's hands in hers. She tugged him to his feet. *This is because of you Margaret, you Reverend Mitchell, and you Mother.* "I forgive you." Her voice was dead.

"Jessie, I don't deserve your forgiveness. I'm not worthy."

Jessie tried to say something comforting, but she felt numb, unable to respond. She felt alone, totally alone.

Her stepfather still wept. "What will we do without your mother?"

Unable to look at his despair, Jessie averted her eyes. She mumbled, "We'll manage somehow."

She felt like a wounded animal. She wanted this man, whom she still hated, to take his grief away. She wanted to mourn alone. How could God have let this hateful man live and let her beautiful mother die? Waves of anger tried to swell inside her. *I forgave him, Margaret. I'll do what I can.* She looked to Lee. Tears dripped from his eyes. But Jessie felt dry, flat, alone.

Then it came.

Soothing warmth poured through Jessie. Over the jagged shards of her shattered heart flowed a healing balm—more wonderful than she thought possible, more healing than she could have imagined. Its intensity gripped her.

Strength . . . peace . . . joy . . . lifted her spirit. She felt summer breezes flutter through her heart. Love, unbelievable love, real love for this man, bubbled up within her and overflowed. The sensations—their force stunned her. Unable to resist their momentum, she reached out and tugged Hiram closer to her.

"I forgive you," Jessie whispered, and soothing tears began to wash her cheeks.

Lee saw the change in Jessie. Her face softened, her embrace of Hiram lost its wooden quality. Reaching out, Lee laid his hand on her shoulder. The smile she gave him was the most beautiful he had ever seen. It reminded him of a Renaissance

Madonna smiling down at the babe, Jesus. Fleetingly he recalled the touch of his own mother's hand, the mother he had lost when he was Linc's age. "Jess," he whispered, his tears falling too.

She stepped closer to Lee, releasing Hiram. The three of them stood like statues. Only their labored breathing and flowing tears betrayed them as human. Uncounted minutes disappeared. They silently absorbed the impact of what had just taken place.

Jessie had heard of miracles, but she had never anticipated one in her own life. Her tears washed away the last traces of the numbness that had gripped her. Her heart and soul glowed pristine, new. When she glanced into the faces of Lee and her stepfather, she saw what she felt reflected back to her.

Finally Jessie spoke, "We will manage, Hiram. We have to take care of the twins. They'll need us the most."

Wiping away his tears with his hands, her stepfather embraced her fiercely. He stepped back. "You're right. They need us. You must come and live with us until you can rebuild."

"I'm sorry. I'll come to help you, but I have to stay with Miss Wright, Susan and Ruby—"

Hiram said eagerly, "I have room for them too. Bring them with you."

Gazing at Lee, Jessie saw her own surprise mirrored in Lee's face. "Do you mean that?"

"Yes, I've been a fool about them before, but I feel so different now. All I can sense is that they need me and I need them. I can't explain it. I feel . . . changed, transformed. I'm not the same."

Jessie kissed Hiram on his cheek. "I feel it too."

"I have to go break the news to the twins," he spoke briskly, his usual take-charge manner returning. "The three of us will get ready for all of you. You, too, Smith . . . I mean, Dr. Smith." He shook hands with Lee, kissed Jessie once more, then hurried away.

Jessie and Lee stood, facing each other. Then Lee said, "I'm stunned. I can't believe what I just witnessed."

"I can hardly believe it myself. I can't explain it, but all my anger toward him left me—completely."

"This is a day of miracles."

The food tent was nearly empty now. Only a few tired volunteers clustered at the back, drinking coffee and talking quietly. The scorched stench from the burned-over land came to Lee on the night breeze. A few brave crickets were clicking cheerfully in spite of the devastation that had come so close.

"Jess, what about me? Has your anger toward me left you?"

"Yes, oh yes." She stepped eagerly into his open arms. "I was a fool to deny my love for you."

"I was a fool to lie to you, but believe me, I can hardly remember the man I was that April morning when I walked up your back steps."

Jessie rested her head on his shoulder and gazed up at Lee. The powerful joy on her face almost made him weak at the knees.

I don't deserve her. "Thank you, Lord," Lee murmured. "I didn't merit a second chance in life, especially with this wonderful woman. I'll try to be worthy of her."

"Don't talk about being worthy of me." Her love for him shone in her eyes. Then she raised her face to heaven. "Dear Father, help me to shine as a light, a witness of your infinite love. Help me to live always in your will and not my own. Keep my heart soft, not stubborn."

Lee joined her in prayer. "Lord, I ask the same of you, but my stubborn heart is a wandering heart too. Keep me close to you."

"Amen."

He smiled tenderly. "I love you, Jessie. Will you be my wife?"

"Yes. God has given us time and love—gifts too precious to waste."